I0669133

Her Tuscan Sister

A NOVEL

Also by E. Louise Jaques:

Dreams of Amelia
Splitters, An Amelia Island Mystery
The Truth Be Told

Her Tuscan Sister

A NOVEL

E. Louise Jaques

Jan-Carol
Publishing, Inc
"every story needs a book"

Her Tuscan Sister
E. Louise Jaques

Published September 2021
Little Creek Books
Imprint of Jan-Carol Publishing, Inc
All rights reserved
Copyright © 2021 by E. Louise Jaques
Front Cover Design: Kristen Jaques
Photographs: E. Louise Jaques
Book Design: Tara Sizemore

This is a work of fiction. Any resemblance to actual persons, either living or dead is entirely coincidental. All names, characters, and events are the product of the author's imagination.

This book may not be reproduced in whole or part, in any manner whatsoever without written permission, with the exception of brief quotations within book reviews or articles.

ISBN: 978-1-954978-19-5
Library of Congress Control Number: 2021946103

You may contact the publisher:
Jan-Carol Publishing, Inc
PO Box 701
Johnson City, TN 37605
publisher@jancarolpublishing.com
jancarolpublishing.com

To my grandsons, Nico and Remy.

You bring love, laughter, and never-ending joy to our family.

Chapter 1

TRUE COLORS

Bam! The screen door slammed behind Cat as she stepped onto the porch of her 1920s cottage. The sound brought back bittersweet memories of the cottage her family had rented the summer before her mother died. She inhaled the heady fragrance of the Tuscany Superb roses that she'd planted in memory of her mom. The tranquility of her home always soothed her soul.

Catherine Emerson picked a jasmine bloom and swung open the picket-fence gate that surrounded the pearl-white, shingled house with ice-blue shutters. A soft breeze was welcome relief from the sultry, southern evening air. She strolled along Ladies Street in Old Town

1

Fernandina, which was on the north end of Amelia Island, Florida. Her destination was the Plaza San Carlos, where she would watch the glorious sunset over the Amelia River. As she passed under the three-hundred-year-old live oak known as "The Wishing Tree," she reached up and brushed the dangling Spanish moss with her hand.

"Hello, Catherine. How are you?" a squeaky voice called from the front veranda of a two-story home on Estrada Street. A diminutive Black woman in an oversized rocking chair grinned at Cat. The elderly lady's shock of white hair stood straight out, like Einstein's in his later years. A tiny head popped up from the woman's lap, and a puppy with the same hairstyle as his owner began to growl.

"Hush, Maddog."

"Hi, Abigail. It's a beautiful night to watch the sunset."

"Sure is, honey. Thank heavens the world is back to normal."

"You're so right," Cat answered. "More than six hundred thousand lives lost was beyond tragic."

"That virus brought out people's true colors. So many kind, courageous, and heroic people," stated Abigail.

"All the nurses, doctors, and front-line workers. It was astonishing," Cat said.

"But, Lordy, there were too many stupid, selfish, and downright evil folks."

"It really was a study in human nature."

"And I still can't get over the fact that a Black woman is vice president. Never thought I'd live to see that day."

Cat smiled. "We're making progress in so many ways."

"Thank goodness. Say, I enjoyed your fiftieth birthday party," Abigail said. "I liked chatting with your brother. He's quite the world traveler."

"Yes, he is, and he loves being on the move again. I was just thinking about Jim. You must have read my mind."

Right then, Maddog began barking like crazy, and Abigail tried hard to shush him.

Cat began to laugh. "By the way, how did Maddog get his name?"

"Well, my granddaughter thought he always had a resting angry look on his face, so she thought Maddog would be a perfect name for him. I had to agree. I'm sorry to say he's living up to his name right now."

"Your grandkids are such a delight, and it's so nice for you that they live close by," Cat said, knowing that Abigail had frequent visits from them.

"My grandkids and great-grandkids are a joy, and they're so good to me. They really fill up my home. It's a shame that neither you nor your brother had children."

After saying goodnight, Catherine strode away, pondering Abigail's words about the pandemic and her reference to the fact that she and her brother did not have children. *Is she right? Did Jim and I miss out because we didn't have children?* Cat wondered.

Cat tucked her chin-length, wavy dark hair behind her ears as she approached the park. She resembled her pretty, olive-skinned mother, and her brother, Jim, took after their father, tall and slim with curly blond hair. Her brother had been her best friend and protector ever since their mother passed away when she was ten and Jim was twelve. When their father died of a heart attack when she was twenty-two, Jim was her only close relative.

As Cat entered the park, she could see several people near the river, aiming their cell phones at the splendid shades of coral and pink in the evening sky. Many people still kept their distance from one another even though it was no longer required. She didn't miss the days when every trip to the grocery store was accompanied by fear.

To capture the radiant colors, Cat pulled her phone from her pocket, pressed the camera icon, and raised the lens toward the descending sun. While doing so, Cat glanced at the top floor of the Victorian house on the edge of the square. She caught sight of movement in the window and wondered if it was the ghost who was believed to haunt the historic home. Before she could take a photo, Catherine's phone rang, causing her to jump. It was Beatrice, her ex-sister-in-law. The woman's voice was worse than fingernails on a chalkboard; Cat was convinced it could literally curdle milk.

"Hi, Beatrice, how are you?" Cat asked, trying to be pleasant.

"Hello, Catherine. I'm fine, but your brother's gone."

"What? Gone where?"

"Gone... He's dead. He had a heart attack an hour ago in a taxi. I was still listed as his emergency contact, so the hospital called me."

Cat's vision blurred, her heart pounded, and a mournful wail escaped her lips. She dropped to her knees, her hand like a vise on her phone. She could hardly believe what she was hearing.

"I'm sorry for your loss, Catherine. I know how close you two were. I'm leaving tomorrow for an African safari. I'm sorry I'll miss the funeral."

Catherine wilted, and her phone tumbled to the ground. She fought for air through heart-wrenching sobs.

* * *

The next few days passed in a blur. Several years earlier, Catherine and Jim had purchased burial plots in Bosque Bello, a cemetery within walking distance of Old Town Fernandina. Her close friend Lisa Benedetto had talked her into making the purchase and had promised that her family would always take care of them. Cat had been anguished that her parents had been cremated and their ashes spread on the ocean, and that had made her want a final resting place in the sandy soil beneath the graceful branches of an oak tree. She did not want to end up as fish food.

Lisa stayed with Cat, and they spent two days making funeral arrangements. As twilight approached the evening before the funeral, the women sat on Cat's porch. A chorus of cicadas sang, each tiny creature contributing to the melody.

"In the darkest days of the darkest year, I still had hope. Hope that we'd defeat the virus—even after all the variants and the pandemic of the unvaccinated. I thanked my lucky stars when we survived and ushered in a new administration," said Cat.

"Me, too," answered Lisa. "The number of people who died is staggering, and it still breaks my heart."

"You know, Lisa, I fully expected to make it to old age surrounded by the people I love. Now Jim is gone. My whole family is gone." The last couple of days had been very hard on Cat, and she was just now coming to terms with the new reality.

4

Lisa gently took Cat's hand. "I'll always be here for you, my friend." The two women had become as close as sisters over the years.

Jim's service was held in a stately funeral home on Atlantic Avenue in Fernandina Beach. Catherine tucked several seashells and mementos into the coffin and gently touched Jim's curly hair a final time before the casket lid was shut forever. After the poignant service, Cat wept as the two dozen cars in the procession made their way up North 14th Street to the cemetery.

A reception at Cat's house followed the internment, and the smell of freshly turned earth stayed with Cat long after she left her brother in the ground. She was grateful that people were once again able to gather together. She was also thankful for the kindness of her neighbors. They filed in with steaming casseroles, salads, and platters of desserts. Standing on the front porch, Catherine greeted each mourner as they arrived. Rodney Simmons, a burly long-time employee of Jim's company, hefted a large cooler of beer up the steps, set it on the porch, and took out a can. His Calvin Klein cologne wafted toward her, overpowering the floral scents from the garden.

"Thanks, Rodney. You're a good man," said Cat.

"No problem, Miss Catherine. You know how much I loved your brother. He was so healthy. I can't believe his heart gave out."

"I can't believe it, either. He had a CT scan a year ago, and everything was fine."

Rodney hesitated. "That's why..."

"That's why what?" Cat questioned.

"There are a couple of things I need to check into. Don't want to talk about it yet."

"Well, I'm always ready to listen when you do want to talk. Come on inside. There's plenty of food to go with that beer," she said as they entered the cottage.

In the living room, several of Jim's friends regaled the neighbors with stories of their worldwide adventures. Abigail sat spellbound as the middle-aged explorers described their antics in exotic locations. Lisa poured Catherine a glass of wine, and they joined the group.

"It sounds like you boys never really grew up, including Jim," Cat said.

"You should have come with us, Catherine," answered Jake, a childhood friend of both Cat and Jim.

"Very funny, Jake. You know I don't fly."

"Our very own 'fraidy Cat."

Catherine ignored the comment. "Can I get anyone another drink?"

Everyone declined, so Cat slipped away to the kitchen and flopped into a chair. She knew that Jake and the others were trying to lighten the mood and celebrate her brother's life, but tears welled in her eyes. She set down her glass and covered her face with her hands.

"Catherine!" a hefty man barked.

"Oh, Bradley, I didn't know you were here." She took a napkin and dabbed her eyes.

"I'm sorry for your loss, Catherine. Giancarlo sends his condolences. He's out of the country right now."

Jim's business partner, Bradley Ritter, pulled up a chair and grabbed Cat's hand. He was portly and had slicked-back hair, beady eyes, and trendy glasses that looked ridiculous on his rotund face. Jim had trusted Bradley completely, but Cat wasn't so sure about him.

"It'll be hard to manage without James."

Cat's stomach churned from his clammy touch. She yanked her hand away and rose from her chair.

"Do you know where he was going? He left the office before I got back from a meeting. I understand he was on his way to the airport."

"No, I don't know where he was going."

Bradley hauled his hulking frame out of the chair. "We have so many irons in the fire right now. It was odd for him to leave and not tell me his plans. And I can't find his laptop. Do you have it?"

"I did get his suitcase and briefcase from the hospital, but I haven't opened them. And I haven't had a chance to clean out his apartment."

"Well, Catherine, I'd like to get his laptop when you find it. I want to make certain I have all the company files."

Chapter 2

OUR MOTHER

A few days after the funeral, Catherine was at home, hunched over her desk. She groaned and threw her pen across the room. She was on the second edit of a hard copy of a suspense novel. The author had ignored most of Cat's previous suggestions about trimming pages of inconsequential backstory that bogged down the action. Since the author was on a tight deadline with his publisher, Catherine couldn't delay the project any longer.

Cat's career in marketing had ended when the company she'd worked for unexpectedly closed its doors. The death of the owner had shaken her to the core. He'd successfully battled the COVID-19 virus, only to later perish in a car accident. It had been a good job, but now there were few jobs available for marketing professionals who'd passed the half-century mark.

She'd been a part-time freelance editor for many years and now found she was able to support herself doing it full-time. Editing mysteries and suspense novels was her specialty, but the fear of failure held her back from writing a page-turner of her own. Several people had used their shelter-at-home time to complete the novel they'd always wanted to write. Some incorporated the pandemic in their writing, and others wrote about a less traumatic time. She'd co-authored a memoir for an acquaintance and had vowed never to do that again. Helping someone air a family's dirty laundry was as unappealing as actually washing dirty laundry.

Catherine had an uncanny ability to get into the heads of her authors and understand what they were trying to say even when their

7

writing wasn't clear. Lisa called her an empath. Cat loved helping novelists turn their stories into saleable books, whether she used her intuition or not. She'd been involved with the local annual Book Festival for many years, which provided thousands of free books to the schools in the county.

She also enjoyed mentoring young writers and worked with high school students by editing their short stories and novels. She encouraged them to write about their experiences during the pandemic, through all the tragic waves of the virus and frightening variants, and the deplorable actions of the governor. Many of the stories were heartbreaking. The deadly insurrection at the US Capitol before the last inauguration was another topic the teens wrote about, as was the guilty verdict of the police officer in the George Floyd trial. She firmly believed her validation of their thoughts and feelings was cathartic for them. They'd suffered from anxiety and social isolation during the pandemic, and many feared for the future of their country.

Retrieving the pen from across the room, Cat walked to the front door and opened it wide. The sweltering, damp air hit her in the face. The cicadas were once again filling the night air with their distinctive song. Thunder boomed in the distance, and flashes of lightning bolted across the darkening sky. When the lightning flashed, she caught sight of a person skulking in the small park across the road, which separated her street from the Tiger's Point Marina. When the heavens lit up again, she saw that the menacing figure was charging toward her house. Realizing what was happening, Cat muffled a scream, slammed the door, and bolted the lock. She put her ear to the door, fearing the sound of footsteps on the porch, but heard only the occasional clap of thunder.

"Okay, Catherine, calm down," she said aloud, breathing deeply to calm her racing heart. "I'm sure I'm overreacting. He probably just wants to get out of the storm."

Since she'd started living alone after her divorce eight years earlier, Cat often talked to herself. She enjoyed the solitude but was lonely at times. She'd tried online dating sites, and friends had set her up with several men, but she'd had no interest in pursuing relationships with any of them. Cat resigned herself to the fact that she'd spend the rest of her days alone. She was of average height and constantly struggled to keep her weight under control. Catherine's narcissistic ex-husband, Robert, often derided her about her lack of exercise and her carb-based diet. The critic in her head was ever present, and Robert had played on those insecurities.

As she headed back to her desk, Cat spotted Jim's briefcase and suitcase and veered into the living room. The overwhelming pain of her loss had caused her to avoid going through his things or even to make arrangements to clear out his apartment and office. Doing so would make his death so much more real. She placed both cases on the plush, white leather sofa and opened the silver hard-sided carry-on first. She rifled through the contents and determined that Jim had been planning a week-long trip. After making so many trips for pleasure, and for his import-export business, he had been an expert at packing. Finding no clues in the suitcase about Jim's travel plans, Cat turned her attention to the briefcase and discovered it was locked. She headed to the kitchen to search through her junk drawer for a screwdriver. Just then, the cell phone on her desk rang, and she walked over to answer it.

"How are you, my friend?" Lisa asked. Ever since Jim had passed away, Lisa made a point of calling Cat at least once a day to check in on her.

"Trying to work, but I'm having a hard time focusing. I had the weirdest dream last night about Jim. He was walking on the beach in a swirling mist, repeating the words 'not natural.' I have no idea what he meant."

"Maybe he meant it wasn't natural for him to die so young."

"You could be right. A wave of sorrow washed over me when I woke up this morning. Jim was the only one who understood what it was like growing up without our mother. When Mom died in that plane crash, in an instant we became different. Our classmates and their parents treated us like 'the children of the crash.' It wasn't only that our mom had died, but it happened in such a dramatic and traumatic way."

"Kids just don't want to be different."

"Exactly. I need to make arrangements to clean out Jim's apartment and office. I finally opened his suitcase a few minutes ago, and now I'm going to pop the lock on his briefcase," said Cat.

"I guess his secrets will be revealed, if he had any."

"I hadn't thought of that. Hmm, will I uncover something mysterious? I doubt it. Jim always confided in me."

Several years earlier, Jim and his business partner, Bradley, had ventured into a new area, and they'd both obtained their commercial real estate licenses. They'd joined forces with Giancarlo Riva of Riva Realty and had been successful ever since.

Jim's and Bradley's temperaments were at opposite ends of the personality scale. Jim was the charismatic face of the business, and Brad was the financial guy who consistently overestimated his skills. As college roommates at the University of Florida in Gainesville, they'd bonded over *Dungeons & Dragons* and Gators football. Catherine had attended the University of North Florida in Jacksonville so she could live at home with her father, but also because she'd been too nervous to move away.

"Well, let me know if you find anything tantalizing," Lisa said. "And don't worry about editing my cookbook. It can wait."

"Thanks, Lisa. See you tomorrow."

Catherine was grateful for Lisa's friendship and unconditional support. With her brother gone, she felt vulnerable, and she needed someone who would always be there for her. Cat walked back to the living room, screwdriver in hand. She could jimmy locks with the best of them, and she easily opened the briefcase. Lying on top of several file folders was Jim's passport, and inside there were two boarding passes for flights departing the night he died. The first was a flight to Miami, and the second was a flight to Rome.

"What the hell, Jim! Why were you flying to Rome and didn't tell me or Bradley?" She didn't receive an answer from the "other side," so she proceeded to empty the contents of the case on the sofa. At the bottom was his laptop, which she carried to her desk. After powering up the computer, it took her several tries before she guessed the correct password—their mother's maiden name, Maria Teresa Rossi. Perusing his emails, she noticed that several were flagged. One in particular jumped out at her because of its subject line: *Meeting in Rome*. It was from L. Bianchi. Cat gasped as she read the content.

Dear Jim,

Thank you for your swift response. This news was a shock for me, as well. I will reveal more about our mother on the 25th. I will drive from Siena to Rome and meet you at your hotel.

Regards,

Luna

"Our mother?" Cat exclaimed. "Our mother? And Luna? Oh my God!"

Catherine went into her bedroom and rummaged through the boxes in her closet. She located her stash of childhood journals and found the one she wrote when she was ten years old. At that time, she'd had an imaginary friend named Luna. After her mother had died, Cat had poured her heart out in her journal. Then, suddenly, she'd started receiving "messages" from Luna. Her dad, Scott, had insisted it was her vivid imagination, and Cat had reluctantly accepted that explanation. Yet deep in her soul, she'd felt as if a real person was communicating with her. Sometimes foreign words had peppered Luna's responses, and Cat had had no idea where they came from.

She brought the journal into the living room, grabbed Jim's laptop, and settled on the sofa. If her brother had been flying to Rome to meet this woman, he must have taken her claims seriously. Cat thought, *Why was he traveling to Italy almost a full week before the meeting with Luna? And why didn't he tell me? Was he concerned about the veracity of Luna's story? Is it a coincidence that this woman has the same name as my childhood imaginary friend? Do I have a sister I don't know about?*

Cat checked social media on the laptop to see if she could discover anything about Luna Bianchi, but there was nothing on any business or social site. She decided she'd call Stella, her mother's best friend from her childhood in Toronto. Cat would talk to her in the morning and ask if there was a possibility that her mother had had another child. She opened the journal she'd written as a ten-year-old following her mother's death. Even after all these years, the agony of the loss seared her heart. Her dad had tried his best to fill the void, but there was always a gaping hole in her life from her mother's absence. She read each entry, feeling again, in real time, every blistering emotion she had felt as a child. The anger, frustration, sadness, and despair jumped out at her from the pages. She'd become a more timid, anxious child from that day onward.

Years later, she had been hesitant about becoming a mother herself, with no mother of her own to guide her. She'd written lists of pros and cons about parenthood, and she'd spent sleepless nights debating in her mind whether she even wanted children. What if something happened to her and she left her children the way her mother had left her? It turned out she hadn't needed to worry. Several doctors had confirmed that Catherine was physically unable to have a child.

"I can't wait for the morning. I'm calling Stella right now." Cat jumped up, found her address book, and called Stella. The elderly woman answered on the second ring.

"Hello?"

"Hi, Stella. This is Cat. I hope I'm not calling too late. How are you?"

"Catherine! I'm doing well. Just the usual aches and pains. Thank you for sending me the note about Jim. I'm so sorry about his passing. He was such a lovely man."

"Yes, he sure was. We're all going to miss him. Stella, I hope you don't mind, but I—I have something important to ask you about my mother. I'm going to come right out and ask. Did she have another baby? I mean, other than Jim and me?"

Stella paused and then said with equal candor, "She did."

Cat dropped into a chair. "When was that?"

"Oh, my dear. She had a baby during the year she was a nanny in Italy. As you know, she went the summer after high school. But tragically, the child died a few hours after birth. She named her Rose."

"Did my dad know about this?"

"Of course. She told him when they began dating. Shortly after arriving in Siena, Maria met a local young man, and soon after she was pregnant. The scoundrel left her as soon as he found out. She was determined to have the child on her own, and her parents supported her decision. Your grandmother offered to take care of the baby when Maria began attending university."

"Is it possible the story isn't true? That she had the baby and gave her up for adoption?"

"Good heavens, no. Why do you ask?"

"Oh, just something I read on Jim's computer. It's probably nothing."

Changing the topic, Stella said, "You should come visit me soon. It's been a long time, and I would love to see you again."

"You're right, Stella. It has been too long. I'll plan a trip to Toronto soon."

"That would be wonderful, but please let me know if you find out anything more. I've told you all I know, which isn't much."

"Thanks again. Take care."

"You, too, sweet Catherine."

Chapter 3

MIA SORELLA

Waves crashed on the shore of North Beach. Massive dark clouds hung over the ocean, and rain threatened to move toward the land. Cat marched up the deserted beach, ignoring the wild weather. Her stormy internal state mirrored her external environment. She was mourning the loss of her brother and grappling with the fact that she might have a half-sister she hadn't known existed. But how was that even possible if the baby had died? Unable to be heard over the crashing waves, Cat said aloud, "Mom, why didn't you tell me? Jim, why did you keep this a secret?"

Her voice was drowned out by the screech of laughing gulls fighting over bait that had been dumped on the sand by a wizened fisherman. The grizzled old man piled his rods and reels onto a cart and gave Cat a toothless grin as he trudged by. Rain clouds swept toward her, and she ran back to the car. She drove down the tree-lined streets of the historic town of Fernandina Beach. Tourist shops, art galleries, and locally owned restaurants lined Centre Street. She loved the quaintness of the town and its cast of characters, which included many locals who imagined themselves as pirates and dressed the part at every opportunity. She was reminded of the annual Shrimp Festival parade, when they would all be out in full costume, along with a massive wooden pirate ship "sailing" down the main road.

The Eight Flags Shrimp Festival followed the parade. In the late 1800s, real pirates had stayed in town during the heyday of Fernandina. The town had served as a major seaport, and they had left their indelible imprint. Amelia Island was the only place in the country that had been ruled under eight different flags, including the French, English, Spanish, and Confederate. Cat had been grateful when Fernandina Beach high school removed the Confederate flag from its logo after the Black Lives Matter protests.

Cat parked in front of Ciao Bistro, her favorite Italian restaurant, to meet Lisa for lunch. The lovely couple who owned the restaurant were kind and generous. They even helped Lisa perfect some of her family recipes. Still mulling over the unexpected revelation of a possible sibling, Catherine ducked inside before the heavens opened up. Lisa was waiting at a window table and was sipping prosecco. A second glass was waiting for her friend. Lisa's curly dark hair was pulled into a high ponytail. She was petite and had what her husband, Dom, called a voluptuous figure. Her two college-aged sons, Dante and Max, towered over her, but she still ruled the house with "the look" that kept all her boys in line.

"Did you sleep at all last night?" Lisa asked.

Catherine laughed, eased into a chair, and took a mirror from her purse. "Wow, I am a sight! I was walking on the beach. And no, I didn't sleep much." She took a gulp of the sparkling wine. "But I did find something shocking on Jim's laptop. There was an email on there from an Italian woman named Luna Bianchi. She asserts that her mother was our mother! He was on his way to Rome to investigate when he had the heart attack."

"No way! Holy shit!" Lisa could not contain her shock and surprise. Several heads turned to glare at her. She lowered her voice and asked, "How is that possible? Why didn't Jim tell you?"

"God only knows. Although, when I got his phone from the hospital, I turned it on and my contact info popped up right away. Maybe he was about to call me when he had the heart attack."

"I bet you're right. Did your mom ever tell you about having another child?"

"No, but I was only ten when she died. I called her childhood friend Stella last night. She said my mom *did* have a child when she was a nanny in Siena. But she also said the baby died a short time after birth. I'm totally confused."

Lisa took another sip of wine. "So, Jim was on his way to Italy to check out this woman's claim?"

"I guess. He obviously took it seriously and was planning on meeting her in person."

"Wow, a real-life mystery. You can be an amateur sleuth! Have you contacted Luna yourself?"

A server came to the table, and the women ordered lunch. Cat drained her glass of wine, then took a gulp of water. "Not yet. I wanted time to digest this possible new reality."

"If it's true, Cat, then you still have family. You're not alone."

"You're right! I hadn't thought of it that way. I'll email her later this afternoon."

The women parted ways after lunch. Lisa went home to work on her cookbook that was based on family recipes, and Cat drove to the Riverside area of Jacksonville to clean out Jim's furnished ground-floor apartment. The three-story building was in a lovely neighborhood on the St. John's River. The area was popular with its contemporary buildings and restaurants set amid historic homes and tree-lined streets. Jim had sought to keep his life simple after his divorce from Beatrice and hadn't wanted to own a house again. Catherine had benefited from his decision when he'd added additional money for the down payment on her cottage.

With a heavy heart, Cat unlocked the apartment door. She was grateful the landlord had kept the air conditioning turned on. She picked up a golf shirt that had been flung over a chair near the door, and drew it to her face. She inhaled the Hugo Boss cologne scent that lingered on the garment. The fragrance always reminded her of her brother. She spied a photo on the desk of the two of them at their favorite beachside bar on Amelia Island. "Why did you leave me, Jim?" Again, there was no answer from the great beyond, so Cat began placing items from the expensive antique desk into one of the large boxes she'd brought with her. She went to open a drawer and discovered the lock was broken. Startled, she glanced around and actually observed the room. Jim wasn't known for his neatness, but there was more disarray than normal. *Someone's searched this room and broken into the desk.*

She ran into the bedroom and saw that it had been tossed, as well. It was definitely not a professional job, as drawers were hanging open and clothes were scattered on the floor. His closet had also been searched, and shoes had been tossed around the room. Anger welled inside her. Cat stormed over to the landlord's apartment and pounded on the door.

The old man answered and gasped. "M-Ms. Emerson. What's wrong?"

"Who's been in Jim's apartment? Someone's gone through his things and left it in a mess."

"N-no one that I know of," he stuttered.

Cat regretted upsetting the elderly gentleman and lowered her voice. "Are there any security cameras near his apartment?"

"N-none that work. Sorry, Ms. Emerson."

"That's okay, Mr. Robinson. I'll let you know when I've cleaned out his things and arranged for his desk to be moved."

"S-sounds good."

She returned to Jim's apartment, loaded up the boxes, and headed home. Cat took a glass of iced tea and Jim's laptop onto the porch and settled into the Adirondack chair—the one her mother called the Muskoka chair. Canadians had a different name for many things; a touque was a knit hat, and a washroom was a restroom. Cat cherished the memories she had of her mom and had made certain they didn't fade over the decades. *But how well did I really know my mother? Could*

Stella be wrong about the baby? I need to find out. Opening the laptop, Cat went to Luna's email and pressed reply.

Dear Luna,

I'm sorry to inform you that my brother, Jim Emerson, passed away from a heart attack. I learned by reading his emails that he was planning to meet you in Rome on the 25th of this month. My brother and I were very close, but I knew nothing about this trip. Would you please tell me why you believe your mother was also our mother? I look forward to hearing back from you.

Sincerely,

Catherine Emerson

Cat went back to the list of emails to read the ones Jim had flagged. Before she had a chance to explore further, though, an email from Luna popped up. Jumping out of the chair with her heart racing, Catherine paced the porch. She opened the email and saw a phone number and a request from Luna that they FaceTime in ten minutes. *This could change everything. Am I ready?*

Each minute seemed like an hour. Back and forth, she marched across the front porch, then pounded down the steps and roamed in her garden. Finally, Cat returned to the Muskoka chair and tapped in the number on her iPhone. There was a short delay, and then a lovely face appeared on her cell—a face that resembled Maria Rossi Emerson and Catherine Emerson.

"Mio Dio! Catherine, siamo sorelle! We are sisters, si?" said Luna.

Cat burst into tears. "Oh, Luna. Yes, I believe we are!"

"But why are you crying?"

Catherine reached over to the wicker table, grabbed a tissue, and dried her eyes. She slid back into the chair and took a deep breath. "You not only look like my mother—our mother—but you also sound so much like her. I never thought I'd hear her sweet voice again."

"That fills my heart with joy, to know what Maria sounded like," Luna said with a broad smile. "My friend, Viola, jokes that she and I look like sisters, but you and I truly do."

"Please, please tell me how this is possible," Cat said.

"I was going to give Jim the explanation. I was not certain if you had changed your surname when you married, so I contacted your brother. I am so sorry to hear about his passing."

"He had a great heart, Luna. But just like our father's, it didn't beat nearly long enough. I—I thought my family was gone when Jim died. But now..."

"Si, mia sorella, we both have a surprise family! And this is my soon-to-be son, Nico. He is fifteen. His late mother was a dear friend. I filed for temporary custody after her passing, and I have been seeking permanent custody."

Another face popped onto the screen. "Ciao. Mia madre was Luna's amico. She took me in and will adopt me, as my mother wished." Nico hugged Luna. "Sono grato!"

"Hello, Nico. It's a pleasure to meet you."

"I am excited to meet you, too!"

"Luna, I called my mother's childhood friend, and she confirmed that my mom had a baby when she was living in Siena. But she said the baby died shortly after birth. Do you know what happened?"

"I had always felt that I was adopted. My parents insisted I was incorrect, and my birth certificate listed their names. I loved my mother and father dearly, but there was something sbagliato—wrong. I was different from them, not so much in my appearance, but in my interests and attitudes. They died several years ago, and I never pursued the issue. Then, a few weeks ago, I received a letter from a nurse named Angelina. She was close to dying and wanted to meet me. She had worked at the hospital where I was born."

"Wow, a deathbed confession," said Cat.

"And when I met her, she told me what happened at my birth. The doctor who delivered me had a cousin giving birth in the maternity ward of the hospital at the exact same time I was born. He knew his cousin's baby was seriously ill, and in fact the baby girl died several hours after birth. The doctor understood that Maria was an unwed teenager, and he made a decision to help his cousin. He switched the armbands and placed the deceased baby in Maria's bassinet, then put me in the one belonging to his cousin. He told no one. But Angelina suspected what he had done and checked the blood types of the babies.

19

We were both O-positive, so that evidence was inconclusive. There were no security cameras at that time to prove her suspicions."

"Angelina didn't confront him?"

"No. She was too frightened to challenge a well-respected doctor. Shortly after I was born, he moved to Milan. He passed away many years ago, so I cannot speak to him."

Cat sighed. "I wonder if he left Siena because he felt guilty and didn't want to be reminded of what he'd done. Did the parents who raised you ever know?"

"I believe they never knew the truth. They always said I was their miracle daughter."

"Maybe they didn't want to know the truth," Cat pointed out.

"Perhaps you are correct. Angelina saw me as a little girl and was certain that I was Maria's child. She kept in touch with the family who had hired our mother, and told them she had a special place in her heart for the Canadian girl whose baby had died. Through the family, Angelina knew when Maria had married and had more children. I guess Angelina wanted to make things right before she met her maker."

"Poor Mom. To have her baby stolen! That's horrible."

"Yes, Catherine, it is unimaginable. It was a terrible tragedy. I was never able to have children of my own, but I can completely understand the trauma of losing a child."

"Don't forget, you have me now," Nico chimed in.

Luna hugged the fifteen-year-old. "Sì, mio figlio, I have you, and I am so grateful. Angelina kept a notebook that tracked Maria Rossi in Toronto, all through her marriage to Scott Emerson, the birth of their children, and her untimely death. After learning the truth, I found Jim's business address and contacted his email. I wanted to tell him the information in person."

Cat smiled at her sister. "I'm so happy you were able to find us, Luna. I couldn't have a baby, either, and Jim never wanted to have children."

"Zia Catherine," said Nico. "Can I call you that? You must come to visit us right away!"

"Yes, Nico, I'd love for you to call me Aunt Catherine. But I'm sorry, I don't fly. Why don't you both come to Florida? I could take you to Disney World or Universal Studios. They aren't too far from here."

"What do you think, mio figlio?" Luna turned to Nico.

"Grande! Let's go!"

"Your English is very good, Nico," Cat noted.

"He studies hard and is an excellent student. His dear mother, Carlotta, made certain he learned English. I will make the arrangements and get back to you. I am so excited to meet you and visit Florida."

Chapter 4

PERSONAL MATTER

"Catherine! Oh, honey, I'm so sorry about your brother." Hazel Sinclair waddled over and opened the front door of Emerson & Ritter, Inc. to greet Cat. In every way, Hazel resembled Mrs. Santa Claus—from her silver hair and vanilla-scented perfume to her jolly laugh. Cat enjoyed spending time with Jim and Bradley's elderly personal assistant, who'd been with the company from the start. There were always freshly baked goodies on her desk, and today it was the aroma of chocolate chip cookies that greeted Cat.

"Thank you, Hazel. It's been hard letting Jim go, but I should clear out his office. Brad dropped off a few things after the service, but I know he has a room full of treasures from his travels."

"I'm sorry I couldn't make it to the funeral. It was my grandson's birthday. My daughter was recovering from surgery, and she needed help. I was very sorry to have missed it."

"I completely understand," said Cat.

"I miss Jim. His smile lit up the room, and he charmed everyone he met," Hazel said. "It's a shame his passing came so soon after the company expanded. I'm not sure how Bradley will manage without him."

"Yes, Jim told me the real estate business was booming and that the income from that part of the company kept them going during the crisis. I'm the executor of his will, and Bradley's the backup executor. I know my brother left his third of the business to me."

"Are you going to sell your share to Bradley? I think that would be the wisest thing to do," said Hazel.

22

"I haven't decided," Cat said. "But I'd better get a move on. Do you have any spare cardboard boxes in the warehouse that I could use?"

"Yes, dear. I'll get some for you after I unlock Jim's office." They walked down the hallway and stopped outside Jim's old office. "It smells like the Lysol factory around here," Hazel said apologetically. "But we're fortunate that Brad is a germaphobe. His actions stopped us from having many cases of the virus."

"Yeah, I agree. Jim told me how fussy Brad was about disinfecting everything. His phobia actually helped. He also said Giancarlo's mother had the coronavirus and was in the hospital for two months. Thank goodness she recovered."

As Hazel began to walk toward the warehouse, Cat said, "Don't worry, Hazel, I'll get the boxes."

Catherine was shocked by how crammed the warehouse was. There was stuff everywhere. Amid the disarray, Cat found a couple of large boxes and the shipping tape. She waved to Rodney as he drove a forklift toward the loading dock. Another worker was opening a massive crate, and Cat went over to investigate. Huge, elaborately framed paintings were being removed from the container and unwrapped. The artwork appeared to be original—the paintings were obviously antique, or else they were excellent reproductions.

Cat returned to the front of the office and found Hazel in the lunchroom. "Wow, there's a lot of inventory back there. What's with the paintings?"

"Oh, Bradley has a new contact in Florence through Giancarlo. The man wants to get into the American market. There is some wonderful artwork there."

"I'm surprised that Jim didn't tell me about all the new acquisitions."

"He'd been traveling so much lately that I didn't have time to let him know about the paintings," grumbled Bradley as he shuffled into the room.

"Good afternoon to you, too, Bradley," Catherine said.

Ignoring her comment, Bradley asked, "Catherine, did you find out where James was going the day he—he left us?"

"It was a personal matter, and I'd like to keep it confidential right now. But on another matter, I'm going to contact our lawyer about

Jim's will in the next few days. I know he left me his part of the business, and I want to get more details about that."

A crimson color flooded Bradley's face, and his eyes bulged behind his silly glasses. "I'm quite aware of the fact that you'll get his share. I'll have my lawyer contact you about a buyout of your thirty-three percent," he growled.

"Catherine," a voice boomed. Cat and Brad both jumped.

Giancarlo Riva, a tall, lean man with a long face and short-cropped hair, stood in the doorway. He wore an Armani suit and glossy leather shoes. He had an aquiline nose and piercing dark eyes. Trotting at his heels was his nerdy assistant, Kirk.

"Hello, Giancarlo," Catherine said.

The imposing man approached Cat and offered his hand. "It is a pleasure to see you again," Giancarlo purred with an accent both enticing and disconcerting. "Please accept my condolences. James was a good man. Bradley is correct in saying that he would want you to have the financial benefit of selling your company shares."

"I haven't given any of this much thought," Cat said. She broke eye contact with Riva and pulled away her hand. "But I will."

Bradley slipped out of the room.

"I am confident you will make the right decision," Giancarlo said, then strode away. Kirk, the obedient puppy, trailed behind him.

"Hazel, what's with Bradley? He's more irascible than usual," Cat whispered.

"Bradley's often cantankerous these days. I let it roll off me like water off a duck's back. He has a rough exterior, but he's a good man. Giancarlo is a bit scary, but he's smart as a whip. He has a good side, too. He even had a private nurse come in and give us early flu shots. And he was quite a handsome male nurse."

"I agree that Giancarlo can be intimidating. Jim rarely ever spoke about the Italian stallion."

Hazel giggled. "Can you tell me where Jim was going? I promise to keep it a secret," she whispered.

Cat went to the fridge and took out two bottles of water. She plunked down in a chair and handed a bottle to Hazel. "He was going to Rome," she began. "It seems that we have a half-sister living in Siena.

Our mother had a baby after high school, when she was a nanny in Italy. There was a switch made by a doctor, and our half-sister, Luna Bianchi, was given to another woman. The other woman's baby died soon after birth. A nurse who was on her deathbed contacted Luna and told her the whole story. Luna tracked down Jim, and he was going to meet with her when he had his heart attack."

"Good Lord! How strange. But how exciting for you! What a shame that Jim passed before he met her. Luna Bianchi. What a lovely name."

"It really is sad that Jim didn't meet her. Luna's parents are no longer alive, so she felt free to investigate the nurse's claim."

"What a tale she had to tell. And you believe her?"

"Yes, Hazel, I do."

Hazel rose and patted Cat's hand. "Well, keep in touch, honey." She shuffled out of the room as Rodney bounded in and grabbed a soda from the fridge.

"Catherine, I didn't know you were coming today. There's—there's something important I want to talk to you about." Lowering his voice, Rodney added, "Brad said you're inheriting Jim's share of the business."

Sensing something was not quite right, Cat said, "Rodney, what is it?"

Rodney gazed up at the security camera, seeming to remember they were being recorded. He leaned in close and whispered, "Can't talk about it here. I'll give you a call. I have to figure out some things first. I'm going to visit Diana this weekend. My granddaughter has a dance recital, and I'm taking my old laptop to my grandson. We can talk when I get back."

"You have my cell number. Have fun with your grandchildren."

25

Chapter 5

SISTERS

A small crowd gathered outside the security area at the Jacksonville airport. Catherine anxiously looked for two passengers arriving from Rome via Miami. She spotted Nico's grinning face among the many passengers as they walked down the hallway beside security. She rushed to meet them.

"Zia Catherine! Ciao," Nico said as he dropped his backpack and gave her a bear hug. He was tall, lanky, and definitely a child of Italy. His curly dark hair was cut short, and his handsome face was beaming.

"My goodness, Nico, you're tall for fifteen! I'm so happy you're here. Welcome to Florida."

Luna joined them. She was a slightly older version of Catherine—similar height, weight, and lovely features. The women smiled, wrapped their arms around each other, and held tight for a long time. It was an exquisite moment neither had ever imagined.

"Family. I have family again," Cat said. She sighed and gently touched the cheeks of her sister and nephew, thrilled that they were really there. "I'll give you a quick tour of the island before we go to the house, but first let's go get your luggage."

Nico picked up his pack, and the three joyfully strode through the airport, arm in arm, to the baggage claim area. While waiting for the luggage, Catherine spotted another familiar passenger, and she gasped. "Zach!" she called out.

The man turned around, and Cat realized it wasn't her high school sweetheart, just someone who resembled him. Zachary had promised his

26

undying love at the senior prom and then dumped her six weeks later. He was her first love, and she'd planned their life together, through college and beyond. The shock of his rejection was almost as painful as the loss of her mother. It had been another crack in her fragile heart.

In the following years, she had often dreamed of Zach and their imaginary life together. This happened even when she was married to Robert. She woke from these dreams with a profound, soul-deep sorrow. After Zach's betrayal, she'd also lost her high school friends. They had sided with him and had locked her out of their world. She'd had three close friends in college, but they'd all moved away, two to the west coast and one to London. Because she wouldn't travel to see them, the friendships had fizzled out.

"Sam!" Nico called out as the handsome Zach look-alike joined them. He was just over six feet and had salt-and-pepper hair and a solid build. He wore an expensive suit, a starched white shirt, and loafers with no socks. He didn't look like he'd flown over the ocean; he looked like he'd just stepped off a photo shoot for GQ.

"Hi, Nico. This must be the aunt you were telling me about," Sam stated, looking at Cat. "She's as lovely as you, Luna."

"Catherine, this is Samuel Lawrence," Luna explained. "He sat with us on the trip from Rome to Miami. He entertained Nico with stories of his world travels."

Sam took Catherine's hand and gently kissed it. She was captivated by his smile, which was so like her one-time sweetheart's smile. She blushed and looked away, shocked by the reminder of how much it still hurt to have lost her true love all those decades ago.

"Nice to meet you, Sam. Do you live in Rome?" Cat questioned.

"No. I live here in Jacksonville. I'm in the import business. I had meetings in Florence and Rome, which is why I was in Italy."

"My brother has—or had—a similar business. His name was Jim Emerson. Did you know him?"

"Why, yes. I didn't know him well, but our paths crossed a few times. He didn't tell me he has such a charming sister. And you said 'had.' Did he sell the business?"

The color drained from Catherine's face. "No. He passed away recently. He had a heart attack."

Sam looked stricken. "I'm so sorry. I hadn't heard."

Seeing the luggage start to arrive on the belt, Nico muscled his way through the crowd of passengers and grabbed his bag from the carousel. He then retrieved Luna's large floral suitcase and rejoined the group.

"Sam, can you visit us on Amelia Island?" Nico asked. "Can he come for dinner, Zia Catherine? I know he does not have a wife to cook for him."

Cat recovered her composure and answered Nico's question. "That's a lovely idea. Sam, would you join us for dinner on Saturday around seven? I'll give you my address. Do you have any family you would like to include, as well?"

"That would be great. Thank you. And I don't have any kids or family, but thanks for asking. I haven't been to the island in a long time. I usually head to Jax Beach."

Cat fished through her purse and found a notebook and pen. "I'll add my cell number in case you need to contact us."

Sam took the paper while flashing a smile that was so similar to the one in her memories. He located his suitcase and headed toward the exit after saying goodbye to his new friends.

Chapter 6

TELEPATHY

Driving over the bridge to Amelia Island, Luna gazed out over the pale-green marshlands and the silver-blue river below. "The Lowcountry is beautiful and so different from Tuscany. I imagined all of Florida was similar to Miami. I am glad you told me it was a marshland on your island, like the movie *The Prince of Tides*. Nico and I watched the film to get a feeling for the landscape."

"I grew up in Jacksonville, which is fifteen miles south of the airport. I always loved visiting Amelia. I'm fortunate this island is my home," said Cat. "The marshes, the ancient oak trees covered in Spanish moss, and the historic town are lovely."

"And the beach!" said Nico.

"Yes. We have a great beach here, Nico," Cat said, seeing the excitement in his eyes. "Many writers and artists make their home here. There's a politically progressive community here, and that's important, too. We have come out of the most incompetent administration in our history, and we need people who share my concern about the future of our democracy."

"Yes, your last president was a classic narcissist, a mad king. But the ship has been righted," Luna said. "Concerns of human nature, power, and politics have befuddled mankind since ancient days."

"You're right. After the election, it helped to know that many Americans put the welfare of the country over their party politics. I'll be forever grateful to those on the right who voted against the last president and his sycophants. And of course, the incredible actions of the African American community turned the tide."

"We do hope societies are moving in the direction of goodness and enlightenment, but the shadowy side of humanity is ever present," Luna noted.

"And not likely to be overcome any time soon," replied Cat.

Their conversation subsided as they drove through the dappled sunlight beneath a canopy of majestic live oaks that were dripping with lacy moss. When they arrived at the south end, they toured the resort and drove through American Beach, which was one of the few beaches in the south that had allowed African Americans from the 1930s to the 1950s. The long-gone nightclub, Evans' Rendezvous, had hosted many famous entertainers of the time, including Dinah Washington and Ray Charles.

Then they headed north along the beach road, driving past midcentury houses and mini mansions. The homes were surrounded by palm trees, crepe myrtles, and colorful oleander. Cat took her guests to the northeast part of the isle, where surfers' pickup trucks lined the road beside eclectic beach shacks and new Lowcountry-style houses. Nico watched as suntanned teens hoisted surfboards from their trucks and jogged over the boardwalk to the beach.

"There are thirteen miles of beach from the state park at the north end to the park at the south end," said Cat. "Would you like to see the beach?"

"Sì, per favore. I would like to see the surfers, too," Nico said.

Cat could tell Nico wanted to try surfing himself. She found a place to park on the side of the road, and they walked over the boardwalk, past the sea oats gently waving on the dunes, to the beach. Massive white clouds sailed over the blue-green water, and a gentle breeze swept across the broad, pale sand beach.

"I have never seen such a wide beach," Luna exclaimed, inhaling the fresh ocean air and removing her shoes to enjoy the soft sand. "Beautiful. And the waves are much louder than I expected."

"Yeah, since we're on the Atlantic coast, we sometimes get powerful crashing waves. There are some good breakers today." Cat looked out over the water and pointed to a sailboat moving quickly in the waves.

"Look at those birds diving in the ocean! You would think they would hurt their heads," said Nico.

"I'm always amazed that the pelicans don't have brain damage," Cat noted. "Oh, Nico! Look to the right. Can you see the dolphin?"

"Bellisimo! There are three dolphins coming out of the water." Nico ran ahead, took off his shoes, and rolled up his pant legs. He waded into the warm ocean, grinning from ear to ear.

Luna and Cat strolled to the water's edge, enjoying this first time being together, and Cat said, "You must be tired after your long journey, but I thought I would drive you home through the downtown area. I'm so thrilled to share my island with both of you and, of course, to meet you. It's such an unexpected joy to have you here."

"We are happy to see your home, Catherine. The pictures do not do it justice. I truly wish that one day you will visit us in the glorious city of Siena."

"I would love to see your home, too. Maybe someday, Luna."

Luna's phone chimed, announcing a text. "Please excuse me." Luna strolled down the beach and made a phone call. She spoke in Italian, her voice hushed but intense. A few minutes later, she rejoined Cat, who suggested it might be time to head home.

"Nico, it is time to go," Luna called out as she waved to get his attention. Cat could tell that Nico would have been happy to remain at the beach all day.

After arriving at the cottage and unpacking, Luna and Nico took a quick nap. A while later, they joined Cat on the front porch. Luna toured the fragrant garden and breathed in the scent of the roses. Lemonade, white wine, and cookies were set out on the wicker table, along with two books. Cat handed a photo album to her sister when she returned to the porch.

"Luna, I thought you'd like to see pictures of our mother. She was sweet and beautiful and was a wonderful mom. We were a very happy family." Cat opened the album to a family portrait. "I love this photo of the four of us. Did you know that she perished on her way home from visiting her family in Toronto?"

"Yes," Luna said with sadness in her eyes. "What happened exactly?"

"Her plane crashed in a blizzard. There were no survivors," Cat explained. "That was such a dark period for Jim and Dad and me. A part of me died, too, that day, and I know my dad and brother felt the same way."

"Sì, Nurse Angelina kept up to date with Maria through her old au pair family in Siena," Luna said. "She gave me a notebook with all the details of Maria's life. That is how I came to know of your birth and that Emerson was your last name. When I return home, I will begin the search for my birth father."

"Ever since our mother died, I've been terrified to fly. I haven't taken one flight. I know it's irrational, but I can't make myself even buy a plane ticket. Jim had the opposite reaction. He wanted to see the world because he believed tomorrow was never guaranteed. He'd been to every continent except Antarctica, and that was on his wish list."

"I understand. Perhaps you could take a ship to Italy someday," suggested Luna.

Nico knelt beside Luna as she turned the yellowed pages of the album. They smiled, pointed to various photos, and chatted away in Italian. Cat poured the drinks and watched her new family embrace her past. Looking at Luna and Nico, Cat said, "My dad did fly, but not very often. When my nonna and papa passed away when I was in high school, Jim, Dad, and I drove to Toronto. And when Stella, our mother's friend, crosses over, I'll drive there again."

A thought popped into Catherine's mind. "Luna, when is your birthday?"

"I was born on the first day of May. Why do you ask?"

Cat stood and leaned against the railing. "Mom was usually a happy person. But every May Day, May first, she was distracted and gloomy. Even as a small child, I thought it was odd because it's the celebration of the Virgin Mary, and she always went to mass at the Catholic church near us. Now I know she was mourning her lost child. She used to say, 'The Rose of May is far away.' I never understood what she meant until Stella told me Mom named her first baby Rose."

"Oh my, Rose is what she named me. Incredible. It does make sense, as Mother Mary is called the 'Rose of May.'"

"I was named after Saint Catherine of Siena, which was the name of the church Mom attended as a child in Toronto. And I had an imaginary friend named Luna when I was young."

"Remarkable, mia sorella! I had a make-believe friend as a child, as well, whom I spoke to in English. Questions would come into my mind, and I wrote them down and then answered them. I believe that a true friend does not have to be in one's sight, simply held in one's heart."

Cat paused for a moment, digesting what Luna had just said. "Oh my gosh!" she said as she picked up the second book she'd brought out. She flitted through the pages of her old journal until she found the right passage. "Luna, look at this."

Luna began to read: "'A true friend does not have to be in one's sight, simply held in one's heart.'"

"I knew it! I knew I was connecting with a real person when I wrote these things, not an imaginary friend," cried Cat. "You and I were communicating telepathically! It all began after Mom died, when I had a strong urge to converse with someone. Amazing."

Nico looked at Cat, then Luna. "Is that possible? Veramente?"

"I can't think of another explanation, Nico. There's so much we don't know about the mind, the soul, intuition, and, yes, telepathy," answered Catherine. "I always had a tingling sensation in my body when I talked to my imaginary friend way back when."

Luna said, "Oh my! I, too, believed I was communicating with a real being. I presumed it was a ghost or an angel. But it faded over time."

"For me, as well," Cat said. "I guess we connected when I was really missing my mom. As I healed, I no longer needed it, and my ability to connect faded away. And now my real 'imaginary friend' is sitting in front of me!"

"Is our bond genetic or spiritual or both? Do you think our mother had this ability, too, Catherine?"

Cat eased back into her Muskoka chair and contemplated the question. "I'm not sure about Mom, but our telepathy could be genetic or simply a part of our souls. I know I can often tap into what people are thinking, especially during a situation when emotions are intense. When I'm editing, I understand what my authors are trying to say in their writing, even when it isn't on the page."

"When I return to Italy, we will have to see if we can use our telepathy once again," said Luna. "We can set up a test."

"That's a wonderful idea!" Cat exclaimed. "We can see if there's still a spark of the connection we had in our youth. There are so many things about getting older that are distressing. It would be great if a tiny bit of the child inside us is still there."

Nico popped a cookie in his mouth. "What kind of books do you edit, Zia?"

"I usually edit mystery and suspense. I've edited an occasional romance, as well. I co-wrote a memoir for an acquaintance, but I don't want to do that again."

"Why is that?" asked Luna.

"The family history included infidelity, criminal actions, and bizarre behavior by family members. I learned way too much about the guy's creepy relatives." Cat said.

Nico laughed. "There are many strange stories in this world other than the supernatural. They say that truth is stranger than fiction."

"That's certainly true, Nico. To date, I haven't edited a paranormal novel, but I've always been fascinated by the subject. Now that I know I have the ability to communicate telepathically, it makes me want to explore the concept. I've thought about writing my own novel, but I'm not sure if I could actually do it."

Nico said, "I love fantasy and science fiction books and movies. You should write a book, and then I can say I know a real author."

"At the moment, I'm editing a cookbook for my friend Lisa. It's a collection of family recipes. She comes from a large Italian family, so she's got a built-in market for the book."

"Mia madre was a chef, the best in all of Palermo. And she taught me very much in the kitchen. But—but we had to leave Sicily," Nico said, looking downcast.

Seeing his sadness, Luna jumped into the conversation. "Carlotta Alessi was an excellent chef. She found work easily when she came to Siena. She and Nico rented the top floor of my house, and we all became grandi amici," Luna said with fondness. "I came to love them both. Then there was the accident, and our dear Carlotta left us."

Nico's shoulders dropped, and he slumped onto the top step of the porch. His face was twisted in pain, as if all the joy in life had vanished in an instant. He was holding back tears, staring into the growing darkness. Luna joined him and placed her arm around his shoulders, trying to comfort him. Nico was still young, and he missed his mother, plain and simple.

"I wish I could have met her, Nico," Cat said. "Knowing you now, I'm sure she was a wonderful mother." Looking at the time, she added, "I'm going to go inside and make us some dinner. Why don't we drive into town afterward and get some ice cream? There's a fudge shop that has lots of yummy flavors."

"A very good distraction," Luna whispered as she walked past Cat on her way into the house. "A treat is often how I handle things when Nico is upset. Most days, he is fine, but his emotions can overwhelm him at times."

Chapter 7

THE FIRE

"How's it going with your visitors?" Lisa asked when Cat answered her phone.

Catherine was snuggled in bed when her friend called. "It's amazing. I have an incredible affection for two people I just met. I've never experienced anything like this. And listening to Luna talk is like being with my mom again. We've had so many things to talk about, but it broke my heart when Nico's mother was mentioned."

"Do you know how she died?"

"Yes. Luna told me about it after Nico went to bed. His mom, Carlotta, was a chef in Sicily. Nico's father, Salvatore, took off shortly after he was born. Then he filed for divorce just before Nico's first birthday."

"That must have been hard on him," Lisa said, knowing that without Luna, Nico would have been alone in the world.

"Nico and his mom lived in Palermo, and when he was ten, a gang of young men who fashioned themselves after the mafia—they called themselves the 'I Demoni'—tried to recruit Nico. When he refused, the restaurant where his mother worked went up in flames. Carlotta and Nico lived nearby and saw it burn."

"Oh my God!" Lisa said. "I thought things like that only happened in the movies."

"Carlotta was so frightened that they left Sicily and moved to Rome. Shortly after, she found a job in Siena, and they rented the top floor of Luna's house. Luna said she was an excellent chef. Then, when Nico was a couple years older, the accident happened. Late one night, as she was closing the restaurant, there was a fight between two drunken patrons. Carlotta tried to break up the fight. One of the men struck her, and she fell and hit her head on the stone hearth. She died instantly."

There was a long silence on both ends of the phone. "What a terrible tragedy," Lisa finally said. "Poor Nico. How old was he when his mom died?"

"He was twelve, and he's fifteen now. He seems quite well adjusted until the memories flood back and overwhelm him. That happened tonight when we spoke about his mom. But he said he often feels his mother around him, which is comforting."

"Luna has been trying to locate his dad in the hopes that he will relinquish custody of Nico so Luna can legally adopt him. Carlotta asked Luna to take care of Nico if anything ever happened to her. She made this request in front of Nico and Viola, Luna's lawyer. Nico's grandparents on both sides have passed away, and Carlotta was an only child. His dad has a younger brother in Sicily who's brilliant but eccentric, so there was no family on his father's side to take him in."

"My heart aches for the child."

"Why don't you and Dominic join us for dinner on Saturday? I've also invited a man from Jacksonville who Luna and Nico met on the flight from Rome. He's in the import business like Jim was, and he actually knew him."

"Sounds good. I'll check with Dom, but it should be fine. Now, turn out the lights and get some sleep, Catherine. You've had a long day."

Cat hung up and turned off the light. She wrestled with the covers and finally threw them to the floor. "How can I help Nico?" she whispered into the night. "I feel as if he's my responsibility, too."

Finally, she drifted into sleep. In her dream, it was her new acquaintance Sam Lawrence who was her husband, not Zach. They were sitting on the front porch of the cottage, sipping wine and listening to an old Nat King Cole album playing on a vintage record player. Sam stood up and took her hand, and they danced to the enchanting melody. The diamond on her left ring finger sparkled in the candlelight, and he softly sang in her ear as she melted into his arms.

Blaring sirens wrenched Catherine from her dream. Flickering light seeped through the venetian blinds. Jumping out of bed, she dashed to the front porch to see what was happening. Fire trucks and police vehicles were racing to the Tiger Point Marina, not far from Cat's house. Luna and Nico joined her as they watched the flames fly into the dark sky.

"What is burning, Catherine?" asked Luna.

"It's the marina. Looks like a main building is on fire."

"I hate fires," Nico said, then went back into the house. The screen door slammed behind him.

Firefighters quickly doused the flames as onlookers gathered near the marina, keeping a safe distance from the toxic fumes. It was obvious that the boats in the building had been destroyed by the fire.

"I think they have it under control," Cat said, referring to the firemen. "The smell of the smoke is making me sick. Let's go inside. I have a nice bottle of Chianti we can open."

"Excellent idea. I do not think I can sleep right now."

Cat brought the wine and glasses into the living room, and the women settled onto the sofa. "Luna, what will happen if you can't find Nico's father?"

"I am still working on that with my lawyer. We have followed all of her advice and will wait to see."

Cat poured the rich ruby liquid into the crystal glasses. "Does Nico want to move back to Sicily?"

"No, I do not think so. The gang of hoodlums is still active, and they are far too dangerous. Two of them even came to Siena, to our home, and threatened Carlotta and Nico. He is happy to stay with me in Tuscany. We laid his mother to rest in the Palermo cemetery with her parents, but we have no other plans to return."

"I'd love to see your city one day. In the photos online, it looks as if it hasn't changed in centuries."

"That is true. There have been glorious times as well as tragedies in my city. It is one of the best examples of civic building in Italy, although there are beautiful churches, too. From the mid-1200s to the mid-1300s, there was much growth. Then the Black Death killed one third of the citizens."

"That's awful," Cat said. "I guess there have always been, and always will be, plagues and pandemics."

"The worst for Siena came two hundred years later. The Florentines placed Siena under siege for eighteen months and defeated the city. All progress stopped, and Siena was frozen in time. But it was a blessing in disguise. The city is a living museum, and progress has not destroyed it."

"Fernandina is old, but it cannot compare to Italy," Cat said. "The Spanish first arrived here in 1562, but that is relatively recent compared to Italy."

"I had no idea the Europeans were in Florida so long ago. I will have to learn more about your island. And learn about Canada, too, since I have discovered that my mother was from Toronto."

Catherine swirled the wine in her glass, then took a large sip. "We're both half Canadian, and Jim was, too. I'd thought about moving north to that wonderful country if our recent election had gone a different way."

"I know what you mean. The politics in Italy can be volatile and frustrating, too."

"I was just thinking, Luna. I miss my brother so much, but it's as if he gave me a final gift: you and Nico. I know you would have tried to contact me if you hadn't heard from Jim. I'm glad you reached out to him first."

Luna leaned over and gave Catherine's hand a quick squeeze. "I am grateful, as well. And I am thankful that I was talking to a real person when I was an adolescent."

"What has it been like raising a teenager? Most parents have many years to prepare."

Luna chuckled and shook her head. "He is a marvelous boy. But there have been stressful moments. As an accountant, I am used to working with numbers. They are much easier to deal with than the hormones of a teenager. I trust him to stay out of trouble. He was frightened by the gang of boys in Palermo. And then seeing the fire at his mother's restaurant had a profound impact on him, as you saw tonight."

"Poor guy. I know how terrible it is to lose your mother at such a young age. At least I had my dad and Jim. But he seems to be doing really well with you as his guardian. I know our mother is smiling down on you."

"Thank you for your kind words. It is incredible being with you, Catherine. I am only sorry I did not get a chance to meet Jim before he passed."

"Me, too. He would have loved you and Nico. I enjoy working with the high school students in town from time to time. But sometimes when I hear of some of their antics and problems, I'm glad I don't have that responsibility full-time."

"The love I feel for Nico completely outweighs the challenges," Luna said.

"That's understandable. He is an incredible young man."

Chapter 8

VERY MUCH IN LOVE

The ringing phone startled Cat. Half awake, she fished around the nightstand for her cell phone, her brain foggy from the late-night wine. The alarm clock indicated it was just after 7:00 AM. "Hello?"

"M-Ms. Emerson? This is Herbert Robinson. Sorry to call so early. Miss Alma, my neighbor, said she saw a man going into your brother's apartment two nights after he died. She didn't see his face but said that he was a thin man and that he might have had a key."

"Did she mention anything else about the intruder?"

"N-no. It was dark, and she was too far away. She lives across the parking lot from your brother's old place. She likes to keep an eye on things around here."

"Thanks for calling, Mr. Robinson. Please let me know if anything else comes up."

"S-sure thing Ms. Emerson."

"And thank you for letting the movers in to get Jim's desk and the rest of the boxes."

"Y-you're welcome."

Cat rolled over in bed and stared at the ceiling. *Someone did break into the apartment, and they might even have had a key. Did Jim get himself involved in something he shouldn't have? What on earth could the intruder have been looking for? And did he find it? One thing's certain: it was definitely an amateur who searched Jim's place.*

Slowly, Cat dragged herself out of bed and opened the blinds. A heavy fog shrouded the street, making it hard to see anything, including the smoldering ruins of the charred marina. *Small mercies. At least Nico won't have to see the results of last night's fire.* After slipping into shorts and a t-shirt and running a brush through her hair, she caught her reflection in the mirror. *I look like Luna, my older sister! I never in a million years thought I'd ever say that. Miracles do happen.*

The heavenly aromas of coffee and cinnamon floated down the hallway and reached Cat before she made it to the kitchen. Luna was seated at the kitchen table, speaking excitedly in Italian on her phone. She quickly ended the conversation and smiled at Cat, saying, "Buongiorno, Catherine. I hope you do not mind. I brought coffee with me, and I found cinnamon rolls in the freezer. Nico loves them."

"The coffee smells wonderful, and I'm glad I have someone to share the rolls with. Sometimes I long to be with people in the morning. I like the freedom of working from home, but I miss the feeling of community I had at the office. I often spend mornings at the coffee shop on Centre Street just so I can chat with other people."

"Do you think you will ever work at an office again?" Luna asked, checking on the coffee.

"Only if the right opportunity came along," Cat said decisively. "It would have to be on the island. I don't want to commute into the city anymore. Financially, I'm doing okay, and now I'll inherit Jim's share of the business. That reminds me, I saw crates of large paintings in Jim's warehouse when I was over there the other day. Jim's business partner,

Brad, said they have a connection in Florence who is hoping to sell them in the US. I thought it was odd that they were into high-end artwork."

"You said they were involved in commercial real estate. Do you think they were looking to decorate the buildings they sell?" Luna suggested.

"Maybe. I hadn't thought of that. Luna, is everything okay? You sounded upset on the phone."

"Si, si, all is fine. Simply a nervous client who is concerned about a government inquiry into his taxes. It was a good time for me to call. It is early here in Florida, but it is the afternoon in Italy."

"Since I don't speak Italian, I was worried that it might be bad news about Nico's birth father."

Just at that moment, Nico bounded into the kitchen. "Yum, something smells good."

The timer on the stove dinged, and Luna took the rolls from the oven. She spread the creamy icing on top and slid three rolls onto plates. She poured two cups of coffee and a glass of freshly squeezed orange juice. She was right at home in Cat's kitchen.

"Would you like to go to Orlando today?" Cat asked her guests. "I could book a hotel online, and we could stay for a couple of nights. Disney World and Universal Studios are both there."

Nico grinned. "You may think I am too old, but I want to see Disney World. My mother promised we would go to the one in France, but we never did."

"Well then, let's go. I'll book a hotel after breakfast. It's foggy right now, but hopefully the sun will be shining when we get to Orlando."

A couple hours later, they began packing up the car. The fog started to lift, and Cat felt better than she had in ages. In all the years she'd mentored teens, she'd never had a maternal yearning and hadn't thought she ever would. Now, when she looked at Nico, a wave of motherly love washed over her. For the first time in her life, she experienced the love a parent has for their child. She imagined she felt how adoptive parents felt.

They were just about to leave when a USPS truck blocked the driveway. "Morning, ma'am. Glad I caught you," the driver said as he hopped out of the truck.

Cat thanked the driver. "I wasn't expecting a package. I wonder who it's from. The return address is a PO Box in Jacksonville." Opening the small box, Cat was surprised to see a brand-new men's leather wallet inside. "Why on earth would anyone send me a wallet? It's nice, but I have no use for it. Nico, would you like it?" She handed the wallet to the teen.

"Si. It is a Borlino wallet. Very nice."

"It's probably from an old client. I'm surprised there isn't a note," Cat said as she dropped the packaging in the trunk. Taking a final look around, she said, "Should we head out?"

As she backed down the driveway, Cat asked, "Would you mind if we stopped by the cemetery before we go? I want to freshen the flowers for Jim."

"That would be lovely," said Luna. "I would like to pay my respects to our brother."

They went down a rutted, unpaved road in Bosque Bello cemetery, driving under the swaying Spanish moss dangling from the massive oaks. Mist swirled around the statues and headstones marking the graves of generations of local families.

"This is an amazing graveyard, Zia Catherine," Nico stated. "It looks like it could be in a scary movie. Can I take photos on my phone?"

"Of course. We'll stop in the old section, then visit Jim in the new area."

Cat parked, and they wandered among the crumbling brick walls and rusted iron fences that separated the family plots. Cat was saddened by the number of small graves. "A hundred years ago, so many children died young."

"Yes, modern medicine has saved countless lives," said Luna as she knelt down and touched a headstone. "This dear little girl was born in 1914 and passed away in 1917."

Nico took a photo of Luna and the weathered stone. "Why do innocent children die young? Why do good people like mia madre die too soon? Why do bad people have long lives?"

"I don't know, Nico," answered Cat. "And why do some immoral people have wealth and the power to hurt others? They break the law and get away with corruption."

"The nature of good and evil is a mystery," Luna stated.

They made their way back to the car, and Cat drove to the newer section and parked close to a plot with freshly laid sod. Catherine took a bouquet of roses and a small container of water from the backseat. Slowly, she approached her brother's grave, holding back tears.

"Zia, may I put the flowers in the vase?" Nico asked.

"That would be lovely, Nico," Cat said.

The three of them spent a few minutes walking among the graves, pondering life and death, and then Cat turned to them and said, "On a happier note, are you ready to go to Disney World? The amusement parks became so busy after the pandemic was over. There was a pent-up need to gather together in a place of fantasy and fun. I'm sure there will be lots of people there today."

A while later, they were on Highway 95 South, and the traffic was light. They took the exit for Highway 4 toward Orlando. Cat hadn't been to the city since over a decade ago, when she had accompanied Lisa and her boys on a vacation to the amusement park.

Cat was interested in learning more about their home in Italy. She looked in the rearview mirror and caught Nico's eye. "Nico, tell me about Siena. What do you like most about it?" she asked.

"My favorite is the Palio. It is the horse race held in the center of the city every year on the Piazza del Campo. The persone go crazy cheering for their rider. So fun to watch."

"I've read about the race," Cat said. "How many horses and riders participate?"

"There are seventeen contrade, or districts, in the city. There is a horse and rider from each. They do not have saddles; everyone rides bareback," said Nico.

Luna added, "There is much pageantry before the race begins, with flag-throwing competitions and a grand procession. The horses are blessed at the church in each contrade, and the riders wear medieval costumes. The winner receives a palio, which is a banner. It is mainly for bragging rights among the districts. And there is a lot of betting."

"That sounds like fun," said Cat. "The city must be packed during the festival. Is the Piazza where that beautiful tower is? I remember seeing a photo of it."

"Yes. It is called the Torre del Mangia by the Palazzo Publico, the town hall. It is the second highest tower in all of Italy. There is also a lovely fountain in the Piazza. The magnificent Duomo, the cathedral, is a short walk from there," stated Luna.

"It must be a magical place to live," said Cat. "Maybe a trip on an ocean liner is in my future. I would love to tour Italy with you both and experience your country."

"It would be wonderful for you to spend time with us. Our mother was in Tuscany for a full year before she returned home to Canada. And then later, of course, she married your father. I wanted to ask you, how did your parents meet, Catherine?" Luna inquired.

"Mom grew up in the suburbs of Toronto, as you know. She was in her final year of university and went on spring break to Panama City Beach. Many students go to Florida for their vacations to get away from school and parents and to enjoy the beaches and the warm weather."

"Is that near to your home?" Nico said.

"No. Panama City Beach is on the west side of Florida, on the Gulf Coast. My dad was from Jacksonville, and he was on spring break there with a group of friends. He said he saw Mom and it was love at first sight. They met every day for a week and exchanged phone numbers. He decided he couldn't live without her and traveled to Toronto a few months later."

"When your heart calls out for another, it cannot be denied," commented Luna. "How romantic. But it must have been hard for her to leave her family in Canada."

"Yes, it was. Yet she knew that Scott Emerson was her true love and that he would never desert her like her boyfriend in Italy had. She hated cold weather, so living in Florida was a dream come true. They were very much in love until the day she died."

"What happened to your mother?" asked Nico.

"Mom was visiting her family in Toronto. She was flying from there to Rochester, New York, to see a friend before returning home to Florida. She was on a small regional jet, and a blizzard came up quicker than expected. They think it was a wind shear. A huge gust of wind caused the pilot to lose control, and the plane crashed into Lake Ontario."

"Così terribile," said Nico. "How sad for your family. So you must know very well how I miss my mother."

"Yes, Nico, I really do. I was ten when she died. You learn to live with the loss, but it has long-lasting effects. As a result of her death, I won't get on an airplane, and I don't like winter and snow. The only blizzard I want to see is at a Dairy Queen. That's an ice cream treat at a fast-food restaurant."

"I would like that kind of blizzard. I love ice cream," said Nico.

Catherine asked, "Luna, were you ever married?"

"Yes, but not for long. I met my husband while studying accounting. He was very kind and reserved. I thought he was shy and naturally not very affectionate. But I learned soon after the wedding that he was in love with another classmate. A man."

"I'm guessing that he was trying to conform to society's norms and marry a woman even though it served neither of you."

"That is correct. A divorce came soon after I discovered the truth. I have dated several men over the years, but I never remarried. What was your husband like?"

Cat chose her words carefully, knowing that Nico was listening. "Robert was charismatic, like most narcissists. He would lure people into his web with flattery, and he had an ability to manipulate them for his own benefit. I fell hard for his charm in the beginning, but that didn't last long. Behind closed doors, he was verbally abusive."

"We are alike in that we chose poor husbands," Luna said. "Perhaps we are not good judges of character."

Nico grinned and stayed silent.

As they got close to Orlando, they drove past a sign for the town of Cassadaga. "That's a small town of psychics, mediums, and healers," Cat said. "Luna, maybe we could stop in Cassadaga on the way home and see if we can communicate with our mother through a medium. If not, we can go the next time you visit me."

"It would be interesting," said Luna. "And of course we will come to Florida another time."

"Maybe I could talk to my mother, too!" Nico exclaimed. "There is much I want to tell her."

They were interrupted when Cat's phone rang. She used her Bluetooth to answer a call from Hazel.

47

"Hello, Catherine. I'm sorry to bother you, but have you talked to Rodney lately? He hasn't come in to work for two days, and his daughter said he isn't answering his phone. Diana's driving in today from Gainesville to check his apartment. She's worried, and so am I."

"No, I haven't heard from him. That is strange. The last time I spoke with him was when I was at the office to pick up Jim's items. I hope he's okay. Let me know if you or Diana hear from him." After a few pleasantries, Cat ended the call.

"Rodney runs the warehouse for Jim's company. He's had some troubles with gambling before. Maybe he fell off the wagon and is holed up in a casino somewhere," Cat told her passengers. "It must be upsetting for his daughter, Diana."

Chapter 9

DISNEY WORLD

The trio was impressed by the soaring ceiling in the lobby of the Disney Animal Kingdom Lodge. Cat had read that the decorations and African artifacts in the hotel were authentic, and they took time to marvel at each one. They were escorted to their savanna-view villa in the Kandini Village, and Nico rushed out onto the balcony.

"Meraviglioso!" Nico called out. "There is a struzzo, an ostrich, out there. So cool."

49

Cat and Luna joined him on the balcony after they sorted out the room arrangements and put their suitcases away. They were sharing a room with two queen beds, and they gave Nico the separate room with the king-sized bed.

Luna was seemingly in awe as she gazed at the scene before her. "This is such an unexpected delight. I thought Disney World was only Mickey Mouse and princesses. This is an adventure within an adventure," she said. "Look, there is a zebra."

Cat suggested they get unpacked and then plan the rest of their day. She and Luna went inside to get organized, leaving Nico on the balcony. He heard a soft sound and looked up to see a giraffe swing his large head toward their balcony. Nico slowly approached and gazed into the big deep-brown eyes of the creature. An overwhelming wave of sympathy washed over the young man as he locked eyes with the giraffe. The graceful neck, stubby horns, and perky ears of the spotted animal delighted him, and he was surprised by the long whiskers around the creature's mouth. He felt grateful that the beautiful giant was here, but he was also sad that it wasn't in the wild in Africa.

Nico quietly called for Luna and Cat. They came outside and were swept into the energy that permeated the area. The three stood silently on the balcony, staring into the giraffe's eyes until he finally swung his patterned head and slowly ambled away on impossibly long legs.

"That was amazing!" Nico said. "Bellisimo! The giraffa was astonishing. Yet I felt sorry for him. Do people have the right to take animals from their natural home, even if they are well taken care of?"

"One more question about humankind," Cat said. "And it involves our place in the natural world. It was a wonderful experience, though," she added. "So, are you ready to meet Mickey Mouse?"

The remainder of the day was a joyful tour of the "happiest place on earth" according to Disney fans. When they first arrived at Magic Kingdom, Cat almost had a panic attack from being in a crowd of people. Even though social distancing was a thing of the past, it was hard to overcome the residual fear of large gatherings.

They strolled down Main Street USA, popping in and out of the shops, enjoying ice cream cones, and drinking lots of water to keep cool. They went on the traditional rides that Nico had read about: Pirates of the Caribbean, the Dumbo ride, It's A Small World, Peter Pan's Flight, and the Haunted Mansion. Cat and Luna accompanied Nico on Splash Mountain and enjoyed watching the story of Brer Rabbit from the movie *Song of the South*. There were short drops on the track, but they weren't expecting the final plunge into the water. After screaming at the top of their lungs, the sisters laughed at their own fear.

"I do not like heights!" Luna stated as they exited the ride.

"I don't, either! Nico, I think you'll have to go on some of the scarier rides by yourself," said Cat.

"I am not afraid of any of the rides," Nico boasted.

"Of course not! You're fifteen, not fifty-something," Cat said with a laugh. "Let's get dinner, and then we can stay for the fireworks."

The following day, they returned to Magic Kingdom. They completed Nico's wish list of rides and attractions, including the Treasures of the 7 Seas and a ride around the park on the train. Nico went on the Tower of Terror on his own, and he finished by taking an elevator to the Astro Orbiter, the Dumbo-like ride with a great view of the park. At Animal Kingdom, they went on the simulator ride called Flights of Passage, which was based on the movie *Avatar*, and Expedition Everest, a roller coaster through the mountain with close encounters with Yetis. Cat and Luna hadn't realized there was huge plunge at the end of the ride, too, and their screams could once again be heard across the park.

Their final evening at Disney World was spent at the Animal Kingdom Lodge. The women sat beside the Samawati Springs pool as Nico headed for the 128-foot-drop waterslide. They dined at Jiko - The Cooking Place, savoring the delicious African and Mediterranean food. Luna and Cat enjoyed specialty wines from South Africa. After dropping their exhausted bodies into bed that night, Catherine, Luna, and Nico folded the joyful memories into their hearts. This was a marvelous family vacation none of them had ever expected, and they would always cherish it.

Chapter 10

FAMILY GATHERING

Catherine's excited energy made it hard for her to put on her makeup before the dinner party on Saturday night. She touched up her lipstick then slipped into her new white eyelet dress with a violet ribbon at the waist. She placed several bangles on her wrist and gold hoops in her ears. She pinned back her hair over her right ear with her mother's pearl-studded barrette.

Earlier in the day, she'd asked Nico to help her unwrap the dishes she'd inherited from her mom. Cat rarely used the Tuscan-made Meridiana ceramic plates and bowls. It had been a long time since she'd had a dinner party. They'd opened the antique art-deco-hope chest that Stella had given Maria and Scott as a wedding present. Cat had run her hand across the cherry wood inlays on the top of the chest that sat at the foot of her bed. After lifting the lid, a gentle rose fragrance from sachets had greeted them. Cat had handed the cloth-covered plates to Nico, who took them into the dining room. She'd followed with the salad bowls.

"These are beautiful, Zia. The pattern is similar to my mother's Meridiana Ceramiche dishes. I have them packed away for when I have my own home," Nico had said.

"I love the blue-and-yellow pattern on these. My mother collected them over the years. I only use them on special occasions. And this family dinner is certainly special to me."

Now Cat checked her reflection in the mirror one more time. The doorbell rang, and she rushed to open it. *Sam's early*, she thought. *Why am*

I so nervous? I'm being ridiculous. There was no one on the front porch, but a package was sitting on the doormat. She retrieved it and brought it into the living room, where Luna and Dominic, Lisa's husband, were comparing stories about their hometowns in Italy. Dom had been born in Lucca, and there was a friendly rivalry between the two cities.

"Oh, another package? Is this from a client, too?" Luna asked.

"I'm not sure. I think the return address is the same." Cat opened it and found a small box inside. "Strange. It's a jar of expensive Parisian face cream. What the heck could it mean? Now I've received an Italian leather wallet and facial cream. I'm not getting the message. And I have no idea who sent them."

Nico's voice called out from the kitchen, "Zia Catherine, would you please come here?"

Cat put the jar of face cream on the hall table and went to stand in the kitchen doorway. She was transfixed by Nico as he prepared food and chatted with Lisa. She felt a wave of love unlike anything she'd experienced before—a profound maternal love she didn't know her heart could feel. She entered the room and gently put her hand on Nico's shoulder.

"This young man is a natural chef. It's a pleasure working with him," said Lisa. "His mother taught him well."

Nico smiled. "It is fun learning from Miss Lisa. She is almost as good a cook as my mother."

Lisa laughed and threw a piece of chopped tomato at Nico. "Almost? Well, maybe you're right, Nico. Luna said your mother was a brilliant chef."

"The best in all of Palermo."

"I love watching you two create a meal together," said Cat. "My kitchen has never been filled with so many wonderful aromas at one time."

"I think I need Nico to test more of my recipes. The cookbook could be improved by his input," said Lisa.

"Did you know that the first ever school for chefs was in Sicily and that the first cookbook published was Sicilian? It was in the fifth century BC in Syracuse, which was then ruled by the Greeks," said Nico. "The philosopher Plato lived for a time in Syracuse, as well."

53

"I remember from a college course that Plato left Athens after his teacher, Socrates, died, but I didn't know he went to Sicily. The whole idea of how democracy was tested then, as it was in our country recently, is fascinating," Cat said.

"I had no idea the ancient Greeks had a cooking school," stated Lisa. "I learned from my nonna that Sicily was ruled by many others over the centuries."

"Yes, the Greeks, Romans, Normans, Arabs, French, British, Spanish, and the Italian state. And most only took from the island, leaving the people in poverty. It is a very sad history, and one that led to the mafia," said Nico. "This is delicious," he added, biting into the food that Lisa had just taken out of a deep fryer. "I would be happy to try more of your recipes, Miss Lisa." He took another bite of his arancina, a deep-fried rice ball filled with mozzarella and Parmigiano-Reggiano cheese.

"I always enjoy Lisa's food," Cat said. "I wish Jim were here to see this. He just loved good Italian cooking." There was a lump in her throat as she spoke, and she forced a smile as she took a small bite of the arancina Nico handed her. "Delicious! We'd better save some for the others."

While preparing a salad, Nico returned to the conversation about Sicily. "I have studied the history of my homeland, Sicily, quite a bit," he began. "Being ruled by many nations did bring some good things. The Normans brought the vines for many types of wine. The Arabs brought rice, sugar cane, and the study of science. The Spanish brought chocolate and tomatoes from the New World. It was not all bad."

"You're right, Nico," Lisa said. "Unfortunately, over the past two centuries, there has been so much poverty and corruption. More recently, the mafia flourished before and after the World Wars. Many Sicilians ended up immigrating to America, Australia, and other countries to find a better way of life, just like my family did."

"Sì, and although it is better, there are new bands of young men who threaten the citizens. Even so, I do love Sicily, and maybe one day I will return to live there."

The doorbell rang again, interrupting their conversation. Cat passed through the living room, noticing that Dom and Luna were still engaged in conversation, and opened the front door. Sam stood there holding a massive bouquet of red and white roses, along with a bottle of wine.

Cat's heart did a back flip, and she grinned from ear to ear. "Please come in, Sam. I'm glad you could join us tonight." Her smile was still glued to her face as they entered the living room. "Sam, this is my friend Dominic, and you know Luna, of course."

"So good to see you again," said Luna.

Dom extended his hand. "Welcome, Sam. Do I know you? You look familiar."

"No, I don't think we've met, Dominic."

"Call me Dom. Can I get you a drink?"

"I've brought a Brunello, if you'd like to have it now."

"How did you know it was my favorite wine?" asked Cat. "Dom, would you please open the wine?" She went into the kitchen to arrange the roses in a vase.

Nico rushed from the kitchen to the living room. "Sam! Ciao. Come see what we are making."

"Sounds great, Nico." He followed the young man.

Dom handed a glass of an exquisite Brunello to both Luna and Cat as they joined him near the bar cart. He poured two more glasses of wine and took them into the kitchen for Lisa and Sam.

"Sam is very handsome," whispered Luna after Sam had gone into the kitchen.

Cat laughed. "He looks so much like my high school sweetheart. It's incredible. They could be brothers. But he also reminds me of the fact that my ex-boyfriend Zach broke my heart."

"There is pain in your voice. Has no one ever replaced Zach? Not even your ex-husband?" Luna asked.

"Luna, I've never thought of it that way, but I think you're right. A part of me loved my husband, Robert, at least in the beginning. But I never had the passion for him that I had for Zach."

Luna grinned. "Perhaps Sam can light a new desire for romance in you."

Before Cat could answer, everyone joined them in the living room. Nico carried an impressive antipasto platter. Sam brought out the arancini and marinara sauce. Lisa followed with paper plates and napkins decorated with sea turtles and starfish.

"The antipasto is Nico's handiwork," said Lisa. "He's a culinary artist as well as an impressive cook."

Nico blushed and thanked Lisa. "Cooking and playing video games are my passions. I think I inherited my love of food from my mother."

"This looks amazing, Nico," Sam said, looking at the platter of incredible food. "I love playing games, too," he added. "It's too bad that you and Luna aren't staying a little longer. We could have a game night."

"That would be fun. I play video games with my friends, and I used to play board games with my mother." Nico took his new wallet from his pocket and retrieved a photo of his mother. "This is who taught me to cook. Cara madre."

Each person looked at the photo, and everyone commented on Carlotta's beauty.

"Nico, may I look at your wallet?" Sam asked as Nico was about to put it back in his pocket.

"Si. It is a Borlino," Nico said as he handed it to the older man.

Looking at it carefully, Sam said, "I'm sorry to tell you, Nico, but this wallet is a fake. You can tell by the stitching. There are a lot of counterfeit products on the market these days. I've been around long enough to know the difference."

"How strange," Catherine said. "I received that in the mail. I don't know who it was from. I thought an old marketing client might have sent it to me. I had no idea it was a knock-off."

"The phony leather products that are imported these days so closely resemble the authentic articles that people are often duped. But this food sure looks authentic!"

Everyone dove into the array of cheese, meat, olives, crostini, and arancini. The wine complemented the food perfectly, and the conversation lagged as they enjoyed the appetizers.

Noticing that everyone was enjoying his rice balls, Nico said, "Did you know that they call these 'arancina' in Palermo, where they are round like an orange? And 'arancino' in Catania, in the east part of Sicily, where they are shaped like a cone similar to Mount Etna. There is much competition between the cities about food and many other things."

"You're so well informed, Nico," said Dom. "I wish our boys took an interest in history like you do."

"Grazie. Since I now live in Siena, I have learned to make a kind of pasta that is special to Tuscany. It is called 'pici,' and we are having Pici all'Etrusca as our first course tonight," said Nico. "My mother taught me to make this when we moved there."

"And we're having panzanella salad and veal saltimbocca," Lisa said.

"Are you planning to be a chef like your mother?" Dom asked.

"Sì. I have many of my mother's recipes, and I will learn much more when I attend scuola di cucina. I also inherited my mother's knives. They are in a special wooden box that Luna gave to me. I will work hard to make her proud."

"I am already proud of you, Nico, my soon-to-be son. I will be happy when you change your name to Nico Alessi-Bianchi. It will be a day of great celebration."

"Maybe we can all be there," Sam suggested. "I'm often in Italy. What do you think, everyone?"

"Dom and I are in," said Lisa. "And if we have enough notice, Cat can take a ship over."

Catherine blushed, knowing that her travel plans were not always convenient for others. "Perhaps a hypnotist can cure me of my fear of flying, but I doubt it. A slow boat to Italy is more likely."

"So the sister of a world traveler like Jim won't get on a plane?" Sam questioned. "That's surprising."

"Maybe in my next life I'll be a pilot and fly around the world. Until then—" A buzzer from the stove interrupted Cat. "Saved by the bell," she said and dashed into the kitchen.

Lisa followed her and took an amaretto cake out of the oven. "Sam's a good-looking guy, don't you think?" she whispered. "Maybe you should ask him out. Nico told me he's single."

"You're right, he's handsome, but he reminds me too much of Zach. It would be weird."

Preparing the last of the serving dishes, Lisa said, "Well, I think the food is ready. Let's call everyone for dinner."

The compact dining room was filled to capacity. The plates of food were carried to the table. They would be dining family style, which was typical Italian fashion. Candles placed on the fireplace and side tables provided a pleasant glow in the room. Dom opened another bottle of wine and filled the glasses as the diners passed the serving dishes around. An Andrea Bocelli CD played softly in the background.

Wow, oh wow! This is what a family gathering looks like. I've never had so many people in this room before. I'm so grateful, Catherine thought. *Mom, Dad, Jim, and Carlotta, are you here with us?*

Chapter 11

LOVE IS LIKE THE UNIVERSE

"What a great evening. Thanks so much for making dinner, Lisa. The food was fantastic, and I'm glad you had a chance to visit with Luna and Nico." Cat hugged Lisa and Dom as they said their goodbyes.

"It was a delightful evening, and Luna and Nico are amazing," said Lisa. "And their English is so good! I'm so happy for you, my dear friend. Call me tomorrow." Lisa and Dom walked down the sidewalk toward their car.

Cat went back inside and slowly looked around her home. Invisible but real, the wonderful energy of the evening lingered in the air. She joyfully strolled into the kitchen, where Sam, Luna, and Nico were stacking up the last of the dirty dishes. She picked up a dishtowel.

"No, no. Nico and I will clean up," Luna said. "You and Sam enjoy this beautiful evening on the veranda. Andare!"

Sam grinned and poured two petite glasses of limoncello liqueur. Cat followed him out to the porch and inhaled the fragrance of the garden roses. She lit a candle on the coffee table and settled into a chair. She was grateful for the soft light, as it hid her nervousness.

"That was a spectacular dinner," Sam said. "Lisa and Nico are true chefs, and I couldn't have had a better dinner in a Michelin-starred restaurant. I'm sure the young man will be very successful someday. Thanks for inviting me tonight."

In the candlelight, Cat noticed that Sam looked even more like Zach. Her heart pounded, and small beads of perspiration dotted her

59

forehead. She dabbed them with a napkin and took a sip of the lemony liquid. "It was so fun to have a full house. I wish Jim could have been here."

"You must miss him. I know he had a business partner. What's going to happen to the company now?"

"I have to meet with our lawyer. I'll inherit his third of the business since he had a prenup with his ex-wife, Beatrice. I'm not sure what to do. Bradley's okay, but his personality is a little off-putting. He wants me to sell them my shares."

"They're exporters as well as importers, aren't they?" Sam asked. "It's a business I've wanted to get into."

"You should give Bradley a call and see if you can do some business together. They merged with the commercial real estate company Riva Realty a while ago. Giancarlo Riva kept them afloat during the crisis, and he owns thirty-four percent."

"I haven't heard of him. I'll talk to Brad before I leave on my next buying trip. I'm going to Milan next week, then stopping in Cyprus. I'm seeing a friend from Florence who married a woman from the island. They're spending a few weeks with her family. Did Jim ever go to Cyprus?"

"Not that I know of. But he traveled so much, and I didn't keep track of all his trips. If you do talk to Brad, would you please not mention Luna? I don't want the staff gossiping about my mother and the fact that she had a baby when she was an unmarried teenager."

"I completely understand. If it comes up, I'll simply say we met through mutual friends."

"Thank you. On a slight change of topic," Cat said, "I hope you don't mind me asking, but were you ever married?"

Sam chuckled. "Twice. Once after college for three years, then again in my early thirties for two years. I loved both women, but my lack of desire for children broke up both marriages. Before we tied the knot, I told my second wife that I wouldn't change my mind. But she thought she was the one who could change me."

"I wasn't sure about having children, either, but in the end I was physically unable to have a baby. At this point in my life, there are days when I wish things were different. I'd be looking forward to being the mother of the bride or groom, then welcoming grandchildren. But it is what it is," Cat said. Her voice was filled with melancholy. "I feel a love for Nico that is totally unexpected and wonderful."

"He's a great kid and a good cook. I've thought about not having children of my own, especially now that I'm in my fifties. But like you said, it is what it is."

Catherine and Sam sat in silence, listening to the cicadas singing in the muggy night. A sudden rush of wind swept across the front porch, giving them a brief respite from the heat. The candles flickered, and a wave of energy rushed through Cat's body. Sam's gentle touch on her hand brought her back.

"Are you okay?"

She took a deep breath and smiled. "I'm more than okay."

"I've had a great time tonight, and I'm wondering if you would like to get together again? Maybe lunch or dinner?"

Cat's blush was hidden in the candlelight. She wasn't really surprised by his offer but was surprised by her instant desire to say yes. "Yes, I'd like that, Sam. Call me when you get back from your trip."

Catherine stood up and walked over to the porch railing. Sam approached and took her hand. He gently drew her close. Her heart started beating like a drum, and butterflies flew in circles in her stomach. He lifted her chin and kissed her on the cheek.

Just then, Nico bounded outside with an ice cream cone in his hand. "This is so good! Would you like some gelato?"

Cat and Sam laughed and said "no thank you" to the young man. Nico shrugged and went back inside, the screen door banging behind him.

"It is fun to have a nephew now. Even though we live a continent apart, we can text and use FaceTime. It's amazing how quickly my heart opened and filled with love. I feel a deep bond with both Luna and Nico. Love is like the universe—always expanding."

"You're right, Catherine. Love is infinite. Well, it's getting late, so I'd better head back to the city. I'll go in to say goodbye to Luna and Nico first."

After Sam said farewell to Luna and Nico, he gave Cat a quick hug, thanked her again, and promised to be in touch soon. Then he bounded down the porch steps, and after a wave from the other side of the garden gate, he got in his car and slowly drove away. Cat smiled and sighed deeply as she blew out the candle and then went inside.

* * *

The next several days rushed by as Catherine, Luna, and Nico explored the island and lounged on the beach each afternoon. They rented bikes and rode through the maritime forest in the state park and toured the nineteenth century Fort Clinch. They took a tourist cruise on the Amelia River and marveled at the bands of wild horses on the largely uninhabited Cumberland Island in Georgia, just north of Amelia. Cumberland became famous when John Kennedy, Jr. and Caroline Bissett were married in the tiny chapel on the island in complete secrecy.

On their final night together, Luna and Nico made a fabulous dinner, and then they all sat out on the porch, enjoying the warm evening air. As they sat and reminisced about their time together, Cat's cell phone rang, and she went into the dining room to answer it, seeing it was a call from Diana, Rodney's daughter.

"Catherine, I'm at my dad's townhouse again. I finally convinced the landlord to let me in. My dad changed the locks, and I didn't have a key. Something's definitely wrong. His wallet, cell phone, and suitcase are all here, but his car is gone. I don't know what to do!"

"Did you call the police?" Cat asked, concern in her voice.

"Yes, and I filed a missing person's report. It's been several days since I've heard from him, and I'm beyond worried."

Catherine hesitated and then asked, "Diana, do you think he went somewhere to gamble?"

"No, I don't! His wallet's here, and it has his ID and credit cards in it. He hasn't gambled for several years, and I don't believe he started again."

"Did he mention any concerns or worries when he visited you?"

"No. He was just happy to be with the kids. He's such a loving grandfather, and with my mom gone, my kids need him. Oh God. What if something happened to him?"

Cat could hear Diana sobbing. "You said his suitcase was there. Did he have another one he may have used?"

"I don't think so. The kids gave him this one for Christmas last year. I know he wouldn't travel anywhere without it."

"Are you staying at your dad's tonight?"

"Yes."

"I'll come over in the morning. I have to drop off my sister and nephew at the airport. I'll join you before I head to the lawyer's office in Jax Beach. Try and get some sleep."

Catherine slumped into a chair and took a deep breath. *What's happened to Rodney? I have a terrible feeling about this. He cares so much about Diana and the kids. I know he wouldn't put them through unnecessary worry.*

Luna entered the dining room and seemed to know right away that Cat was upset. She closed her eyes, took a deep breath, and appeared to focus. "Is this about your friend, Jim's co-worker?"

"Yes. Good guess," Cat said. "I'm as worried as his daughter that foul play is involved in his disappearance. He's much too good a grandfather to vanish and leave them hanging. It's so out of character. I'm going to go over to her place in the morning after I drop you and Nico at the airport. Maybe there's something I can do."

"No respectable parent would desert their family like that. It sounds troubling to me," Luna said. "That is what most concerns me about Nico's father. He has never once tried to contact his child in all these years."

"He may have had good reasons for his neglect, but I'm not sure what they could be," Cat said. "It's one thing to divorce a spouse, but leaving a child in the lurch is a terrible thing."

Chapter 12

FAREWELL

Cat, Luna, and Nico strolled through the picturesque town of Fernandina Beach early the next morning. They wanted one final visit before heading to the airport. The shops were not open for business, but the sisters enjoyed the window displays of beachwear and the coastal artwork in the galleries. They walked along the city marina boardwalk at the west end of Centre Street, marveling at the yachts and sailboats moored in the harbor.

Nico stopped and peered into the water. "What was that?"

"What did you see?" Cat asked.

"It looked like a big gray lump. There it is, over there," he said as he pointed to the far side of a fishing boat.

"I see it," said Cat. "It's a manatee. They call them sea cows. They slowly graze on plants, just like cows do. They can grow up to thirteen feet in length and weigh a thousand pounds."

"Wow, I have never seen such an animal," Nico exclaimed.

"The closest relative to the manatee is the elephant, believe it or not. In some places in Florida, you can swim with them, but that's usually in the winter months."

"You could call them gentle giants," Luna said. "But I would rather swim with the dolphins. It was incredible to see them in the canals of Venice during the pandemic. In a way, that was a wonderful time for Mother Earth to rest and heal from man's activities. And it is fortunate that they no longer allow massive cruise ships to enter the canals."

A gentle breeze cooled the tree-lined street as they made their way to a coffee shop. After grabbing an outside table in the sun, Cat went inside, ordered their breakfast, and then returned to the sidewalk.

"I'm going to miss you, Zia Catherine! My heart has been filled with joy being with you," Nico said.

Tears welled in Cat's eyes. She tousled her new nephew's dark curly hair and hugged his shoulders. "I'll miss you, too. But it's been fantastic to have you both here. We're connected for life, Nico."

"We are so fortunate to have text and FaceTime. And I am happy that we set a weekly time and day for our telepathic communication," said Luna.

"It would be crazy cool if it actually worked," said Cat. "Let me know if there's any news about Nico's dad and your birth father, Luna. Wow, your two father stories would be good material for a novel."

"You should try your hand at writing fiction, Catherine. You should not be afraid to attempt to write a novel. Besides, you know how to edit," said Luna.

"Maybe I will someday. I can begin with my journals from childhood and our messages across the miles. I could write about family—genetic relatives and others who become our family. I think I'd like to write a fictional book rather than a memoir."

After breakfast, Cat drove her guests to Jacksonville International Airport and escorted Luna and Nico to the security area. Tears flowed freely as they said their goodbyes. Cat's emotions fluctuated from joy and love to a profound sadness. *A sister found. And a nephew as a bonus! Life is full of surprises.*

"Have a safe flight. Text me when you arrive home. I love you both!" Cat called out, and Nico and Luna gave her a final wave.

As Catherine headed back to the parking garage, a text on her phone shifted her attention. It was Diana asking when she would arrive at Rodney's townhouse. *On my way,* she typed in reply. Fifteen minutes later, she arrived at her destination, her stomach in knots. Diana opened the door before she could ring the bell. *She looks as if she hasn't slept in days.* Diana was attractive and tall, with a solid build like her dad. She was always stylishly dressed, and she carried herself with poise. But at the moment, she was disheveled and frantic with worry.

"Thanks so much for coming," Diana said. "I need a fresh pair of eyes to see if something is amiss or if there's a clue about my dad's disappearance. I've searched all the rooms and haven't found anything that helps. I'm worried that something terrible has happened. I just can't lose him!"

"Any word from the police?"

"No, nothing. They sent Dad's photo to the Seminole Casino near West Palm Beach. I know that's where he went when he fell off the gambling wagon a few years ago. They checked their security videos and said he hasn't been there."

"Did he have any—any girlfriends he may be staying with?"

"I don't think he was seeing anyone. Oh, dear Lord! Where could he be?"

Cat hugged the younger woman, then swept her strawberry blond hair from her heart-shaped face. "Did you find his laptop?"

"No. Maybe he has it with him." Diana's hazel eyes, full of sadness and fear, peered into Cat's.

"Hazel! What about Hazel? Did you learn anything from her or from Brad?" Cat questioned.

Diana pulled away and paced the living room. "They're both concerned, but neither of them have any leads. I just don't know what to do now. I have to get back to Gainesville. Molly has a dance recital tonight. I just can't believe her grandfather won't be there, too. He never missed one of them."

"Why don't you head home? I'll stay here and take a look around to see if there are any clues. I'll lock the door on my way out and text you when I'm leaving."

"Thanks, Catherine. Please let me know if you find anything." Diana wiped a tear from her eye, picked up her purse, and headed out the door.

Cat stood quietly, surveying the townhouse. "Okay, Rodney. What's happened to you? Lisa claims I'm an amateur sleuth, so let's see what I can find. And I'm talking to myself again!"

Cat hunted for clues in each room. Elaborate, colorful costumes from his amateur theater performances were scattered throughout the townhouse. She was unable to determine if someone had ransacked the place or if Rodney normally lived in disorganized confusion. His distinctive cologne lingered in each room. The search revealed nothing until Cat investigated the bedroom. On a small corner desk was a familiar box. It was exactly like the two Catherine had received in the mail. *Rodney sent those boxes! What was he trying to tell me?* The box was empty. *What the hell does this mean? And why did he use a post office box for the return address?*

Chapter 13

DARTH VADER

After a final sweep of the apartment, Cat locked the door and headed to Jacksonville Beach so she could meet with her lawyer and discuss the terms of Jim's will. Jerome Farnsworth greeted her at his office door with a bear hug. The large man was a dead ringer for James Earl Jones, and he even had the same resonant voice. Cat always felt as if she was meeting Darth Vader when she went to Jerome's office.

"Come, Catherine, have a seat. You must have been busy considering you haven't made this journey out to see me before now. Most people are anxious to read a will. Is everything okay with you?"

Taking a seat, Cat said, "I had some unexpected visitors, which delayed my seeing you. I discovered I have a half-sister living in Italy, and she came to visit. We had a wonderful time together. But back to the business at hand. As you know, Jim and I updated our wills last year, so I think I know what to expect."

"I met with Jim two weeks before he passed away. He dropped off this letter for you and said to give it to you at the reading of his will."

The look on Cat's face most likely told Jerome she didn't know about the letter. "Strange. I wonder why he didn't just give it to me."

Jerome handed her the envelope marked with her name and the notation *For Cat's Eyes Only.*

"Thanks. Are there any other surprises?"

"There were no recent changes to Jim's will," said the voice of CNN. "Bradley Ritter remains the backup executor for both of your wills. Let's go over everything now."

Cat and her lawyer reviewed the documents and were satisfied that all was in order. Sitting back in her chair, Cat said, "I know I can get E & R's financial reports from Bradley, but I'd rather have an independent accountant review the books."

Jerome assured her, saying, "I'll hire a top-notch CPA to assess the company's financial reports. I'll let you know when her work is completed."

"Thanks, Jerome. Brad keeps texting me about selling my third of E & R to him. He's also anxious to get his mitts on Jim's computer. I want to make sure the financials are in order before I give the laptop to him."

"I agree that you should be cautious even though Bradley is the backup executor. It is always best to follow your instincts."

"As we just discussed, I'll email the changes I'd like made to my will in the next day or two. Now that I have a sister, I plan to make her the beneficiary of my estate. If you don't mind, just FedEx the documents to me, and I'll sign and have them notarized on the island. I'll FedEx my signed copies back to you."

Jerome smiled. "It's always a pleasure doing business with you, Catherine."

While driving up highway A1A to the Mayport ferry, Cat mulled over the strange disappearance of Rodney and his cryptic gifts. She pulled into the line and drove onto the boat moments later. She paid the attendant and exited her car as the horn announced their departure. She inhaled the fresh air, which was tinged with the smell of fish from nearby docks. She enjoyed watching the pelicans take flight and the screeching sea gulls circle the ferry as it traversed the short distance across the St. Johns River.

Catherine took Jim's letter from her purse, read it, and pondered the contents. One mysterious sentence kept repeating in her mind. Then she opened a folded document that was included with the letter and gasped in shock. She quickly tucked the papers into her purse and hurried back to her car as the ferry pulled into the dock.

Cat continued the drive north past Little Talbot Island and Big Talbot Island state parks, then crossed the bridge to Amelia Island. She took the AI Parkway and headed over to Lisa's home. The gray, Lowcountry-style stucco house had a metal roof and a large veranda. Her friend was lounging on a chaise on the front porch, a cocktail in her hand.

"I know it's not quite five o'clock, but I needed a pick-me-up," Lisa called out.

Catherine chuckled and pulled up a chair. "Okay, what's up? It's not like you to get into the libations before five."

"I have a perfectly good reason. My cousin—my bitter, neurotic cousin in St. Louis—is threatening to sue me!"

"Good heavens! Why?"

"It's about my cookbook. She says my grandmother's recipes were stolen from her grandmother, my nonna's older sister. Serena thinks that she's the rightful inheritor of my great-grandmother's recipes and will sue me if I publish them."

"But wouldn't they both have gotten the recipes from their mother and therefore both have rights to them?" Cat asked reasonably.

"That's what I asked her. She insisted that her grandmother updated and refined the recipes and that they belong to her. Her son's a lawyer, and she said he'll take legal action on her behalf. I'm glad my nonna isn't alive to see this."

"That's crazy. What are you going to do?"

"Put the project on hold for now. I can't afford to hire a lawyer and possibly get tied up in a lawsuit. I thought that after the trauma we all went through when our uncle died from the virus, we'd be a united family. But my cousin has disregarded the pain of losing him and has reverted to her selfish ways."

"How many nights did we cry as the tragedy unfolded? The suffering was unimaginable, and each story of courage and loss touched our hearts. But for some people, there was only momentary empathy. When the crisis was over, their true colors came through again. Their compassion was a mirage," stated Cat.

"So true. Sometimes family can be an awful burden."

"It's funny, I rarely think about the downside of family, only my lack of it," Cat said. "I hope my sister, now that I've found her, doesn't hurt me in some way."

"Luna seems wonderful, and so does Nico. I'm sure they'd never intentionally harm you. How did it go with the lawyer today?"

"There were no surprises in the will, but Jim gave Jerome a letter for me just days before his heart gave out. I'll tell you about it later, after I figure out what it means."

Lisa looked at Cat. "That sounds mysterious."

They were interrupted when a car pulled into the driveway. Dominic joined the ladies. "What's up, my lovely Lisa? Cocktails this early in the day always signal a problem."

"Oh, no big deal," Lisa said, sarcasm in her voice. "My favorite cousin, Serena, has threatened me with a lawsuit over the recipes in my cookbook. I'll give you the full details later. Right now, I think Catherine and I deserve a glass of prosecco."

"At your service, my lady," Dom said as he entered the house. He returned a few minutes later with two glasses of prosecco. "I'm going to start dinner. Catherine, would you like to join us?"

"That would be wonderful, Dom."

"I'll let you two chat," Dom said as he went inside.

"So, what's happening with Rodney's disappearance?" Lisa asked.

"No news. I met his daughter, Diana, at his townhouse this morning, but there were no clues whatsoever about where he might be. Diana had to get back to Gainesville, so I stayed to look around. What I did find was a box in his bedroom that was just like the others I received in the mail, but the box was empty. Rodney must have sent me the wallet and face cream, but I don't get what he's trying to tell me."

"Or why he didn't just talk to you."

"Maybe he was afraid of something. And maybe he was right to be scared. It could be something from his gambling days, or maybe he somehow got himself in trouble. He has been on the straight and narrow for the past few years, but he does have a flare for the dramatic, which is obvious from the strange packages he sent me. After he stopped gambling, he became obsessed with a theater group in

Jacksonville. His large physical size is great for certain roles, and he has a very good singing voice."

"Do you think he ran off with another thespian? Or could it be about something at work?"

While she sipped her wine, Catherine's wheels were turning. "I doubt it was anything to do with his acting. But it could be work-related. Speaking of the company, Brad has been so insistent that I give him Jim's laptop. He said something about wanting to make sure he had all the company files. When I looked at it, I noticed there were several email files that Jim had flagged. I haven't had a chance to look at them. But now that my visitors are gone, I'll do it soon and see what I can find."

Chapter 14

MADONNA DEL VOTO

The timeworn taxi passed the magnificent Duomo and drove to Luna's home in Siena. The travelers were weary but happy and were glad to return to their medieval city. Luna and Nico lugged their suitcases into their bedrooms before heading to the kitchen for a glass of sparkling water and orange soda. Before Luna could take a sip, her cell phone rang.

"Ciao, Viola. Your timing is perfect. Nico and I just got back from Florida. What have you discovered?" Luna asked. She listened carefully as her lawyer shared some important information. She listened a little longer, and then her eyes opened wide. "Sì, sì, that will be fine. Ciao."

"What is it?" Nico questioned.

"Viola has located your father in Greece, and he would like to see you. He's traveling here to Siena in three days, departing from the island of Crete."

"Oh! It is happening. So soon. My dream of meeting my father is coming true! But I am nervous, too. What will he be like? What will he think of me? Why did he abandon us? Why did he not contact me after my mother died? I have so many questions for him."

"We both have many questions for him. We will write everything down and prepare for his visit."

"I want to understand his point of view. And I want him to be in my life, if that is possible. I will make a photo album. Then he can see what I looked like as I grew up."

"Excellent idea, Nico. There is an empty album in the bookcase. Let me know if you need help."

Nico grabbed his soda and ran into his room to search through boxes of photographs. Luna sighed, amazed at his energy.

As Luna unpacked, thoughts about Salvatore swirled in her mind. The call with Viola had shaken her, but she knew she had to welcome Nico's father regardless of what he had done in the past. She took out a pad and paper to record the questions she would ask Salvatore when he arrived. She'd seen a few pictures of him with Carlotta, along with one of him holding Nico as an infant. Salvatore was handsome, and Nico looked very much like him—the same dark curly hair and slim physique.

Carlotta had told Luna that her ex-husband was charismatic and charming. He could spin amazing tales that, more often than not, turned out to be fabrications. He claimed he had numerous talents and abilities that he didn't actually possess. The next get-rich-quick scheme was always around the corner. Carlotta said the reality of a screaming newborn didn't fit into his grandiose plans, and so he left. She was determined her son would never lack for anything even though she was a single mother, and she worked hard her whole life to ensure both she and Nico had everything they needed.

Luna retrieved her computer and emailed Viola to request all the background information she had on Salvatore Alessi. Any man who would desert his wife and child, and never inquire about them in fifteen years, required investigation. Fortunately, Luna did not have long to wait to hear back from Viola. The documents that she forwarded revealed a man who had lived in numerous cities in Italy and Greece and who had had several run-ins with the police. He'd been arrested for disorderly conduct and writing bad checks, and in the second case he was imprisoned. He would move on after he became a persona non grata in each location, and he ultimately landed in the coastal Crete town of Agios Nikolaos. He was presently employed as a waiter at a seaside restaurant.

Luna padded down the hallway and looked in on Nico, who was sleeping soundly after their long journey. Photos were strewn on his bed, but he'd given in to slumber. After quietly closing the bedroom door, she decided to call her sister and discuss the situation.

Cat picked up on the second ring. "Luna! I didn't expect to hear from you so soon. You got home safe and sound? What's up?"

"I needed to talk to my sister," Luna replied with a smile. "What a lovely thing to say!"

"I'm happy you called me. So, what's wrong?"

"It is about Salvatore, Nico's father. He is traveling to Siena from Greece to meet us in three days. I heard back from my lawyer, Viola, just after we arrived home. She had an investigation done on Salvatore, and I am sorry to say he is an unsavory character. He has had problems with the law, and he spent a short time in prison for writing fraudulent checks. I am not certain how much I should tell Nico."

"Wow, that is a problem. Nico's very smart, but he's also a fifteen-year-old boy with a sensitive heart. I've talked to a lot of high school students over the years. The one thing they tell me is that they don't want to be lied to or treated like children."

"Yes, he is very intelligent. I am just not sure how to present the information to him," Luna explained. "But I am certain that he needs to know the truth."

"I think you should write a synopsis of the reports. You can give Nico the basic facts, including the arrests and imprisonment. He can let his father explain what happened and answer any other questions he has, like why Salvatore left them and why he hasn't bothered to contact Nico. That way, Nico can make up his own mind."

"That is good advice. Better that he has all facts in hand, and he can refer to them before and after the meeting. The investigation my lawyer conducted was money well spent."

"I agree, Luna. Call me after your meeting with Mr. Alessi. And let me know how Nico handles meeting his father for the first time."

Luna and Cat chatted for a few more minutes, and then they ended the call. Luna thought about all the new information she was trying to process and realized that, as tired as she was, she would not be able to sleep right away. She wrote a note, placed it on Nico's pillow, and kissed his forehead. She went outside and wandered the streets of her hometown, watching the throngs of tourists conversing in several languages. She did a complete tour of the Piazza del Campo and ended at Piazza di San Giovanna. She shook her head at the restaurant selling "American" pizza with French fries and hotdogs on top. She hadn't seen anything like that in Florida.

She found herself drawn to the majestic Duomo and stared at the Sun Symbol over the center door of the Gothic cathedral. It had been created to bring the Sienese together and end the feuding among the Contrades, or seventeen districts. In the fifteenth century, St. Bernardino hoped to unite the people under the symbol of the risen Jesus.

Entering the hallowed place, she marveled at the white-and-black striped marble columns, the magnificent soaring ceiling, and the intricate frescoes and statues. She slipped past two groups of tourists and made her way to the Bernini-designed Chapel of the Madonna del Voto. The incredible beauty of the church always left her in awe of the artisans, architects, and laborers who had created the medieval masterpiece.

Luna had not attended a church service in a very long while, but she felt drawn to the energy of Mother Mary—the Rose of May. She closed her eyes and began to pray for guidance in dealing with Nico's father. Her main concern was Salvatore's potential refusal to sign over his parental rights so that she wouldn't be able to adopt his son. And even more worrying was the possibility that Nico would want to move to Greece to be with the man who had abandoned him so long ago.

A silent prayer filled Luna's mind: *Dear Mother Mary, give me the strength to face the challenges ahead, give me the wisdom to know what is best for Nico, and let me approach every situation with love. Amen.*

Chapter 15

BIRTHDAY CARD

"Catherine! I heard from my father," Diana cried when Cat answered her phone.

Cat was sitting on the wide sand beach near Seaside Park, enjoying the sunshine. The number was unfamiliar, but she'd intuitively felt she should answer it and not let it go to voicemail. She was glad she did when she heard Diana's voice.

"Oh my God. What a relief. That's great! Did he call you?"

"No, he didn't call. He sent a birthday card to Molly even though her birthday isn't until next month. On the inside, he wrote, *Happy Birthday, Diamond Girl. Sorry I can't be there right now. I'm staying with friends. It's super hot here. My love for you is genuine, unlike so many other things. Hope to see you soon. Love, Nana.* I think he's in trouble."

"Nana?" Cat questioned. "Are you sure it's from your dad?"

"Absolutely. His nickname for me growing up was diamond girl. My mom passed away two years ago, and Dad would never use her name or refer to her as Nana if it wasn't important. The fact that he has done so means he doesn't want anyone to know he's contacted me."

"Was there a return address?"

"No, but it was postmarked in Miami. I've already called his two friends in the Miami area, but neither of them has heard from him. Whenever he was in trouble with gambling, he always said things were 'super hot.' I don't know how he's living without his ID and credit cards. And the police said he hasn't touched his bank account."

77

"Are you going to tell the police about the birthday card?"

"I'm not sure. If I tell them, they might stop looking for him. They could help him, even if he doesn't want help. I just know he's in danger. Why else would he use snail mail and not call or text? And if Dad's worried about electronic communication, then so am I. I'm actually calling from a friend's phone. I'm also monitoring my computer. I find myself looking in the rearview mirror when I'm driving and watching through the blinds to see if there are any strange cars parked near the house."

"Diana, this is concerning, and you're right to be cautious, especially when details are so scarce. Let me know if you want me to do anything, and please let me know if he gets in touch with you again or if there's any more news."

"I will. Thanks for listening."

The word "genuine," which Rodney used in the card, was bouncing around in Cat's mind. She took the iPad out of her beach bag and typed *counterfeit goods* in the search engine. Instead of the FBI site popping up like she expected, she discovered it was the Customs and Border Protection arm of the Department of Homeland Security that was responsible for fake goods. She read on the DHS website that civil or criminal penalties could be levied and "Purchasing counterfeit goods supports criminal activities such as money laundering and trafficking in illegal guns and drugs." *Wow, this is serious stuff.*

A young family of five—loaded down with chairs, coolers, and toys—marched by Catherine. The smallest child picked up a cream-colored oyster shell, ran over to Cat, and handed her the treasure. Cat thanked the little girl as she sped away to catch up with her parents. *Maybe I'll play with Nico's baby one day. That's as close to being a grandmother as I'll ever get. I hope that everything works out with Salvatore and that he lets Luna adopt Nico.* She closed her eyes and listened to the rhythmic waves crash on the shore. The sound soothed her nerves and calmed her mind.

Her phone dinged, and a text from Sam popped up. *Things are going well in Italy. Can't wait to see you.*

Me, too, she replied. A Cheshire cat grin crossed Catherine's face as she gathered her belongings and headed to the car. When driving up North 14th Street, she caught up with the vehicles in front of her and

78

was surprised to see police cars and the bomb squad from Duval County. She followed them into Old Town and ended up on Garden Street. Rolling down her window, she called out to a bystander, "What's going on?"

An elderly gentleman walked over. "They were digging a hole for a concrete piling at that new house. They found a cannonball and called in the bomb squad from Jacksonville."

"Oh yeah, just like the two that were found at the History Museum, and then someone realized they were live and dangerous. I guess they'll detonate this one, too."

"Something from the past that you don't expect," the man said, "can blow up in your face."

While heading home, Cat questioned whether something from Rodney's past had reappeared and blown up in his face. Once inside the cottage, she decided it was time to investigate Jim's computer files and see if there was any link to Rodney. She wondered if she should be worried about her phone and computer being compromised. *Jim loved conspiracy theories, and maybe I'm more like him than I thought.*

Settling in the chair behind Jim's antique desk, which had been delivered to the cottage from Jim's apartment the week before, Catherine opened his laptop and forwarded each flagged file to her email and Lisa's. There were six in all, and she began her investigation with the earliest ones. These were from two separate people who were identified only by the initials KH and GY. She had no idea who these contacts were or what the emails meant. Some seemed to be about shipments, and others merely contained addresses. There was no mention of Rodney in any of the messages.

Frustrated, Cat roamed around the house, then returned to the living room. *There has to be a clue among these messages. But what is it? Jim, help!* Her pearl earring dropped from her earlobe and rolled under the desk. When she went to retrieve it, she noticed something she hadn't seen before. To her surprise, she discovered what appeared to be a secret panel on the bottom of the desk. There was a tiny keyhole, and she quickly searched through the desk drawers for a key small enough to fit the lock. But there was nothing like that in them.

Cat headed into the kitchen to find the small screwdriver that had come with an eyeglass repair kit. Within minutes, she had popped the

79

lock, and the panel flew open. A single piece of paper fluttered to the ground. On the note was a single word and a series of numbers. *Come on, Jim! I want answers, not another mystery. Did you knock my earring off so I'd find this?* Catherine took a photo of the paper with her phone, placed the note in the lockbox in her bedroom, and then flopped on her bed. Her ringing cell phone startled her, and she darted into the living room.

"Cat," Lisa said when she answered, "what's the meaning of Jim's emails? I couldn't make heads or tails of them."

"Me neither. Did you notice that they were forwarded from two people who only appeared as initials? Weird."

"Maybe Jim had insiders on the lookout for certain communications and had them sent to his work email. Does that make sense?"

"Nothing makes sense. And totally by mistake, I found a secret compartment in the bottom of his desk. When I popped the lock, a piece of paper dropped out. There was one word on it and a series of numbers."

"Wow! Another mystery. What was the word?" Lisa asked.

"It was Nicosia, like Nico with 'sia' at the end. I have no idea what that means."

"Okay, I typed it into my search engine, and Nicosia is the capital city of Cyprus. Did Jim ever go there?" Lisa questioned.

"I don't think so. But Sam is going to the island after he leaves Milan. He has a friend he's seeing there, but I don't think he does any business in Cyprus."

"Have you talked to Sam since he asked you out?"

The color rose in Cat's face again. "He sent me a text saying he's looking forward to seeing me. Maybe he can help me figure this out when he gets back from Italy. I don't want to send the information on the note via email or text. Diana's worried about electronic communication, and so am I. Rodney sent her daughter, Molly, a very cryptic birthday card. She was relieved to hear from him, but she thinks he's in trouble."

"That's crazy," Lisa said."The mysteries keep piling up. I don't know what to suggest. Maybe you should talk to Brad. He might know what the emails and the note mean."

"I'm not sure about that, Lisa. I've got my lawyer, Jerome, checking into Bradley and the financials at E & R. I'm not feeling totally comfortable about him. He keeps talking about me selling my shares of the business to him."

"Are you going to sell them to him?"

"I haven't decided yet. Listen, if you get any ideas about these emails, let me know. Thanks for your help with all this. See you tomorrow."

Catherine was about to research Nicosia and Cyprus online when there was a loud bang outside. She ran to the front porch. A young man with a buzzcut, who was dressed in camouflage, was in the park across the street. He had a shotgun and was firing toward a massive oak tree. He fired again, and a large hawk took flight, screeching until he was out of sight. Before she had a moment to be frightened, Cat yelled at the man, "What are you doing?"

The menacing man spun around and pointed the weapon directly at Cat. She ran into the house, slammed the door, and turned the bolt. She grabbed her phone and called 911. After locking herself in the bathroom, Cat heard footsteps on the porch and the door handle rattling. She began to shake uncontrollably but continued to talk to the dispatcher, who encouraged her to remain calm. The police were on the way.

She held her breath and prayed that she'd remembered to lock the back door. *What made me yell at him? I found a speck of courage at the wrong time.* Police sirens wailed in the distance, and she let out a sigh of relief. Soon after, there was a banging on the door, and a deep voice identified himself as a police officer. Cat splashed cold water on her face and went to talk to the police.

Chapter 16

TURTLE RIVER

"Ooom... Ooom..." Catherine adjusted the headphones attached to her iPad and listened to a serene meditation. She dug her toes into the warm sand and settled in the beach chair. She was alone on the shore and was preparing for her first attempt at telepathy with her sister, who was waiting across the pond.

Luna, if you can hear me, please answer this question: What was the name of your best friend from childhood?

Cat repeated the question several times in her mind, but no answer came. After half an hour, she decided to let it go. She slipped her iPad into her beach bag and retrieved her phone. She sent a text to Luna saying she would call later and tell her what she had been trying to communicate, just as they'd planned. She was also anxious to hear if there was any news on Luna's birth father. Through the family Maria had worked for in Siena, Luna had obtained a name and possible location for their mother's Italian boyfriend.

Cat drove down winding Centre Street into town to meet Lisa for lunch. Her friend was waiting at Leddy's Porch in the historic Florida House Inn. The reportedly haunted hotel had been built in the mid-1800s to accommodate railroad workers, and it seemed as though some of them had never left.

"Catherine!" Lisa called. Their preferred seat beside the window had been reserved, and the waitress brought out their favorite lunch as Cat slid into her chair.

"Now that's what I call service. Chicken and waffles. The best in Fernandina," said Cat. "Thanks, Tamara, this smells wonderful." The friends toasted one another with iced tea and started eating while the food was still hot.

"So, has there been any news about your cousin and her plan to sue you over the use of those recipes?" Cat asked.

"No, not yet. But I'm expecting a letter from her son's law firm. I'll decide what to do after I see what he has to say. Maybe they'll just drop the whole thing," Lisa said. "How did your telepathy session with Luna go this morning?"

"I didn't get any impressions or direct answers like I did as a child. We'll arrange another time to try. Right now, I'm anxious about her meeting with Nico's father. He's drifted from place to place and has been in trouble with the law. He's even spent some time in jail for a non-violent crime. Salvatore obviously isn't a dependable man. I just hope against hope that he signs the documents and lets Luna legally adopt Nico."

"Poor Nico. I'm sure he has mixed feelings about meeting his dad. He must be hurt that he never bothered to find him in all these years. Nico has an inner strength that will serve him well, but he's still a boy."

As the women quietly enjoyed their lunch, a raucous group of teenagers bounded in and sat at a table near them. Lisa and Catherine eavesdropped on their conversations, marveling at how quickly the teens jumped from one subject to another. All of them were on their phones comparing tweets and Instagram photos.

Cat whispered, "So much has changed in the world, and yet so much remains the same as when we were kids."

"I see that with my own boys."

Cat's cell phone rang, and she checked the number. "I think this is the phone Diana called me from before." She answered the call. "Hello?" She listened in silence for several minutes. "Oh, I'm so sorry, Diana. Thanks for letting me know. Since it's too far for you to drive home, please stay at my place tonight. Okay, see you at seven."

"What's happened?" Lisa asked.

"They found Rodney's car in the Turtle River in Jacksonville. And he was inside. They'll do an autopsy after Diana identifies the body.

There was no driver's license or other ID with the body, so they need her to come in person. She is completely distraught."

"Oh my God!" Lisa yelled. "I bet he was murdered!"

The teens all stared at her, then chatted excitedly among themselves.

"We don't know that for sure," Cat said. "It could have been an accident. I doubt it was suicide. Diana's driving in tonight, and she's going to stay with me. I don't think it's good for her to be on her own, not just because she'll be upset, but it might not be safe."

"So you *do* think there's a chance he was murdered!" Lisa whispered.

Cat asked Tamara for the check and took out her credit card. "I simply don't know. But we should have an answer soon."

When Diana arrived at Catherine's that evening, it was obvious she'd spent most of the drive crying. Cat took her to the guest room and then went back to the kitchen to put the chicken soup she'd made into a tureen. Even though it was hot outside, she thought that comfort food was in order. She poured two glasses of wine and took the tureen of aromatic soup into the dining room, along with two ceramic bowls. Her guest joined her just as she was putting the wine on the table.

Diana's sad smile and raw pain were understandable, especially under the disturbing circumstances. The "not knowing" part of the tragedy was the most difficult. At least Cat had known immediately how her brother—and her father, for that matter—had died. But for Diana, there was the added worry that foul play could be involved.

"I hope you like chicken soup and Pinot Grigio," Cat said as she served the soup with a freshly baked baguette and butter.

"Perfect. Thanks for letting me stay here. I feel like I'm going crazy. I dread going to the morgue tomorrow."

"I can go with you if you like."

Diana stirred her soup over and over again and then finally took a few bites. "Thanks, but I think this is something I need to face on my own." She took a big gulp of wine before continuing. "I often worried about my dad when he was gambling, but never once did I think he wouldn't come home. I knew his love for his family would always bring him back. Something's different this time. I'm not sure if gambling had anything to do with his disappearance and now his death."

"Do you want to tell me what you do know?"

"Dad's car was found submerged near a boat ramp on the river. It wasn't completely underwater, and some kids found it. The obvious answer is that he drowned after he accidently drove into the water. They're checking the brakes on the car. There was a duffle bag with clothes in it and a shaving kit with six hundred dollars in cash. His laptop wasn't in the car."

"I guess the coroner will see if there was another cause of death, other than drowning," Cat noted.

"Yeah. They'll do the autopsy tomorrow. Because a crime is a possibility, they're moving quickly."

"You must be worried about the outcome."

"You bet I am. Jason has taken Molly and Mason to his parents' place in Destin. We've been communicating with burner phones and have stayed offline just in case we're compromised that way. It's strange that Dad was driving without his license. And he didn't have his credit cards with him, nor did he take money from his account, yet there was cash in the car. It's so unsettling and so unlike him. And something else is preying on my mind. I'm an orphan."

Diana began to sob, and Cat placed her hand on the younger woman's trembling hand.

"I'm not really hungry, Catherine. Do you mind if I skip dinner?"

"Not at all. Maybe you should try and get some sleep."

Diana refilled her wine glass and went to the guestroom. Cat had lost her appetite, too, and she put the soup in the fridge. She topped off her glass of wine, walked out to the porch, and plunked down in the Muskoka chair. There wasn't a breath of air, and the mugginess weighed on her almost as much as the sadness she'd absorbed from Diana.

"Hello, Catherine. How are you this evening?" a squeaky voice called from the sidewalk.

"Hi, Abigail. I've been better. Do you want to come up and have a glass of wine?"

"A half a glass of wine would be lovely, dear. These old legs are wobbly enough these days."

A few minutes later, Abigail and her dog were settled on the porch. Handing the wine to Abigail, Cat said, "Did you meet Rodney at Jim's wake?"

"Yes, I sure did. He was a lovely bear of a man."

"Sadly, he passed away yesterday."

Abigail put her wine down and gently tugged on Maddog's leash as the dog growled. "Oh heavens! How terrible. What happened?"

"They think it might be an accidental drowning." *Or something worse.*

"Good Lord. Too many young people are leaving us these days."

The women sipped the Pinot Grigio and chatted for half an hour. Sensing that Maddog wanted to get going, Abigail took her leave. "Take care, dear."

Cat watched her slowly amble away, with her yappy puppy trotting beside her. *I guess to someone who's ninety, people in their fifties do seem young. Jim, were you there to meet Rodney? Can you tell me why he was back in Jacksonville? And how he died?*

Chapter 17

SALVATORE

The doorbell sounded unnaturally loud as it rang through the house. Nico was a jumble of nerves. He was well aware of the written report on Salvatore Alessi, including his transgressions. He had been upset at first but had decided to suspend judgment and let his father explain himself. Like any child who searches for an unknown parent, Nico's curiosity was mixed with high expectations and a measure of anxiety.

Opening the solid mahogany door, Nico stared into the eyes of the man who had given him life. Before him, he saw an older version of himself.

"My son! My beautiful boy. I'm so happy to see you," Salvatore said as he grabbed Nico and wrapped his arms around him. "I should not have stayed away from you for so long."

Luna joined them and saw the uncomfortable look on Nico's face. She welcomed Sal into the front parlor, where the table was set with an almond cake and a local red wine. She fussed with the dessert and poured the Chianti while Nico chattered nervously.

"I have many friends who share my love of cooking," Nico said. "When I am older, I want to go to culinary school and be a chef like my mother."

"Your mother was perfection in the kitchen," Salvatore exclaimed. "I have no doubt you have many talents, too. I'm part owner of a restaurant in Crete. You must come and cook with me!"

Nico and Luna quickly glanced at one another. They knew this was a lie, but neither said a word. Nor did Luna mention the paperwork she had sent Salvatore that included her request that he give up his parental rights. Her lawyer had confirmed that he'd been served the papers.

"So, tell me, Salvatore, how long have you lived in Greece?" Luna said, knowing the answer before she asked.

"For six years now. I have lived in four cities in Greece. That's why I haven't been back to Italy. I'm so sorry I didn't go to Carlotta's funeral. I didn't have the funds to return. There have been times when my career did not go as I had hoped. But all is well now. Nico, tell me more about your life since you left Palermo."

Nico ran upstairs to his room and grabbed the photo album that held the history of his life in Sicily and Tuscany. After bounding down the stairs, he excitedly told his father about every photo and the people in each one. Sal was engaged and complimentary of his ex-wife and his son. He commented on how tall and handsome Nico was. He teased his son about attracting the attention of many girls with his good looks.

"As a young man, Nico, I hope you can understand why I couldn't stay with you and your mother. I was too young to take on the responsibility of a wife and child, though I loved you both. I wasn't much older than you are now, and I was too immature. I'm so very sorry."

Nico's head dropped. "I do understand, Papa. And I forgive you."

Salvatore stood, as did his son. The two held each other tight. Luna had been frightened that Sal would break Nico's heart and not apologize for deserting the young man. She was also terrified that Sal would want Nico to move to Greece, causing her to lose him. She hadn't mentioned this to Nico, because she wanted the decision to be his. Salvatore described his life and the various places he'd lived. Neither Luna nor Nico asked Sal about his run-ins with the law.

"I'm a man who likes to be on the move. It's something in my nature, like my father before me. As I think you know, he left my mother soon after I was born. I'm sorry that I didn't attend my mother's funeral, either. It was—it was a difficult time in my life."

Nico asked his father, "Did you ever get married again? Do you have any other children?"

"No, and no. You are my only child, Nico. That's why I would like you to think about visiting me in Crete. Maybe even move there and help me at the restaurant."

Luna and Nico stared at each other. They'd known this request would be a possibility.

"Nico is very settled in his school here and has plans to attend a culinary institute in Italy. Uprooting him again is not a good idea," Luna stated.

Salvatore began pacing. "I believe it's his decision and mine to make. I am his father, after all. I should have a say in where he lives."

Luna planted herself directly in front of Sal and said, "Yes, you are his father, but it should be his decision. Carlotta asked me to care for Nico if anything ever happened to her, and I agreed. I wish to honor her request."

"Papa," Nico said, "I would like to visit you in Greece, but this is my home. Luna is my guardian, my second mother. I can join you on my holiday in December. We can get to know one another then."

Sal glared at Luna. She could suddenly feel his hatred like a blast of cold air. He turned and smiled at Nico. "Certainly, Son. You can come and visit on your holiday. Then you can decide where you would like to live. I understand your hesitance, because we don't know each other well. But given time, we will."

"That would be good, Papa. I would like that."

"Well, I'll be on my way. Thank you, Luna, for your hospitality. I will leave the signing of any papers until after Nico has come to Crete." Salvatore gave his son a quick hug and then left. The meeting had lasted less than an hour.

"Well, what do you think, Nico?"

Nico slumped in a chair, then picked up the photo album and flipped through the pages. "This has been my life. My mother and you have been my parents. Papa lied about owning the restaurant. I know he's only a waiter."

"I'm concerned that he would take you out of school and make you work. Your future may not be your own. But you should be with him if that's what you choose. I do think you shouldn't make any firm plans

89

until you finish school. You still have three years to go before you can attend culinary school."

"Yes, I agree. Thank you for everything you have done for me."

"I will love you always, wherever you are. Let's go to our favorite restaurant tonight and take our minds off all of this."

Chapter 18

MORGUE

The morning sun warmed Cat as she gathered roses from her garden. The fragrant red, pink, and yellow flowers were dotted with morning dew. She rushed inside when she heard her cell phone ringing, but missed the call. Her lawyer left a message stating that the accountant hadn't completed her audit of Emerson & Ritter's financials due to some lingering questions. Jerome said he would contact her as soon as the report was finished. *I wonder if Jim's flagged emails have anything to do with the accounting problems. Maybe I should talk to Brad, but I'm not sure if he'll give me a straight answer.*

Catherine arranged the sweet-scented flowers in a crystal vase. She took a pecan coffee cake out of the oven, placed a couple slices on china plates, and poured two cups of coffee. Diana joined her in the kitchen and gratefully accepted the mug.

"Are you sure you don't want me to go with you this morning?" Cat asked, knowing Diana had a challenging time ahead of her at the coroner's office.

"I'm sure. I'm going to head back to Gainesville after I identify my dad. I've got a lot to do, including making arrangements for his funeral. I'll let you know when they release him to me. I hope you'll come to the funeral."

"Of course I'll come, Diana. I'll contact Hazel, and we can drive together. Let me know if there's anything I can do."

"Telling the kids that their grandfather died was the worst. They both cried nonstop, especially because my mom passed away so recently.

91

They think I've shipped them off to their other grandparents because I don't want them around. But the truth is, I'm still really worried about our safety. They'll come back to Gainesville for the funeral, but then I want them to return to Destin for another few weeks."

"I guess you can't tell them why you're worried. You're right that they don't need to be afraid when we don't actually know what happened."

Diana bit into the cake and refilled her coffee. She was clearly nervous, unable to relax. "A part of me hopes that Dad had car trouble and his death was an accident. But deep down, I know that's wishful thinking. I guess I'll find out this morning. I'll text you when I get the results of the autopsy."

Catherine wrapped a large slice of cake, poured coffee into a travel mug, and handed them to her grieving friend. Diana hugged her host, placed her suitcase in her car, and drove away. She was heading to the morgue in Jacksonville for one of the most tragic things a person can do: identify the body of a loved one. Cat went inside and turned on her computer to try to make sense of Jim's flagged emails. She decided to talk to Hazel about the recent shipments to the company so she could understand why Jim was interested in them. She would also ask Hazel if she could identify the initials of the people who wrote the emails to Jim. But before she could make the call, she received an email from Luna.

Hello Catherine,

I want to report on Salvatore's meeting with Nico and me. He is very handsome and charming, as expected. I can understand why Carlotta was attracted to the man. There is no doubt that Nico is his son. The resemblance is undeniable, and I know it unsettled our dear boy.

Salvatore has asked Nico to join him in Greece, and we will make arrangements for him to go at Christmas. I was grateful that Nico did not want to travel back there with his father immediately. He understood that Salvatore lied to us about his current job when he said that he was part owner of a restaurant. We know he is only a waiter. And he was not forthcoming about why he did not attend Carlotta's funeral. He was in jail at the time.

I did not confront him about his criminal record, but Nico is fully aware of his father's past. My lawyer will reach out to Salvatore and request that he sign the papers soon instead of waiting until Nico has been to Crete, as he suggested. I do not want to wait for several months to have this matter resolved.

I also have news about my birth father. I will tell you about it when we next talk.

Love, Luna

Mystery upon mystery, Cat mused. The mention of Nico reminded Cat that she hadn't completed her searches on Nicosia and Cyprus. Her conversation with Hazel could wait. But before she could start that, there was a knock at the door, and Cat jumped up to answer it. A police officer was standing on her porch.

"Hello, Ms. Emerson. I'm Officer Reynolds with the sheriff's department." He showed Cat his badge. "I have a photo I'd like you to show you. May I come in?"

"Yes. Please come in, Officer Reynolds." Cat settled on the sofa, and the policeman sat in a chair across from her. "Is this about the 911 call I made concerning the young man who was in the park with a gun?"

"Yes. There have been other complaints about an armed individual who has threatened several people on the island." The officer took out a photo from a folder. "Is this the person you saw?"

Catherine peered into the face of the young man who'd pointed his weapon at her. "Yes, that's him."

"In addition," Officer Reynolds continued, "the suspect, nineteen-year-old Terrence McAllen, posted on Facebook that he planned to shoot students at the high school. Two people out of state notified the FBI, and he was arrested yesterday. He's been processed and released into his parents' custody, and they have removed all the firearms in the house. They live in Old Town, as well."

"Couldn't they hold him? He probably thinks I'm the one who informed on him. What if he comes after me? I don't feel safe in my own home."

"They could have held him for a short time, but the judge decided to release him. His parents are keeping an eye on him. Not much we can do at this point." The officer rose to leave. "I'll let you know of any new developments."

"Thanks," Cat said as she showed him out. After closing the door and locking it behind her, she flopped into a chair. *There are too many crazy things happening right now. A fire, a cannonball, and a homicidal kid, all in Old Town Fernandina. What's next?*

Her phone dinged, and Cat read a text from Sam: *Can I take you out for dinner next Saturday?*

She responded, *Perfect. I'll make a reservation at a restaurant on the island.*

I'm way too excited about this date. Take it slow, Catherine. He just reminds you of Zach, she thought.

Her phone dinged again with a text from Diana: *Just leaving the morgue. My dad was murdered.*

Chapter 19

VIRTUES AND VICES

Catherine asked Lisa to go with her to Gainesville for Rodney's funeral. Hazel was planning on visiting friends in Orlando after the service, so she drove separately.

"I had so many great weekends in Gainesville at UF with Jim. It was exciting to go to Gator football games. I don't regret going to UNF, and I'm glad I had that time with my dad," stated Cat. "Living at home during college wasn't always easy, but I'm happy I did it, especially because Dad died so soon after I graduated. It was shocking."

"It must have been a terrible time for you. We met...what? Two years after graduation?"

"Yes, and I'm so grateful we did. You've been a true friend, and I've enjoyed watching your boys grow up. Have you ever been to the University of Florida?" Cat asked. "I don't think I've ever asked you that before."

"No, I haven't, and the Florida State Seminoles is still my team. I only went to home football games. I feel like I'm going into enemy territory," Lisa said, laughing.

Cat grinned. "I have all these wonderful memories mixed in with the overwhelming sadness of why we're going to Gainesville. I never thought I'd be attending another funeral so soon after Jim's. And the fact that Rodney's death wasn't an accident is frightening. The coroner said it was a single blow to the back of his head. I wonder if Rodney knew he was in mortal danger."

"I hope he didn't know what was coming. He was such a big guy. You'd think he'd be able to fight back," Lisa said. "He must have been ambushed. And then to dump his car and him into a river. That's sick."

"And serious. I pray they find out who did this and whether it was tied to his gambling or not. Either way, Diana has a right to be worried about her safety."

"Do the police have any leads?"

"Nothing concrete at this point. The last time I was at the office, Rodney said he wanted to talk to me in private, but we never had a chance to have that talk. It sounded like something related to the company. I asked Hazel if she had any idea about what Rodney was worried about. She said she didn't."

Cat drove through the University of Florida, pointing out the highlights to her friend, including the Ben Hill Griffen Stadium, Lake Alice, the Florida Museum of Natural History, and Mark Bostick Golf Course. The campus was quiet, but soon it would be swarming with students beginning their semester. College towns were a tale of two seasons—serene quiet and jubilant chaos.

Checking the GPS on her phone, Catherine drove southeast to Diana's house, which was in the Idyllwild area of Gainesville. They were surprised that the street in front of Diana's house was jammed with cars since the funeral service was taking place at a church several miles away. Cat decided to go directly to the church. They entered the house of worship and sat in the back row. There were floral arrangements beside every second pew, and the intense fragrance of lilies greeted them.

The amateur detectives wanted to watch the people as they filed in. Catherine surreptitiously photographed interesting attendees with her phone. Some she recognized from Jim's company, including the profusely sweating Brad, the genial Hazel, and several men who worked in the warehouse. Giancarlo Riva strode in with a grim expression on his handsome face. Families who were Diana's local friends and neighbors filled the room, as did numerous theater members from Jacksonville who had become Rodney's friends. A petite woman and a well-built man, both dressed in black suits, entered the church and sat in the last row, right across the aisle from Cat and Lisa.

"Are those two police officers?" she whispered to Lisa.

96

"I think so," Lisa responded in a hushed voice. "They're here in addition to the uniformed police we saw outside."

"An unsolved homicide brings out law enforcement in force."

Diana, her husband, Jason, and the children tearfully walked down the center aisle. The polished oak casket was rolled into the church, accompanied by six older gentlemen. A young woman with an angelic voice began to sing and the congregation became silent. Father Ralph began his sermon, and several speakers extolled the many virtues and a few vices of Rodney Simmons. Understandably, no one mentioned the gruesome murder of the man lying in the coffin.

A short time later, they stood in the intense Florida heat at the graveside. Molly and Mason held their mother's hands and sobbed. The priest kept his remarks brief, and family and friends placed white roses on the casket. Cat observed the faces of the mourners. *Is there someone here involved in Rodney's death? I'm not even sure what I'm looking for.*

Afterward, the grievers gathered at Diana's house for the wake. There were constant whispers about Rodney's untimely demise and speculation about "who done it." Conspiracy theories swirled like tumbleweeds in a tornado. In the kitchen, Cat and Lisa joined Diana, who was making a large pitcher of lemonade. Father Ralph was in a heated debate with a woman about the nature of good and evil. He insisted that because of Satan's fall and original sin, people have an innate defect that makes them succeptable to bad influences from other people as well as demonic forces. Only the church could save their souls from eternal damnation. Even the person who ended Rodney's life could be saved through repentance and absolution, but non-believers would not enter the gates of heaven.

The woman was arguing that religion was a superstitious, manmade mythology first created by unsophisticated people who couldn't explain the physical world. They invented gods, gave them human character-istics and emotions, and developed rituals and rules to appease these divine beings. She stated that the universe is random and conscious-ness is the product of our biology. There is no heaven or hell, and the lights go out when we die. There is no before life or afterlife.

Cat and Lisa left the debaters in the kitchen and moved into the living room. They sat with Molly and Mason, who looked like zombies as they nibbled on cookies. Cat empathized with their shock and grief, having experienced a loss so recently herself. Hazel joined them and spoke lovingly to the children about their grandfather. She told several funny stories about the big man and got the children to crack a smile. Catherine nodded to Bradley as he waddled through the living room and out the front door. She was surprised that she hadn't seen Giancarlo since the mass at the church.

She spied Diana slipping into her bedroom, looking very upset. Cat followed her. She hugged the younger woman and gently held her. "We'll find out who did this, Diana. I'm sure the police are giving it their full attention. Have they been able to share anything new?"

Diana pulled away and flopped onto the bed. "Nothing new. I can't stand not knowing what happened to Dad! He didn't deserve to die and be dumped in a river. I'm not sure if I'm more angry or frightened or heartbroken. At least he and my mom are together again."

"I have faith that they're together. I'm not someone who believes we cease to exist when we die, unlike your friend in the kitchen. I *know* we have souls that continue on after death. I've felt my parents around me, especially during hard times."

"I've felt my mom near me, too. Sometimes I smell her perfume, and I know she's close. I wonder what sign my dad will use to let me know he's around. Do you think it matters that he died suddenly and violently? Will he still be able to connect with me?" Diana questioned.

"That will probably happen...in time."

"I wish he could tell me right now who killed him and why!"

Chapter 20

TAILED

Cat and Lisa began the long drive back to Fernandina Beach. "I'm glad there were so many people at the funeral to support Diana and Jason. There were a few of Rodney's old buddies in addition to the folks from work and others from his theater group," Cat said. "I wish I knew what he'd wanted to talk to me about. And if it had anything to do with his death."

"And what about those strange things he sent you? A knock-off wallet and facial cream. It's weird."

"It still blows my mind that he was murdered. Having the police at the funeral was unnerving. I'm afraid for Diana and her family."

They drove in silence for the next half hour.

"I meant to ask you about the letter Jim gave to your lawyer. Do you want to talk about it?" Lisa asked.

Catherine sighed. "It was quite short. Basically, he said that I should stop being afraid of life. I should face my fears and embrace adventure. I believe he was referring to my fear of flying. And I should open my heart to love. I think he meant I had better find a man!"

"I agree with that!" said Lisa.

"But he also warned me not to have blind faith in people. That there are unscrupulous wolves in sheep's clothing. I have no idea who he was talking about."

Lisa thought for a moment. "I don't think he meant Beatrice, so maybe it was something to do with his company."

"That's possible. He also wrote that if I was reading the letter, he would be gone physically but would always watch over me."

"It sounds like he knew he wasn't going to live a long time. Do you think he was worried about having a heart attack like your dad?"

"He always took good care of himself, but it's likely he feared that his heart would give out someday. And after the virus swept the world, he knew no one was ever physically safe. The biggest surprise of all was that he had a life insurance policy for four hundred thousand dollars, and I'm the beneficiary."

"Catherine! Why didn't you tell me?"

"In a way, I feel guilty that I'll profit from Jim's death. When he helped me buy the cottage, I knew he had a good income and could afford it as an investment. But this felt different. I know it doesn't make sense."

"It's a gift he wanted you to have. Don't feel guilty. And now I understand why you haven't rushed to sell your shares in Jim's company."

Catherine's phone rang, and she answered on her Bluetooth. Lisa giggled as she heard Darth Vader speak to Cat.

"Hello, Catherine. The accountant has finished her audit, and all questions were answered. I'll overnight the documents to you. Contact me if you have any questions. You can proceed with the sale of your shares of Emerson and Ritter if you wish. Let me know, and I can contact Mr. Ritter and get the ball rolling."

"Thank you, Jerome. I'm not sure what I'm going to do at this point. I think I'll hold off for now. I want to keep my foot in the door until I know what happened to Rodney."

"That could take a long time, or the crime may never be solved, Catherine. Perhaps it's best to make a clean break. Did Jim leave instructions in the letter he left for you?"

"No. It was related to personal matters, not his business."

"Let me know if you change your mind. Good day."

Lisa laughed out loud. "Good heavens! I could barely keep from laughing. He sounds just like Darth Vader. And you said he looks like James Earl Jones?"

"Yes, he does! Definitely his doppelganger. Lisa, take a look behind us. Can you see that beige sedan a couple cars back? I think it's been following us since we left Gainesville. Every time I change lanes, they do, too. And they keep the same distance behind us."

Lisa turned around to check out the car. "Why don't you get off at the next exit and see if they follow. If Diana thinks she's in danger, maybe you are, too."

Seconds before the exit, Cat swerved onto the ramp, then made a sharp right turn at the stop sign. She floored the pedal and, with screeching tires, peeled into a parking lot behind an abandoned building, where they could see the service road. A short time later, they watched the beige car speed by their location.

"Wow, I think you were right. Let's get out of here before they come back."

The remainder of the trip home was uneventful, but Cat's nerves were on edge. She pulled into Lisa's driveway. "It could be a coincidence that the car got off at the exit..."

"Or whoever killed Rodney thinks you might be a threat, too. I wish Jim had been more specific in his warning about unscrupulous wolves."

"Me, too. Then I'd know for sure if Rodney's death was related to the business. I hope the police find out who did it, and why, very soon."

"Do you want to stay with us for a few nights, Cat? It might put your mind at ease."

"No, but thanks. I'll be fine. I turn on the security system now whenever I'm at home. Ever since that crazy guy was firing his gun in the park, I realized I should use it regularly."

The sky was darkening by the time Catherine pulled into the driveway. Normally, she would take a glass of wine out to the front porch and watch the sunset turn from coral to midnight blue. Tonight, however, she stayed inside, closed all the drapes and blinds, and activated the security system. Roaming aimlessly around the house, she felt lonely.

She turned on her computer with the intention of editing a new manuscript she'd just received. Instead, she checked her emails and grinned when she saw there was one from Nico. He chatted away about his summer and his friends. He detailed his text messages with his new American friend, Sam. In her mind's eye, she could see Nico talking animatedly to her, a great big grin on his face and his hands gesturing with excitement.

A wave of longing swept through her, and she began to cry. *How can I miss Nico and Luna so much? I barely know them, but my heart breaks that we're so far apart. A slow boat to Italy. Maybe that's what I should do. Get away from here for a while.* She went to her browser and typed in *Cruises from Florida to Italy.*

Chapter 21

LAVENDER

"I was just about to call you, Luna! You must have read my mind," Catherine said as she answered her phone. "I have some news."

"I do, as well. Viola, my lawyer, called and informed me that Salvatore has filed for sole custody of Nico. I am not certain how he can afford a lawyer, but he wants our boy to live with him in Crete. I am not even sure where Salvatore is staying at the moment."

"Oh God, no! Do you have anything in writing from Carlotta stating that she wanted you to care for Nico?"

"No, but Viola is writing affidavits for her, Nico, and me to sign that indicate Carlotta told us that she wanted me to be responsible for Nico. I am grateful that Viola was a witness to that conversation."

"Where do you think Salvatore got the money for a lawyer?"

"It is most likely that he received it from his brother, Riccardo, in Palermo. To my knowledge, this brother never offered any financial help to Carlotta, or to Nico since his mother passed. He has a successful computer company that makes games and security software. I want to meet with Riccardo to ask him to support my adoption of Nico," Luna said.

"Can I go with you?"

"Of course, but I do not understand. How can you be there?"

"That's my news, Luna. I've booked a cruise to Italy! It leaves a week from this coming Saturday and takes fourteen days to arrive in Civitavecchia, near Rome."

"What? This is fantastic news! What made you decide to come now?"

"I miss you and Nico so much that I don't want to wait any longer. Also, I have other news. I didn't mention this before, but Jim took out a life insurance policy and made me the beneficiary. It will be a while until I receive the money, but all the paperwork is done, and I thought I might as well come right away."

"Oh my! Nico will be so excited! He talks about you daily. Please send me your itinerary, and we can plan a trip to Palermo while you are here. We will meet with Riccardo, tell him about the situation, and hopefully convince him to withdraw his financial support for Salvatore's lawyer. Perhaps if he meets his nephew and understands Nico's sincere desire to live with me, Riccardo will assist us."

"I pray that happens, Luna. It's surprising that Riccardo has chosen now to come into Salvatore's and Nico's lives."

"I do not understand it, either. But if we all talk to him, perhaps he will be persuaded. So, Nico and I will come to Civitavecchia and meet your ship. Then we will drive to the ferry in Calabria that will take us to Sicily. We will meet with Riccardo, then tour the island before returning to Siena. I am so excited for your visit!"

"Me, too. I also want to see Rome and Florence, and Siena, of course."

"This is such a wonderful surprise. I will tell Nico right away."

As soon as Luna hung up, Cat's phone rang again. "Hi, Lisa. I was just about to call you. How would you like to drive with me to Fort

Lauderdale a week from this coming Friday? We can take my car, and I'll pay for a hotel for the night."

"What's up?"

"I'm taking a cruise to Italy. I booked it last night."

"That's great! I assume you're going to see your sister and nephew. I'd be happy to go with you and drive your car back. How long will you be gone?"

"I'm not sure, but it's two weeks there and two back for starters. I'm thinking I'll spend a week in Sicily and at least a week around Siena. There are a couple of options for my return cruise, so I'll decide once I'm there. I can't believe I'm actually going! I think that Jim would be proud of me even though I'm not flying."

"I know he's proud of you!" said Lisa.

"It turns out to be a good time to go. Nico's father, Salvatore, wants full custody and for them to live in Greece. Luna thinks Salvatore's brother in Palermo is paying for the lawyer, and she wants to meet with him and convince him that Nico should be with her, not his deadbeat dad. I'm glad that Luna has a good lawyer. It could be a nasty fight. And I'm grateful I can be with them when they confront Riccardo, Sal's brother."

"The timing is amazing. Maybe you got a nudge last night from Jim to book the trip. Your family needs you."

"Thank you for saying that," Cat said while choking back tears. "The joy of having a family comes with obligations. I'm happy to be a part of the battle to help Nico."

"Oh, by the way, do you have a passport?"

"Yes. I've always kept it up to date in case Stella became ill or passed away. I wanted the ability to drive to Toronto at a moment's notice."

"Always thinking ahead!"

* * *

Downtown Fernandina Beach was bustling the following morning when Catherine headed for The Book Loft on Centre Street. She walked up the creaky steps beside the exposed red-brick wall to the second floor. She perused the travel section and selected a book on

Italy, along with one on Sicily. After returning to the main floor, she bumped into an old friend who worked in the store.

"Catherine, it's good to see you," said Nancy. "Travel books! Don't tell me you're going to Italy."

"Yes, I am! I'm taking a cruise ship out of Fort Lauderdale and heading to Rome soon. Since I'll be at sea for two weeks, I'm stocking up. What new novels do you recommend?"

"The latest bestsellers are on the table over here. Isn't it nice that we don't have to read books about tyranny anymore? Thank goodness our democracy is back on track," Nancy said.

"Very true. Yet I learned so much about politics, psychopaths, authoritarians, and the cult of personality."

"Me, too! So, does that mean you don't want to read any political thrillers?"

"Mystery, humor, and women's fiction are on my list today."

Cat paid for the books, dropped them in her car, and walked across the street to an upscale boutique. She was on the hunt for something fabulous for her date with Sam on Saturday. She spotted a lavender-colored dress at the back of the shop. The knee-length chiffon frock had delicate flowers in white and yellow printed on the soft fabric. She took it to the change room and gasped at the price tag. After slipping on the dress, however, she smiled at the image in the mirror. *Beautiful! It's expensive, but damn, I look good!* Remembering that a large sum of money was coming her way, she put her T-shirt and shorts back on and paid for the dress.

Her phone rang as she was pulling into her driveway. "Hi, Hazel. How are you?"

"Quite well, thank you. I found a box of Jim's things in the warehouse. Would you be able to pick it up?"

"Sure. I'll come a week from Wednesday if that's okay. By the way, I'm leaving on a trip to Italy that following Saturday."

"Oh heavens! I'm so glad you're going. But I thought you didn't fly," Hazel said.

"I'm taking a cruise across the Atlantic. Luna is picking me up near Rome, and we're driving to Sicily before returning to her home in Siena. Please don't say anything to Brad about my sister."

"Of course not, honey. That's between us."

"Any news about Rodney?" Cat questioned. "I haven't talked to Diana since the funeral."

"I haven't spoken to her, either, and Bradley hasn't mentioned any updates. It's all so terrible. I still can't believe he was murdered."

"Me, either. I've got to go, but I'll see you soon, Hazel."

There was a package on the front porch when Cat got home. She scooped it up and brought it inside with her purchases. She hung up the dress and dropped the books beside her suitcase. When she opened the FedEx envelope, she gasped as her eyes skimmed over the pages.

Chapter 22

FIRST DATE

A gentle breeze greeted Catherine and Sam as they settled into the chairs at a candlelit table. The enchanting gardens at Espana, Cat's favorite Spanish restaurant in Fernandina Beach, were the perfect place for their first date. The fragrance of jasmine filled the night air as the royal palms swayed. The restaurant owner welcomed Catherine, and they talked about the recent events on the island. He mentioned once again that Mick Jagger and the Rolling Stones ate at the restaurant twice when they were staying on Amelia Island. He then recommended a superb new Rioja wine on the menu, and they ordered a bottle.

"You look beautiful tonight, Catherine."

The color rose in Cat's cheeks. "Thank you. And you always dress so nicely. Is that a new watch?"

"Yes. I've been wanting to get this one for a long time."

"It's striking."

"I'm surprised we didn't go to an Italian restaurant tonight in honor of your Tuscan sister," Sam stated. "I'm still remembering that great dinner Lisa and Nico made."

"It was incredible. I loved having a house filled with people, wonderful food, and conversation. I miss Luna and Nico so much that I've decided to take a cruise to Italy."

Sam's jaw dropped open. "That's amazing! I assume you've never been to Europe. It will be a great adventure for you. When are you going?"

108

"There's a ship leaving next Saturday from Fort Lauderdale. It stops in the Azores Islands, then Málaga and Cartagena in Spain. It docks in Civitavecchia, near Rome. Luna and Nico will pick me up there, and we're driving to Sicily. Nico wants to show me his homeland, and we'll tour for a week or so before heading back to Siena."

"That sounds fantastic! Are you traveling around Italy, too?"

"I'd like to see Rome and Florence. I'm not sure where else. I'm excited and a little nervous."

"Maybe I can meet up with you. I'll time my next business trip to Florence when you're there, or I can meet you in Siena."

Their server arrived and poured the wine, and they ordered sangria salads and the seafood paella for two. They tapped glasses and sipped the wine.

"Let's toast to the world traveler Catherine Emerson!" Sam said.

Cat grinned, and they clinked glasses one more time. "This has been a summer of great contrasts—both wonderful and awful, astonishing and painful. Thinking back on it now makes my head spin. And things keep happening."

"That's just typical of life in general, don't you think?" Sam said. "Always something unexpected waiting in the wings."

"You're so right. When we're in Palermo, we want to meet with Riccardo Alessi, Nico's uncle and Salvatore's younger brother. Sal has filed for custody of Nico, and we want to convince Riccardo to support Luna's desire to be his guardian."

"Yes, Nico sent me a text about it. It's a lot for a young teen to deal with. He belongs with Luna. There's no doubt in my mind. Even though you've only known them a short time, you must love having a sister and a nephew."

"It's amazing that I have a true family even after Jim's passing. And it was so much fun taking Nico to Disney World. He had to go on some rides by himself because both Luna and I are afraid of heights. We're real sisters."

Sam reached across the table and took Cat's hand. Her heart throbbed for the first time since high school. Every inch of her body tingled with excitement. *This is the feeling I've been missing. I didn't think it was possible at my age!* Sam squeezed her hand, then released it.

"I can't wait to have paella in Spain," Catherine said. "Have you been to Málaga?"

"No. I've never traveled in the south of Spain. Madrid and Barcelona are great cities. Maybe we can go together sometime."

"A few months ago, I wouldn't have imagined doing that in my wildest dreams. But who knows! If I enjoy the cruise, maybe I'll go to Europe more often."

"On another matter, I spoke with Brad this week, and he's anxious to move the company forward. I also talked to Giancarlo and was impressed with their operation and the commercial real estate side of things. I have foreign contacts who may want to invest in property here. We all do whatever it takes to succeed."

Catherine sighed. "I think I'll wait until I get back from Italy to decide if and when I want to sell my shares. As long as Rodney's death is unresolved, I don't feel comfortable cutting my ties to E & R. I'll talk to Brad on Wednesday when I go over to the office. They have a box of Jim's souvenirs I need to pick up. I want to take a few of them to Luna and Nico. But enough about me. How was your trip to Cyprus?"

"I ended up not going. My friend had a family emergency in Italy and didn't go. Catherine, when we first met at the airport, I thought I heard you call out the name Zach. I don't know why, but I turned around."

Catherine blushed again, and she sipped her wine. "Yes, I did. You look amazingly like my high school boyfriend, and I thought you were him."

"Is that a good thing or a bad thing?"

"Well, I almost didn't give you my address and phone number. I was unnerved by the resemblance. Zach promised his undying love at the senior prom and then broke up with me a few weeks later."

"So, do you see me as a replacement for your old boyfriend?"

Cat laughed. "Not at all. I closed that door long ago. I have no idea where he is, and I don't really care."

Their salads arrived, and the conversation turned to the getting-to-know-you-better stage. After a delicious dinner, they strolled down Centre Street and followed the music to The Green Turtle bar. A raucous crowd overflowed onto the patio at the Florida House Inn next door. The Honey Badgers, a favorite local band, had the patrons singing along to hits from the 70s. Gen Xers joined Boomers in exuberant dances to a thumping beat. Cat and Sam edged their way to the bar and ordered drinks. They squeezed their way to the far end of the patio, delighting in the spectacle.

The evening ended with Catherine and Sam sitting in the Muskoka chairs on Cat's porch, sipping Pellegrino. Cat had never ended a first date with more than kisses, but tonight she thought it might be different. *I have a pounding heart and butterflies in my stomach. How far will we go tonight?* The sound of music overwhelmed the song of the cicadas. The crooning voice of a young Frank Sinatra was carried through the air from a neighbor's house. Sam stood and offered Cat his hand. He drew her close, and they slow danced to the music. *This is almost like my dream! Except for Nat King Cole and a diamond ring on my finger.*

A loud bang came from the park across the road. Cat and Sam jumped in unison. "Let's go inside," she said. "It might be that crazy McAllen kid. He could have gotten ahold of a gun again."

"I haven't heard about him," said Sam as he opened the screen door. "After you."

A short time later, Sam told her he should be going. "I've had a wonderful evening, and I hope we can do it again." He looked into her eyes and gave her a tender kiss on the lips.

After Sam left, Cat tucked herself into bed, a smile on her face. The next morning, her ringing phone woke her from a deep sleep. "Good morning, Lisa," she said after looking at the caller ID.

"Tell me all about your date! Unless Sam is there with you."

"I'm alone." Catherine got out of bed and headed to the kitchen to make coffee. "We had a lovely evening, but it ended with a moonlit dance and a goodnight kiss."

"Was that your choice or his?"

A joyful laugh escaped Cat's lips. "I wasn't sure how I wanted the night to end. But Sam made the decision for me. I guess he wants to take this relationship slowly."

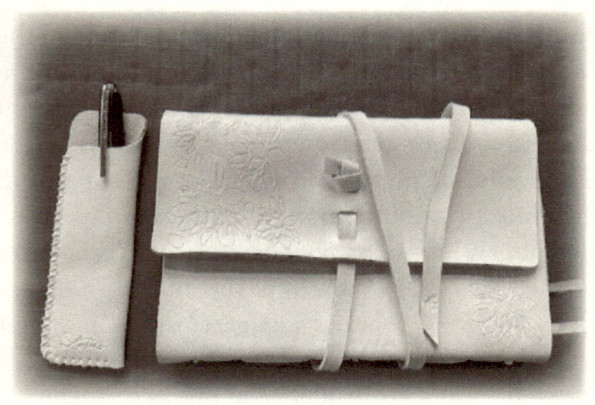

Chapter 23

JOURNAL

Before Catherine left for Emerson & Ritter on Wednesday morning, she deleted all the personal emails and photographs on Jim's laptop. She also deleted the business emails her brother had flagged, which she had forwarded to her computer. On her way to the office, she stopped by a luxury riverfront condo that was managed by Riva Realty. She wanted to take a peek. The CPA's report, which she'd received from Jerome, listed this property, among several other high-end properties in Jacksonville, as one in which E & R had a financial stake. But the most shocking information in the report was that the company was worth 19.4 million dollars.

She parked and entered the ornate building to take a look around, and she was surprised to hear the residents conversing in several languages. She explained to the security guard who she was, then commented on the diversity of people who owned condos in the building.

"Yes, Ms. Emerson. We have a large number of foreigners living here. Some from Italy and lots from Russia. Several of them are young women expecting babies. I guess they come here because we've got great doctors and medical care here in Jax, and it's more affordable than Miami."

I bet there is another reason these women are having babies here: so their newborns will automatically become American citizens.

Catherine thanked the guard and then got back in her car and drove to the E & R office. She hoped that Brad would be out when she arrived. She pulled into the parking lot and immediately walked to the loading dock at the rear of the building. A truck was being unloaded, and she spied Peter, an elderly Black man who had replaced Rodney.

"Ms. Catherine, nice to see you. We sure do miss your brother and Rodney."

"Hi, Peter. I do, too. It's been a hard time for all of us. I'm here to see Hazel but thought I would stop by and say hello. It looks like you have a full warehouse. What's new in the import section?"

"Lots of nice stuff from Europe. Paintings and purses and other things for ladies."

"I'm glad business is good. Have a nice day." *Business is astoundingly good. Especially the real estate division.* Cat walked around the building and bumped into Hazel at the front door.

"There you are. I thought I saw your car drive in."

"Hi, Hazel. Here's Jim's laptop. Brad wanted it. I've deleted his personal emails and photos."

Hazel took the computer and placed it in Brad's office, then returned with a large box, which she dropped on her desk. "This is the last of Jim's treasures. You know, some days I come into the office and expect to see his smiling face."

"Sometimes when my phone rings I expect to hear his voice on the other end. It's going to take a while to accept the fact he's no longer with us. And the same goes for Rodney. Has there been any news from the police about Rodney?"

"We haven't heard a thing. The police have interviewed everyone here in this building twice, but if they discovered anything, they're keeping it to themselves. I think his disappearance and death had something to do with his gambling. There can be no other explanation."

Cat sighed. "You could be right. I just hope the police get to the bottom of this soon. Not knowing is very hard on Diana and her family. Is Brad here right now?"

"No. He'll be back in an hour, if you'd like to wait."

"It's okay. I'll be in touch when I get back from Europe. Please tell Brad I'll be out of the country for a while. Say I'm driving to Toronto if he asks. By the way, how's your daughter doing?"

"Much better. She's recovered from the surgery, and the experimental drug is doing wonders."

"I'm so glad to hear that."

Hazel smiled and said, "I have a little gift for you. It's a leather-bound journal, so you can write about your first trip to Europe."

Cat hugged Hazel. "Oh, that's so thoughtful. You're very kind. Thank you."

"I wanted to give you something before I retired. I've decided to leave the company. Next week will be my final week."

"That's a surprise, but good for you, Hazel. It's time for you to take some time for yourself. You deserve it. Any plans for what you're going to do now?"

"Other than spend time with the grandkids, I'm not sure what's next."

Catherine inhaled the scent of the leather and then dropped the journal in her purse. She picked up Jim's box and said her goodbyes to Hazel, who walked with her to the door, a warm smile on her face.

When she arrived home, Catherine looked through the box of Jim's souvenirs and took out several for Luna and Nico. After placing them in her large suitcase, she began to pack for her unexpected adventure. She included her two new dresses, bathing suits for the Sicilian beaches, and everything else she could cram in the bag. She emptied Jim's carry-on suitcase so she could use it for her overnight stay at the hotel in Fort Lauderdale.

Her phone chimed, and she read the text from Brad: *Hazel informed me you are leaving for Canada. I will email the papers so I can buy your shares, and you can print, sign, and FedEx them back to me before you leave. It's vital for E & R to move forward ASAP.*

What's so important about me selling my shares now? It really annoys me that he's being so persistent. He can wait until I get back. She texted back, *I'll look at the papers when I return home.* Then she went to the contacts section of her phone and blocked Brad's number. On impulse, she called Diana.

"Oh, Catherine. I was going to call you tomorrow. I got some news from the police. There's a gas station near my dad's place that's been closed for a while. The cops were trying to track down the former owner, and they finally did. Luckily, they got the security video from the time around my father's disappearance," Diana said.

"Was your dad on the video?"

"Yes, he was. The day before he went missing. He bought gas, then pulled in front of the convenience store. A light brown sedan pulled up beside him, and he walked over to the driver's window. Dad could be seen arguing with someone, but the tinted window was only open a bit, so they couldn't see the person's face."

"Did they get the license plate number?"

"Yes, and they're trying to track down the owner. I finally have some hope that this nightmare will be over soon."

"Please email me with any info. I feel bad leaving the country when your dad's case is still open, but I'll keep in touch."

"Don't worry, Catherine. We'll be fine, and the police are making progress."

A few minutes later, Cat was putting the final items in her suitcase when the doorbell rang. It was a FedEx delivery again, but this time it was a different kind of parcel. She opened the package, and inside there were two small boxes, along with a note. She opened one of the jewelry boxes, and inside was a quarter-sized gold pendant in the shape of a rose. It hung on a delicate gold chain.

Dear Catherine, I had a friend design the necklaces. There's one for you and one for Luna. Two beautiful flowers! Can't wait to see you again. Sam

Cat was momentarily speechless. What a thoughtful gift. *I can't wait to see you, either!*

After a busy day preparing for her trip, Cat had an early night. Then, just before midnight, the sound of gunshots jolted her from her sleep. She froze for a moment, then tumbled out of the bed and moved away from the window. When the firing stopped, she crawled to the window and peered through the blinds at the front garden. There was no movement. Cat scurried back to her nightstand and grabbed her phone. Before she could dial 911, however, sirens wailed in the distance. She waited until she saw lights flashing through the blinds and heard a car door slam, and then she rushed to the front door and saw a police officer examining the fence along the front of her garden.

"A neighbor called 911. Are you okay, Ms. Emerson?" Officer Reynolds asked.

Shaken, Cat walked down to meet him. "Yes, I'm fine. What happened?"

"It appears that someone shot up your picket fence and the garden. Weirdest thing I've ever seen."

Cat looked around and noticed that the front porch was untouched. "Why on earth would anyone do that? Do you think it was that McAllen kid?"

"Could be, ma'am. I'll go by his house next. It looks like someone wanted to send you a message. Is there anyone who'd want to threaten you?"

A name popped into her mind, but she immediately rejected it. "No. No one I can think of."

"Is there someone you can stay with tonight? Just as a precaution."

"Yes. I'll call my friend and ask her to pick me up. I'm too rattled to drive. My poor rose garden."

Chapter 24

THE SHIP

The grand adventure began early on Friday. Catherine and Lisa loaded the suitcases into the car and headed down Highway 95 toward Fort Lauderdale.

"Don't worry about your picket fence. Dom and the boys will repair it for you, and we'll keep an eye on the place while you're away. I've got a house key, so I will swing by every week just to take in the mail and make sure everything is okay. I'm still freaked out about what happened. Thank goodness the crazy person didn't hit your house or shoot into your bedroom. Do you think it was the McAllen boy?"

"Maybe. His parents said he was home all night, but I guess he could have slipped out. The officer suggested it was someone wanting to send me a message, but I don't know who would want to scare me like that. It's bizarre, and I'm glad I'm leaving for a while."

"Do you have any news about Rodney?"

"I spoke to Diana last night, and the police are following up on some information. I hope they solve the murder soon. It's been so hard on her family, especially Molly and Mason."

"While you're away, I'll keep in touch with Diana. I'll work on Jim's emails, and if I need any computer help, I'll ask Max. My son became an impressive hacker—I should say 'a computer whiz'—during the lockdown."

"That would be great," said Cat. "You can be an intrepid private investigator probing into a murder case."

117

They were making good time on Highway 95, and the traffic was not bad at all. Cat glanced in the rearview mirror and screamed. A black pickup truck sped up behind her, inches away, and barely missed smashing into her rear fender. She let out a sigh when the truck raced past.

"Too much testosterone," Cat said. "My nerves are frazzled enough without some idiot almost hitting us. What were we talking about?"

"The investigation into Rodney's death. I like the thought of being a PI. I think I'd be good at that. Oh, hey, I forgot to ask if you booked yourself an ocean-view room on the ship."

"Even better. I booked a veranda room. I'd get claustrophobic if I couldn't be in the fresh air for two weeks and still have my privacy. I'm not used to being confined in a place with thousands of other people. The thought of another virus is in the back of my mind. I hope I'm not freaked out on board."

"Was the cruise expensive?" questioned Lisa.

"Yes, but I found out from Jerome's accountant that E & R is worth 19.4 million, which is incredible. Most of it is from the real estate business. If I sell my shares, and that's a big if, I'll be set for life. But apart from that, since this is my first big trip, I thought I would treat myself."

"That's incredible, Cat! Did Jim ever talk about their financial success?"

"No, not really. I always assumed they did all right, but I wonder if he really knew what was going on in the real estate part of the company. Maybe that's what all those flagged emails were about. I never fully explored them, but I'm going to try and figure it out on the trip."

"How else are you going to fill your time at sea?"

"I have two manuscripts to edit on my computer and lots of books to read. I've been reading about the history of Sicily, especially during the Greek era, and the time that Plato lived there. It's crazy. Democracy hasn't evolved as much as you'd think in twenty-five hundred years."

"That was made obvious by the deadly insurrection at the Capitol. The horror of that day is seared in my brain," said Lisa.

"Mine, too. But for now, I'm looking forward to the pools and the spa on the ship. And there are nine restaurants on board, including an Italian one, an Asian one, a seafood one, and a fine-dining one. I plan to try them all. With wine, of course."

"Sounds wonderful."

"The ship also has a rock-and-roll club, a blues club, and a theater with entertainment," Cat said. "And a wine tasting room where you can blend your own vino. I'm sure I'll keep busy."

"And maybe meet a nice man?"

"I highly doubt it. But Sam said he might be able to meet me when we get to Siena."

"So, you're saving yourself for a little Tuscan romance?"

"Very funny!"

"I put a small safety kit in your purse. There are band aids, a whistle, and a few other things."

"Thanks, Lisa. You're always prepared."

"And you will be, too."

The women drove in silence for a long while, and then Lisa said, "Cat, I'm really happy that you found Luna. You've been like a sister to me. I hope we'll always be close even though you now have a real sister."

Catherine reached over and took Lisa's hand. "We are best friends and soul sisters. Nothing, and no one, will ever replace you in my heart."

* * *

Chaos reigned in the hotel lobby on Saturday morning. Dozens of gray-haired travelers shuffled in, rolling their suitcases behind them. Elderly couples and gaggles of women in colorful cruise wear lined up to enter the shuttle buses. There were only a few families with chattering children.

Lisa gave her friend a final hug as she held back tears. "Why am I so sad? I know I'm going to see you again soon. Please be safe, Cat."

"I will. Call or email any time using the new Outlook address I gave you. I bought a cell phone data package for the entire time. I have to say, it's fun not worrying about money."

"I have a bad feeling about this trip, Cat. I know it doesn't make any sense. I didn't want to say anything before. Maybe it's just because you've never done anything like this and I'm worried about you."

"I promise not to fall overboard. And I'll be with Luna and Nico as soon as I land in Italy."

Their goodbyes were cut short when a silver-haired woman with a shrill voice began instructing the excited passengers to take their suitcases to the buses.

"I guess that's my cue to go. I'll miss you, Cat."

Catherine gave her friend a final hug. "I'll miss you, too. I'll email you and let you know how things are going."

Cat boarded the bus and sat beside a nattily dressed gentleman. His white hair was neatly trimmed, and he smiled at her with his entire face. She smiled back. The bus lurched forward and began the trip to the Fort Lauderdale port.

"Is this your first cruise across the pond?" he asked.

"Is it that obvious? I'm Catherine Emerson, and you are?"

"Doctor William Hawkins. But I'm not a medical doctor, so I won't be able to help you with sea sickness."

Cat chuckled. "I brought lots of medicine to deal with that. Where are you from, and where are you going, if you don't mind me asking?"

"I'm a history professor at the University of Toronto. I was visiting a friend in Miami before leaving to begin a sabbatical in Italy. It's a pleasure to meet you, Catherine. Where are you from, and where are you going?"

"I was born and raised in Jacksonville, Florida. My mother was from Toronto. Small world. I'm going to visit my sister. She lives in Siena, but we're touring Sicily before she shows me her city. I've never been to Europe before."

"Did your sister recently move to Italy?"

"No. I recently discovered I *had* a sister. A half-sister, actually. I didn't know that my mom had a baby when she was a nanny in Siena after high school. And Luna just found out we have the same mother."

"How exciting for you both. Technology is making the world smaller every day. Do you live in Jacksonville now?"

"No. I have a home on Amelia Island."

"I've heard of the island. Wait, is that where the Republican National Committee was holding its annual meeting when the insurrection at the US Capitol happened?"

"Yes. It was a tragic day for the country. The president actually called into the RNC meeting the day after the riots, and people cheered him. It's taken a long time for all those responsible to be held accountable. I hope nothing like that ever happens again."

They continued chatting, and soon the shuttle bus pulled into the loading area of the port and the noise level reached maximum decibels. People poured out of the bus and retrieved their luggage. Huge white tents were set up, and sign-in tables were arranged in alphabetical order. Photographs were taken for picture ID cards, and bracelets for the different meal plans and drink packages were handed out.

Catherine put the baggage tags on her suitcases, handed them over to a crew member, and joined the line to board the ship, which snaked down the pavement. They went through a metal detector, and their personal items were scanned just as they would be at an airport. As Cat was about to step on the plank, she gasped and observed the floating city for the first time. The behemoth—the white vessel—loomed above her, and a mini earthquake overtook her body. Her knees began to buckle, and her feet were glued to the pavement.

William came to her side and gently held her arm. "Are you okay, Catherine?"

Lowering her eyes, she began to breathe deeply to calm her nerves. "Fine. I'm fine. I knew I had a fear of flying, but I guess huge ships give me anxiety, too."

"It's probably the lack of control of your environment that's causing the apprehension. Very common, actually. Come on, I'll walk up with you."

Slowly, Cat began to move her legs forward as a chorus of disgruntled passengers behind her complained about the delay. Once on board, William led her to her stateroom and got her a bottle of water from the mini-fridge. He opened the doors to the veranda and beckoned for her to join him.

"Thank goodness I can get outside," Cat whispered. "I don't think I'd survive the journey if I couldn't get fresh air."

"It can be quite overwhelming. This experience is unusual for me, as well. Thousands of people in close quarters for two weeks can be unnerving. In the back of my mind are the ships that were impacted by COVID-19. They were literally floating incubators for a highly contagious virus."

Cat shivered. "Oh, it's been on my mind, too."

"I'm sure we'll be fine, and thankfully everyone on board has been vaccinated. Let's explore the ship while we wait for the luggage to arrive. Coincidentally, my room is right down the hall."

An hour later, Cat and William had done an admirable job of getting their bearings and locating the restaurants and theaters. They went to the uppermost deck as the announcement came that they would be departing soon. Leaning against the railing, they watched as families waved goodbye to the travelers.

Catherine laughed. "Now I'm thinking about the Titanic! Lord, I hope I survive this cruise." The blare of the ship's horn announcing their departure made Cat tremble once again. "This is it! There's no turning back."

"Let's meet for dinner, shall we?" asked William. "I think the Italian restaurant would be an excellent choice since Italy is our final destination. I'll make a reservation for eight."

"Perfect," answered Catherine. "I'll see you there. I'm going to unpack and get settled in."

With a slight bow, William left Catherine as she watched Fort Lauderdale recede from view. She looked below into the churning water and felt a wave of fear and regret. *Why am I putting myself through this? Luna and Nico, that's why. Pull yourself together, Catherine.* Finally, she loosened her grip on the railing and returned to her room.

Chapter 25

TIRAMISU

The stateroom looked as if it had been renovated, and Catherine was impressed. The walls were painted a soft gray, and there was a matching tufted headboard. The king-sized bed was covered with a winter-white comforter and navy and sea-foam-green pillows. A large mirror hung over a narrow desk, and a flat-screen television was mounted on the wall across from a small sofa.

Her luggage had been delivered, and her large suitcase was on the stand, waiting for her to unpack it. She flopped on the feather-soft bed and took several deep breaths. Inadvertently, she drifted into a deep sleep. The sound of boisterous voices from the hallway jolted her awake. *Where am I? Oh yes. My home for the next two weeks.* Catherine dragged herself out of bed and unpacked her suitcases. She arranged her cosmetics in the tiny bathroom and placed her laptop and books on the desk. She slipped into a sundress and silver sandals.

Her phone chimed, and she rummaged through her purse to find it. A text popped up from Lisa: *Are you settled in?*

Cat answered, *I'm getting there. Lovely room. Heading to dinner soon to meet up with a professor from Toronto.*

Lisa wrote back, *Wow! A date already.*

Catherine smiled and typed, *Just dinner, not a date.*

William waved to Cat as she entered the restaurant. The décor was elegant—Roman trattoria—with black-and-white photos of famous Italian actors on the walls. The soft background music included selections from Frank Sinatra and Dean Martin, and the aroma of garlic

123

hung in the air. William's engaging smile soothed her nerves, and she was thankful she'd met him on the bus.

"You look lovely, Catherine. And a tad calmer than earlier."

"Thanks. A quick nap helped," Cat said as she eased into the chair. "I'm grateful you can barely feel the movement of the ship. I was afraid I'd be seasick."

"I have been sick on small boats, but these massive ships are incredible. If we hit a major storm, you'll feel the swaying, but I checked the forecast before we left, and we should be fine. Do you like red or white wine?"

"Red, white, and sparkling. But I think I'll have seafood tonight, so white would be great."

"May I order one of my favorites from Orvieto?"

"That would be delightful. Wow, this menu looks amazing."

Their conversation was light and airy as they ordered wine and appetizers, then dined on Caesar salad and linguini alla vongole.

"I had expected to dine alone most evenings," stated William. "Meeting you has been a pleasant surprise."

"I'm glad we met, too. I had no expectations for this voyage, but I'm used to being alone. The social distancing we had to go through wasn't that hard for me. I was able to see my brother, who was alive at the time, and my dear friend Lisa. I live alone, but I'm good on my own."

"I'm quite the loner myself. I've never been married, though I came close a few times."

"I was married once, but not to the right person. And children were not in the cards for me," Cat said.

"My students are like my children. I've cherished every year I've spent teaching. But it's wonderful to take a break like this. Especially when I can spend six months in Italy researching my next project."

"What are you working on?"

"I'm writing a paper on Italian society from the time of Mussolini to the present. There have been more than sixty-five governments in the past seventy years in Italy. The instability has caused many to embrace authoritarian leaders. 'At least Mussolini made the trains run on time' was a favorite saying on the political right. And students today are more fascinated by recent history than ancient times."

"Technology has changed the world, and ancient history to kids today is the time before iPhones," Cat said. "It's so important that the younger generation understands the danger of tyranny and wannabe dictators like the last president."

"Yes. Whether its fascism or communism, authoritarian governments are dangerous."

"I read about the idea of 'authoritarian predisposition,' which is a mindset on the far right or left that craves simplicity. It's fueled by emotion and can disregard objective truth, the law, justice, and rational thought."

"That was obvious when the US Capitol was attacked," William noted. "Both Hitler and Stalin used the new technology of radio to whip up emotions and spread conspiracy theories. The internet and social media spread the small, medium, and large lies, like the 'Big Lie' when your previous president said that he'd won the 2020 election. Social media is addictive, and so many people became radicalized during the lockdown."

"Tyrants also need intellectual elites to channel the anger, fear, and resentment of the masses. The volatile far right found that in the Ivy League senators and journalists who spread propaganda for power, money, and ratings. Humans crave camaraderie and purpose. It's a shame when they follow autocrats who create an alternate reality that inspires hatred for people not like them," said Cat.

"A radicalized mind is difficult to reach with objective truth," William added.

"Way too many Americans renounced the use of reason. It was evident after the second impeachment trial, when the former president was acquitted. It was party over country and personal careers over law and honor. It's such a shame. Oh well. Now, William, what would you like for dessert?"

"I'd love some tiramisu."

"Then tiramisu it is."

Chapter 26

CABIN FEVER

Cat slipped into a comfortable routine as she started to relax and enjoy the journey. Each evening, she checked the activities for the following day on her television. Mornings began on the walking track on the top deck, followed by a breakfast with delicious coffee and pastries, then several hours of work. Lunch by the pool and pleasure reading came next, or lectures and trivia games. This was followed by a late-afternoon tropical cocktail. In the evenings, she dined with William or alone, marveling at the quality of each restaurant. Dinner was followed by a variety of entertainment at the clubs or theaters. Her favorite was the blues club, which had accomplished musicians and exceptional singers.

Early one morning, Cat awoke from a disturbing dream. Jim was standing on the upper deck of the ship, a heavy fog surrounding him. Once again, he repeated the words "not natural." Cat shivered. *Jim, what are you trying to tell me? I'm not getting the message.* She snuggled under the covers and listened to the sound of rain pelting against the glass doors. She could feel the incessant rocking of the ship and rushed to take her seasickness medication. She was grateful for the tea and crackers in her room, which helped ease her stomach.

Catherine decided to take the morning off from editing, instead checking her emails from both her old and new accounts. Mail from Luna and Nico described their excitement about her arrival, which filled her with joy. She read a report from the Fernandina Beach police regarding the damage to her property, and it made her glad she was far away. They were convinced the McAllen boy had not committed the act, but they had no other suspects. Diana's email gave her an update on Rodney's case. They'd identified the person of interest from the gas station security video. The car belonged to a local health care worker named Anson Cassidy. The police indicated that he'd been investigated for stealing narcotics from the hospital where he had worked as a nurse, but charges were never pressed. He continued to work at the hospital through the pandemic and had quit several months ago. The police had an APB out for Cassidy, and Diana was hopeful he'd be found. Cat emailed back to thank her for her message and to encourage her to stay strong and safe.

An email from Brad, which included attached documents for her to sign so she could relinquish her company shares, was immediately deleted. There was a second email from Giancarlo requesting action, but she wasn't going to be pressured by him or Brad. There was also an email from Dorothy, an acquaintance in Jacksonville, about editing a novel she'd written based on her experiences as a nurse during the pandemic. It was a mystery novel in which a murder took place during the crisis but was covered up by the bedlam at the hospital. She skimmed the manuscript, and one passage Dorothy had written made Catherine stop.

The patient's name was Maggie. She told me she was a grandmother, forty-seven years old, and was in perfect health before the invisible evil came into her body. She had a raging fever, severe body aches, and had lost her sense of smell and taste. Her lungs were filling with fluid, and she fought hard for every breath.

Shortly after I met Maggie, she was intubated, and her pale-blue eyes were filled with fear. You never get used to seeing the anguish in someone's eyes when they understand they may die soon. I tried to comfort her and called her daughter, Karen, on her cell phone so she could hear her daughter's voice.

As her condition worsened overnight, Maggie's fear turned into resignation. I called Karen and let her know that time may be short. In the background, I could hear a little girl, and I suggested that she talk to her grandmother.

"Hi, Gram, it's Lily. Your silly Lily. I miss you. When can we plant more flowers in your garden?"

I had to answer the child and say that her gram would always love her but that she may not be able to work in the garden again. I heard Maggie's daughter sobbing and choked back tears of my own. When Lily left the room, Karen told me the story of how Maggie had contracted COVID. Maggie had followed the guidance of her pastor and had continued to attend services at her church, believing that Jesus would protect her. Blind faith had won out over science and common sense. Soon Maggie would be seeing Jesus in person.

"Ahhhh!" Cat shrieked. "This makes my blood boil. I can't believe people died because they trusted their clergy. Not to mention the ignorant politicians who denied or downplayed the virus!"

There was a firm knock at the door. Cat slowly got up to answer it.

"Are you all right, love? I heard a scream," said an attractive woman with an Australian accent. She was tall and slim and had short white hair. She was clothed in a flowing multi-colored caftan.

Catherine smiled at her visitor. "Yes, I'm fine. I was just reading something upsetting. I often talk to myself, but I usually don't yell out loud. I'm Catherine. Would you like to come in?"

"I'm Charlotte. That would be grand. There are very few areas to sit at when the weather is nasty. Every indoor chair is quickly taken, and I was getting cabin fever."

"Are you traveling alone?" Cat asked her neighbor. "Australians seem to vacation in groups."

"A pleasure to meet you, and yes, I'm on my own. You're right about the Aussies. They're often in a gaggle, and a raucous one at that," she said, settling on the sofa.

Cat went back to her computer and turned it off. "Since I've been on the ship, I've learned not to join in the trivia game when they're playing. They sure are competitive," she said. "Would you like a cup of tea?"

"Yes, please. What upset you so, if you don't mind me asking?"

"I'm an editor, and I was reading a novel written by a nurse in my hometown of Jacksonville, Florida. I thought I'd managed my anger over how the pandemic unfolded in the US, and I thought I'd found a place of internal peace, but obviously the rage is just below the surface. It infuriated me when deplorable people in my state said wearing a face mask was killing people, or that it was Satan's work."

"The response in America was shocking," said Charlotte. "The denial of reality by the former president was hard to fathom."

"I understood the 2016 election. People wanted an outsider, or they followed their party or religion when they voted in a conman. But in the 2020 election, they knew what they were getting, and there was no excuse. When he was first elected, it was like an arrow through my heart that pierced my soul."

"We Aussies were dumbfounded by the words and actions of the man. And even more shaken by what happened on January 6, 2021. The whole world trembled as your Capitol was attacked by the homegrown terrorists. And more distressed that there was no accountability for the man, that he was acquitted of starting the insurrection."

Cat placed two cups of tea and chocolate chip shortbread cookies on the small table beside the sofa.

"In my country," Charlotte said, "the virus came so soon after Australia was devastated by the wildfires that we barely had a chance to mourn one tragedy before the next one arrived."

"Very true. Our own wildfires in the west were terrible and they keep getting worse every year. Thankfully, my nation is once again being run by rational, competent leadership, and we're addressing climate change. How did you end up on a cruise out of Fort Lauderdale?"

"My late husband owned a medical supply company in Sydney that became very successful. That was our silver lining. He was the love of my life, and we were together for thirty-four years. When he passed away last fall, I was at a total loss. Our best friends convinced me to travel and join them on this cruise. I flew to San Francisco and toured California before meeting them in Florida."

"I'm sorry about your husband. Was it the virus?"

"No. Complications from Type 1 Diabetes. It was hard on our son, too. He's done an admirable job of taking over the company. He asked me to move in with him and his girlfriend, but blimey, that would be a bad idea. I'm fine on my own."

"Me, too. I've been divorced for eight years, and I enjoy living alone. For the most part."

"What's your story, Catherine?"

"Long story short, my parents passed away many years ago. Then it was just my brother and myself, but he recently had a fatal heart attack. But just before he died, he was contacted by a woman in Siena who turned out to be our half-sister. She and her soon-to-be adopted son visited me in Florida, and now I'm going to Italy to spend time with them. I don't fly, so a slow boat to Italy was the best option."

"That's fascinating. Did you have any idea she existed?"

"None at all. My mother passed away when I was ten, and my dad never mentioned that she'd had a child before he met her. Mom was told the baby died shortly after birth, but what she didn't know was that her baby was switched, and my sister was given to another woman to raise. I'm so grateful I have family again."

"Family is so important. I'm happy for you."

The women spent the next hour comparing life stories, and then there was another knock at the door. Cat opened the door and was pleased to see William. "Three's company. William, come in. This is Charlotte from Sydney."

Chapter 27

PONTA DELGADA

The sun broke through the massive charcoal-gray clouds late in the afternoon. The pool deck began to fill up, and Cat, William, and Charlotte nabbed chairs and ordered cocktails. There was a gentle breeze in the post-storm air, and the passengers were joyful as they drank in the sunshine. Catherine flipped through a Sicily travel book she'd brought with her, and stopped at the description of the city of Syracuse, saying, "I can't wait to see the Greek ruins in Sicily. It's so cool that Plato lived in Syracuse. I'll be standing on the ground where one of the founders of democracy stood."

"Actually, Catherine, Plato came from the democratic city-state of Athens, but he wasn't a proponent of democracy as we know it. It's generally accepted that in his mind the death of his mentor, Socrates, was caused by the rule of the masses. He thought that when Socrates was forced to drink a cup of poison for dubious charges, it showed the defects of democracy. The judge in his trial had not condemned Socrates to death; it was the large jury of average citizens, the mob, who determined he should die," William said.

"Who did Plato think should rule if not an elected leader?" Cat asked.

"He supported rule by the wisest, most enlightened men and proposed that a philosopher king govern. He attempted to educate such a person while in Sicily. During Socrates's time, Athens had been run by thirty tyrants, and the oligarchy killed five percent of the population and

131

confiscated property. They were finally banished, but one of the leaders of the tyrants was a student of Socrates. His fate had been sealed."

"So, the rich and powerful should be in charge?" questioned Charlotte.

"No. Plato and Socrates believed that politicians should be disconnected from economic power because of mankind's innate greed. The most moral and intelligent should rule."

"At least in our last election the masses did the right thing and removed the tyrant and his enablers," said Cat. "Even voter suppression and Russian interference couldn't stop the blue wave. What distressed me most was realizing that so many of the leaders had an insatiable lust for power, putting themselves above all else, including the country, and continue to do so. The quest for power, money, and fame has corrupted way too many."

"William, it's wonderful that you know so much about the ancient Greeks," Charlotte said.

"As a history professor, it's my job and my passion. I was telling Catherine that the focus of my new work will be on Mussolini and Italian society since World War II. Ancient history to my students."

Charlotte laughed. "You're right about that. Well, Professor, do you know the history of our first stop on the cruise?"

"Yes. I've been reading about the capital city of Ponta Delgada on São Miguel. It's the largest island in the Portuguese Azores. I've decided to take the walking tour of the city, not the bus tour, when we're there. I don't care to bathe in the volcanic thermal springs. But it's fascinating that they use the ninety-three-degrees-Celsius springs to cook food, like in a slow cooker. That's two hundred degrees Fahrenheit for you, Catherine."

"Thanks for the conversion," said Cat. "I plan to walk the city, too. It's my first taste of Europe, and I want to feel the vibe of the city on foot, not on a bus tour. The map and information the ship has provided will be enough to get around."

"I hadn't decided what I'd do in Ponta Delgada, but I'd like to walk the city with you two. I have a private tour arranged in Málaga. A friend in Sydney recommended a tour guide. Would you both like to join me there?"

"Yes!" Cat and William said in unison.

"Then it's settled. Now, does anyone have dinner plans?" Charlotte asked.

* * *

A steady west wind greeted Catherine, William, and Charlotte as they left the ship to tour Ponta Delgada. The glorious sunlight bounced off the white-washed buildings. Each had a red-tiled roof, which was typical of Portuguese architecture. Black bricks and trim contrasted with the white structures, and the colors were replicated in the black-and-white-patterned sidewalks. The rolling green hills surrounding the city were similar to the highlands of Scotland or the knolls of Ireland.

They strolled from the marina to the Old Town Center and went through the city gate to the São Sebastião Church. The church, which was erected in the mid-1500s, boasted the tallest clock tower on the island. The bells chimed ten times as they approached.

"I love the black-and-white pattern on the sidewalks and cobblestone streets. It must be like the city of Catania, Sicily, I was reading about," Cat said. "The black pavers and stone on the buildings are made from lava rock."

"You're probably correct. These are volcanic islands, and although the general architecture is reminiscent of Portugal, the Azores has a distinctive style. They also have more cows than people on the nine islands altogether. They make incredible cheeses and have tea fields and a coffee plantation, which is very unusual for Europe," William said.

They sauntered down the narrow streets of the historic district, enjoying the riot of flowers spilling from boxes on wrought-iron balconies. Some homes were painted beige or pale yellow, but most were white. From there, they headed to the Conceição Palace.

"Oh my gosh," Cat exclaimed. "The palace is painted the same ice-blue color as the shutters on my house."

"Good heavens, it sure is a bold change from the white buildings in the city. It's a lovely shade of blue, though," Charlotte said.

William looked at his map and his watch. "Would you ladies prefer to see the Forte de São Brás or the museum. I'm not sure if we have time to visit both and fit in lunch, as well."

"Let's get lunch first and then go to the museum, if that's okay," said Catherine.

"Perfect. There's a restaurant on the map that's not too far from here," said Charlotte.

They found seats at a small round table at A Tasca Restaurant. The décor was simple and fun, and the diners were lively. The menu was in Portuguese, English, and German, so ordering was effortless. The trio dined on seafood tapas, smoked Azorean sausages, and a delicious cheese, honey, and walnut dish baked in puff pastry. A carafe of branco wine was an excellent complement to the meal.

"Catherine, did you know that it was Plato who first recorded the existence of Atlantis? Some scholars believe that if it did exist, the Azores was a part of the land mass," said William. "At this moment, we could be dining on Atlantis."

"No, I didn't know that," Cat answered.

"What else do you know about Atlantis?" asked Charlotte.

"Well, it's all speculation, of course, but in addition to Plato's account, there are beliefs garnered from the mythology of populaces around the globe and metaphysicians like Edgar Cayce. There are theories that during the utopian phase of Atlantis, it was a flourishing society."

"In what way?" asked Cat.

"They had advanced technology based on crystal energy, sonics, and magnetics. They could power ships and buildings using energy from what they called the Firestone. It transmitted invisible beams similar to radio waves. And they had low-flying aircraft."

"That's incredible, if it's true," said Charlotte.

"It was socialism that was successful. Supposedly, during the eras when the female energy was dominant, priests and priestesses were the final authorities. All basic needs of citizens were taken care of, including food, shelter, and health care. People who did wrong were submitted to healers rather than prisons, and they performed community service as reparations. There was equality between the sexes."

"That's exactly what we need today instead of the one percent controlling the vast amount of the wealth on Earth. And then there's the misogyny and the prison culture in the US," said Cat.

"Agreed. Your country continues to be dominated by the patriarchy that founded the nation."

"There's still so much left to do," Cat added.

"You're correct. It's been speculated that when the masculine energy overtook the Atlantean society, there was misuse of the Firestone for destruction, punishment, torture, and war began. Ultimately, the nation was destroyed."

"That's so interesting," said Charlotte.

"Yet, I've recently encountered another theory that places Atlantis in the Mediterranean Sea between Crete and mainland Greece. In this theory, the island of Santorini is what is left of the main city of Atlantis. The Cyclades Islands are the mountaintops of the lost island, and the Cyclades Plateau is the submerged remainder of the lost island. If it's correct that the sea level was several hundred feet lower in ancient times, this is a distinct possibility."

"It's a fascinating story. I guess we'll never know for sure.

The trio finished their lunch and paid their bills, and William announced, "On to the next part of our tour."

They walked off their lunch while strolling to the Sacred Art Museum housed in the Igreja do Colégio. The highlight was a spectacularly carved wood altar that's beauty rivaled any altar on Earth. The long trek back to the ship was a great time to experience the loveliness of the port city, and it was a chance for them to get to know each other better.

Chapter 28

COSTA DEL SOL

The next port of call was the southern Spanish city called Málaga, where Charlotte had arranged a private car tour. Exiting the ship, they located their local guide, Estrella, a lovely young woman with an engaging smile. Her wavy dark hair flowed down her back, and she strongly resembled the actress Penélope Cruz.

"Ms. Charlotte, I'm so happy you contacted me and said you were bringing two friends. Welcome to Costa del Sol." Her English was excellent, and her melodious voice was a joy to listen to.

"Thank you, Estrella. This is Catherine from Florida and William from Toronto. We're excited about touring your city. Where will we begin?" Charlotte said as they hopped in the car.

"Our first stop is Alcazaba, a Moor castle on the mount of Gibralfaro, which is set above the city. I will give you a short history of Málaga as we drive."

Estrella explained that the city was founded in the eighth century BC and was one of the oldest Mediterranean seaports. The Moors who built the castle were Muslims who had ruled much of North Africa and southern Spain, and their influence on architecture was everywhere. Oftentimes, it was incorporated into later construction by the Catholic Spaniards and others.

"I'm surprised by how large and modern this city is, and the surrounding mountains are lovely," said Cat as they arrived at the hilltop fortress. "It's so exciting to see ancient buildings. Nothing in the States is this old."

"So, this is your first visit to Spain?" Estrella asked.

"Yes. It's my first trip to Europe, and it's incredible."

"I'm pleased to share in your adventure. Come and see the archaeology museum inside the castle," said Estrella. "There are many Roman antiquities."

They toured the fortress and gardens under the blazing sun, then went to the nearby Roman amphitheater, which was built in the first century BC.

"Why didn't I travel before?" Catherine asked. "Now I know why Jim was so passionate about seeing the world. It really connects you to the history of humankind. It makes your imagination run wild. I can almost see the gladiators and cheering crowds."

"That's why I embraced the study of history and why I still enjoy teaching young people. The view from here is marvelous," William said.

"Education is so important," said Charlotte. "I'd love to be in one of your classes, William. You're so intelligent and interesting."

Catherine could see the color rise in William's cheeks, and she wondered if he was as smitten with Charlotte as she was with him.

The next stop was the Mercado Central de Atarazanas, the largest and liveliest market in the city. The beautiful stained-glass window depicted historical landmarks of Málaga, and the sights and smells of exotic spices delighted the sightseers. A walking tour of Old Town was followed by a stop at the renaissance cathedral. Estrella took them to one of her favorite restaurants and had pre-ordered salad and seafood paella for them.

Cat's phone chimed, and seeing who it was, she excused herself from the table. She grinned as she read Sam's text, which said, *How are you, and where are you?*

She responded, *I was just thinking about our dinner in Fernandina. I'm having paella in Málaga.*

That's great! Are you with a tour?

No. I'm with two new friends I met on the ship: William, a professor from Toronto, and Charlotte from Sydney. And our tour guide, Estrella.

Is William a good guy?

He's very nice. I think there are sparks between him and Charlotte.

So we're still on to meet in Tuscany?

Absolutely. I'm looking forward to seeing you.

Me, too. Enjoy your paella

After lunch, they explored the museum and birthplace of Pablo Ruiz Picasso, then took a driving tour of the city. Cat sat in the front seat with Estrella, and William and Charlotte sat in the back, chatting amicably. As they passed the Plaza de Toros de la Malagueta, they all agreed that bull fighting was not something they wanted to see. The end of the day included a Tapas Walking Tour, which included sampling tapas at five different restaurants, and a stroll through the gardens near the port. Happy and satisfied, the weary travelers thanked Estrella profusely, and she returned them to the ship.

Chapter 29

REUNION

Catherine delighted in watching the blossoming romance between Charlotte and William. Some nights, she joined them for dinner, and other times she gave them their space. She skipped the next port on the itinerary—a tour of Cartagena, Spain—because of a stomach ailment, but she enjoyed the final days of the cruise. Two weeks had passed much more quickly than she'd anticipated, and she had barely had time to finish editing the two manuscripts she'd brought with her. She had declined to edit Dorothy's novel but had recommended another editor in Jacksonville.

On the final evening, Cat, William, and Charlotte met for cocktails by the pool, then dined in the superb seafood restaurant. Instead of partaking in the prearranged last-night entertainment, they returned to the upper deck to gaze at the starlit sky.

"What have you learned on this journey?" William asked Cat as they sipped licorice-flavored sambuca. "You appear to have changed since we first met on the shuttle bus."

Catherine laughed and gently touched William's arm. "I want to thank you again for your kindness and encouragement. I'm so glad I overcame my fear and embraced the voyage. It's awakened a passion in me to see and experience the world. I feel more alive than I have in years, and the adventure has just begun."

"I gave you a little nudge, but you're the one who opened the door, or more accurately, walked up the ramp. Let me know when you arrive in Siena. You and your family can visit me in Montalcino. It's not far from where you're staying."

"Thanks, I will. I meant to ask you, is renting a villa expensive?"

"I'm renting the villa's carriage house, but it has a full kitchen, living room, office, and bedroom. There's a pool, and the entire property is surrounded by olive groves and vineyards. Homemade wine and olive oil are supplied, too."

"That sounds amazing."

"I'm also doing research on the owner's family history as partial payment. The good old barter system. Then I'll write a narrative about their ancestors."

"Very nice. And, Charlotte, what are you going to do after your two-week bus tour of Italy?"

"Actually, I'm going to join William for a while. Then I'll have a base to come back to, and I can revisit any places in Tuscany that I enjoyed. I've postponed my tour of France."

"That's wonderful! A Tuscan romance," said Cat. "Between an Aussie and a Canuck." She expected her new friends to deny the suggestion, but they only grinned at each other. *Love affairs later in life tend to proceed quickly*, Cat thought. *Maybe Sam and I will follow a similar path.*

Before going to sleep, Catherine checked her emails. She'd sent a message to Luna confirming her arrival time in Civitavecchia. There was an email from her sister stating that they would meet her at the port and that they were very excited. Next was an email with the heading *Warning*. Cat clicked on it and gasped at the message.

Stay away from the Rodney Simmons case. You've been warned.

A chill ran up her spine, and her hands shook as she grabbed her phone. Cat texted Diana, telling her about the threat and asking her if she'd received one, too. Diana replied that she hadn't but that she would forward the message to the detectives responsible for her father's case. Cat sent the email to Lisa, her PI on the home front. She also sent it to the Fernandina Beach police in case the destruction of her fence was related to Rodney's death and her role in the investigation.

How did they get my email? Probably from my website.

She was just about to turn off the computer when a message from Jerome popped up. He'd been contacted by FinCEN, The Financial Crimes Enforcement Network, who told him of questions arising from the CPA's audit of Emerson & Ritter and Riva Realty. The Financial Intelligence Unit of the Department of Treasury was investigating irregularities in the real estate part of the business, and there was possible money laundering. Although the accountant Jerome had hired couldn't find direct evidence of wrongdoing, she'd flagged some of the transactions. Her husband had previously worked in the fraud unit at the Jacksonville office of a major European bank, so she did have some inside knowledge. She'd contacted the commercial bank that did business with Riva Realty, and they notified FinCEN. Jerome said he would keep her apprised of the situation.

* * *

Catherine put all worries out of her mind as she exited the ship the following morning. She raised her face to the warm sunshine and inhaled deeply. It was her first breath in Italy, and her heart beat swiftly in anticipation. She waved goodbye to William and Charlotte, who were following behind her. She retrieved her luggage then scanned the port and saw Luna and Nico. She squealed with delight and rushed to greet them.

"I cannot believe you are here!" Luna said as she hugged her sister. They embraced for a long time, and then it was Nico's turn for a hug.

"Oh, Zia! It is magnifico to have you here. There is so much I want to show you. Come, the rental auto is over there."

"Luna, you rented a car?"

"Yes. My Fiat is perfect for the narrow streets of Siena, but it would not hold the three of us and the luggage. I rented one that will be comfortable for our journey."

Arm in arm, the women walked to the parking lot, with Nico following behind with Cat's suitcases. They began the eight-hour drive down the west coast of Italy. The trio chatted excitedly the entire way and watched the scenic countryside speed by. They drove past the exits for Rome and Naples and arrived in Reggio di Calabria, which was at the toe of the Italian boot. They would spend the night, and the following morning they'd take a car ferry to Messina, Sicily. They checked into the hotel and located a Napoli-style pizzeria down a narrow side street. Prosecco, sparkling water, and Margherita pizzas were ordered, and Cat couldn't stop smiling.

"I can't believe I'm in Italy with you. My life has changed in so many ways, and I'm so fortunate."

"We are lucky, too," said Nico. "I cannot wait to show you my city of Palermo."

"And I'm so excited! It's a shame we won't see your uncle right away. It's bad timing that he's in Rome."

"Yes, it is," Luna agreed. "I have made an arrangement for us to see him when he returns." Then, changing the subject, she said, "Catherine, I've been noticing that lovely necklace you're wearing. Is it new?"

"Oh my gosh! I forgot to give you this," Cat said as she rummaged through her purse and retrieved a small box. "The necklace is from Sam. He gave me one for you, too." Cat handed the box to Luna.

"What a wonderful surprise! We have matching jewelry. I will think of you every time I wear it," Luna said as she put on the necklace. "This was so kind of him."

Chapter 30

VOLCANO

Catherine's excitement grew as the crowded ferry took them across the Ionian Sea to Messina. While driving through the unremarkable city, Luna told her sister that Messina had been leveled by an earthquake in 1908, and two-thirds of the citizens had been lost. They had successfully rebuilt, but it was flattened once again when the Allies bombed the city in World War II. As a result, a lot of the historic charm of Messina had been lost.

The first stop on the Sicilian tour was the spectacular hillside town of Taormina, the playground of the rich and famous. The tourist-filled town had incredible views of the cobalt-blue sea and Mount Etna, an active volcano. They checked into their hotel outside the main gate, then toured the historic town on foot. The cobblestone streets were lined with expensive boutiques and restaurants, including the "Wunderbar," a favorite haunt of actors Elizabeth Taylor and Richard Burton. The highlights of the morning were a visit to the ancient Greek theater that was built in 300 BC and the public cliffside garden that was donated to the city by an aristocratic Englishwoman.

In the afternoon, Luna drove up the north side of Mount Etna, through picturesque towns, olive groves, vineyards, and forests of poplars, birch, and Corsican pines. They parked at the visitor stop called Rifugio Sapienza, and Nico took a photo of an unusual statue—a five-foot Mr. Potato Head sporting a mustache and driving cap. They joined a guided walking tour of the lower section of the volcano rather than taking a gondola ride to a higher point on the mountain.

"Zia, look!" Nico called out. "There is smoke coming from the vent over there. I can smell it. I hope the volcano does not erupt while we are here."

"The guide said there were eruptions during the pandemic. The whole world was in a state of turmoil," Cat said. "It's cool that people are able to ski here in the winter, when old Etna isn't spewing fire into the air."

"It is wonderful that plants grow on the lava after a time. Nature finds a way to renew even after a catastrophe," said Luna. "Look, you can see the city of Catania over there. Fortunately, it is on the opposite side from the cone that is emitting smoke. I understand that many eruptions have reached the town over the centuries."

"And I read that much of Catania was built with volcanic rock," said Cat. "We can check it out tomorrow."

"Catania has always been a rival to Palermo," said Nico. "I visited one time, and it is no match for my city."

Later that evening, their hotel was offering a Sicilian buffet featuring local specialties and music performed by singers in traditional attire. Tables of delectable food were set up on the terrace overlooking the pool and the Ionian Sea. The conical arancini, shaped like Mount Etna, was featured, as were dishes with eggplant, pasta, and shellfish. Luna and Nico joined in when the performers, accompanied by an accordion, belted out Italian folk songs. Catherine delighted in the performance, and sharing it with her family made it even more special.

Cat closed her eyes and listened to Luna singing. The glorious sound brought back memories of her mother singing Italian classics as she prepared dinner. In her mind's eye, Cat could see her parents, Maria and Scott, as they slow danced in the kitchen, her mother serenading the love of her life.

When they returned to their top-floor hotel room, Nico grabbed his laptop and flopped in a chair on the balcony, which was under a starry dome. Cat poured a glass of local Nero d'Avola wine and joined him. A gentle sea breeze that reminded Catherine of home was a welcome respite from the heat of the night.

"Nico, what are you working on?"

"I am writing a record of our adventure. It is off to a great start. I toured Mount Etna with my mother when I was eight years old, and it was nice to revisit the volcano. Before we came, I tried to write a short story about my life in Sicily, but it was not very good."

"I'd love to read your story."

"Oh, it is in my spazzatura."

"Your trash? See, I am learning a few Italian words."

"Yes, my trash," Nico said, laughing. "I will teach you many words. And *maybe* I will retrieve my story for you."

Cat grinned at her nephew's playfulness. "That would be great."

Nico typed while Catherine sipped her wine. "Oh my gosh! I just thought of something. You know how I've been investigating the death of my brother's co-worker?"

"Sì, Zia."

"When you said you'd retrieve your story from the trash, I remembered that Rodney gave his old laptop to his grandson shortly before he disappeared. His new computer was never found."

"So you believe there may be evidence on his old computer that he would have moved to the trash?"

"Exactly. I'm going to text Lisa and ask her to get in touch with Rodney's daughter, Diana. Lisa's my private eye on the case, and she can get Diana to check her dad's old computer."

Chapter 31

PLATO

After a short drive the next morning, they stopped in Catania, a city shaped by lava from Mount Etna and the massive 1693 earthquake. They walked through the heart of the city, which included the Piazza Duomo. It was surrounded by the Baroque Town Hall and the Cathedral. Nico pointed out a famous fountain with a lava-stone elephant, topped with an obelisk and globe. He'd remembered the fountain from his visit with his mother.

The nearby market was jammed with visitors and offered an enormous selection of meat, seafood, fruits, and vegetables. Vendors called out to passersby, and animated discussions ensued amid the odor of fresh fish. Luna pointed out a menu posted on a restaurant wall. "What do you think, Catherine? Would you enjoy a sandwich made from organic Sicilian horse?"

"Ugh! Absolutely not. So, you two, are you ready to visit Syracuse? I've been looking forward to seeing the ancient Greek city."

Their first stop was the island of Ortygia, on the southern tip of Syracuse. As they were walking past the Roman ruins of the Temple of Apollo, Nico stopped to take a selfie and said, "I will send this to Sam. Let me take a picture of the both of you. And he will see that you are wearing the jewelry he gave to you."

The sisters obliged the young man, standing with their arms interlocked. Nico sent the photos, and Sam responded right away.

"Sam says you are beautiful sisters, and he is looking forward to being with us in Siena. I think he has romanza on his mind, Zia."

Cat blushed and hugged the young man. They walked to the port, then followed the tourists to the Castello Maniace. The castle sat on the site where the Roman temple of Hera once stood.

"The book says that much of the stone used in the walls around the island was taken from the Greek amphitheater in the 1500s. It's incredible that so many different conquerors occupied Sicily and repurposed various sites," Cat said.

When they stopped for lunch at a restaurant in the Piazza del Duomo, they marveled at the sunlight bouncing off the elegant ivory-colored cathedral across the square. Referring to the guidebook, Cat explained that the church was built on the site of a monument to Athena, the Greek goddess of wisdom and warfare.

"The world needs more wisdom and less warfare," said Luna.

"Look, Nico. There's a couple on the Duomo's steps, and I think he's asking for her hand in marriage. There's a photographer taking pictures," Cat said.

"That is grande! The people in the piazza are all cheering for the couple."

"There is once again hope for the future, and young love will always be a beautiful reminder that life goes on," said Luna.

The next stop was the Museo Archeologico Regionale Paolo Orsi, which housed extensive artifacts from digs in the southeast part of Sicily. Nico was fascinated by the rare coin and medal collections from the Medieval and Greek eras. The final stop was the Greek Theater, where the ancient playwright Aeschylus premiered his tragedies.

Walking through the ruins, Cat could imagine the amphitheater filled with patrons and the actors strutting across the stage in elaborate costumes.

"I can't believe my feet are on the stones where Plato once stood. My shipmate William explained to me that the great philosopher was not a proponent of democracy as we know it. But I'm still excited to stand here."

"Yes, we learned about Socrates and Plato in school. What we understand as factual is not always correct. Plato wanted leaders to be moral intellectuals, not those elected by the masses," said Nico.

"That's why it's important to have accurate records of history and to teach students the truth, whether it's about ancient or recent history. Some of the American textbooks weren't honest about slavery and the reasons for the Civil War. Thankfully, many of the Confederate statues, monuments, and places named for the generals are being removed. The last president even said he liked the uneducated. I guess it's because they're easier to deceive and manipulate."

"That is true, Catherine. And people readily believe things that support their preconceived ideas."

"And we're back to a discussion about human nature. My friend William also told me about Plato and the legend of Atlantis, along with the advanced civilization that may have lived there. There's so much we don't know about past societies and the story of mankind before recorded history."

They wandered around the stage, then climbed the sixty-seven tiers to the top of the theater. They peered into the grotto, where water once flowed from an aqueduct.

"It is a shame the summer program of classical theater is over for the season. It would have been a joy to see the plays in this magnificent setting," said Luna.

"Yes, it would have been lovely. Do you think it's time to find our Airbnb in Noto?" Cat asked.

"Let's go, Zia!"

After driving south and then west, they arrived at the hillside town of Noto. They checked into the Airbnb, which was nestled in a lemon grove. The fragrance of lemon blossoms filled the air, and there was a resort-like pool where several guests lounged under the shade of the trees.

"This is amazing," said Cat. "We'll have to go for a swim later. You did a wonderful job finding this place, Luna."

They decided to go into town for dinner and attempted to locate a parking lot using GPS. Cat gave the directions to Luna as she drove through the narrow streets. They were more like alleyways, with cars parked bumper to bumper along one side.

"Oh, I am not used to this large car!" Luna said as the tire rims scraped against the sidewalk. "This is not good."

In the backseat, Nico stifled a laugh. "This may turn into an expensive car rental."

Eventually, they found the parking lot and walked through a small market near Noto's city gate. Vendors displayed souvenirs, handmade goods, and various sweet treats. They walked down Corso Vittorio Emanuele and went past baroque churches and civic buildings that were erected after the earthquake of 1693. The street was overflowing with tourists and multi-generational families strolling arm-in-arm. They dined al fresco on excellent seafood, pasta, and local wine. They were at a café next to the Palazzo Ducezio, which was now the town hall. The final stop was for pistachio and chocolate gelato as they sauntered back to the car.

"I feel totally immersed in Sicily here. The ageless beauty of this town makes me feel suspended in time," said Cat, completely enthralled by their visit.

"It is very much like Siena in that way," said Luna. "There is always a delicate balance between preserving the historic buildings and meeting the needs of a modern society."

Chapter 32

VALLEY OF THE TEMPLES

"There is no major autoroute across the south of the island," explained Luna. "We will be passing through small villages on our way to Agrigento. There is a lot of agriculture in this region, though the countryside is dry at this time of year."

"It's beautiful in its own way," said Cat. "Except for the trash that's strewn beside the highway. What a shame."

"Sì, Zia. It is awful that people litter the landscape."

They drove in pleasant silence as the countryside zipped by, rolling hills of grain to the north and the sparkling Mediterranean Sea to the south. The coast of Africa was a quick boat ride away. Their destination was the tiny coastal town of San Leone, where they checked into a hotel with water views. There was a small crescent-shaped beach across the road from the hotel, so the travelers unpacked and jumped into their bathing suits. Cat and Luna laughed when they realized their new swimsuits and cover-ups were almost identical.

They wove their way through the sunbathers, the men wearing skimpy speedos and many of the women in bikinis. Children played with pails and shovels under rainbow-colored umbrellas. The trio placed towels on the pebbled shore and waded into the warm, deep blue water. Nico ran out into the sea and dove under the surface several times.

"Nico reminds me of the frolicking dolphins back home. I love to see him so full of joy," said Cat. The women sat on their towels, delighting in the scene before them.

"Returning to his first home has been good for his soul. I believe this trip will be healing for him. We have not come back since Carlotta was laid to rest. And the conflict with Salvatore has been weighing heavy on his mind."

"Understandable," Cat said. "I pray that Riccardo sees the light and stops supporting his brother in the fight for Nico. The anxiety about that is with me all the time, so it must be doubly worrying for you."

"It is with me, as well. It looms in my mind when I go to sleep at night and when I first awaken in the morning. I have also prayed each day that we resolve this matter quickly. I pray to Mother Mary and to our mother, Maria, for help. I cannot imagine my life without Nico."

"It has to work out, Luna. It just has to."

Nico ran back and plopped down on his towel. Water dripped from his curly dark hair, and he shook his head like a puppy, flinging droplets on the women. "This is grande! I love being in the water. I miss living close to the sea. But I do enjoy our home in Siena, too."

"You are right, Nico. We should visit the shore more often. It will be a part of our future together."

Nico nodded. A darkness swept across his face. "The closer we get to seeing Zio Riccardo, the more I am afraid."

"Try not to worry, mio figlio. We will convince your uncle, and your father, that your home is with me. Viola has given me copies of the affidavits stating your mother's expressed wish to have you live with me."

"We'll figure it out," said Cat. "I have no doubt."

"So, i miei amori—my loves—I read that there is a charming town not far from here where we can have dinner," Luna announced.

"One more plunge, Luna?"

"Of course. Have fun!"

Nico ran into the water and continued his dolphin moves through the gentle waves. It seemed that with each dive, he was shedding a little more worry about what his future might hold.

* * *

The following morning, they drove the short distance to the archaeological site on a hillside below the unappealing town of Agrigento. The spectacular Greek ruins in the Valley of the Temples was an UNESCO World Heritage site. The city the ancients called Akragas was one of the wealthiest of the Greek colonies. In its prime, it had two hundred thousand citizens, and the ruins of nine temples were all that remained on a ridge below the original city.

"This place is breathtaking! I never imagined that such a massive historic site outside of Greece existed," said Cat as they parked, paid at the entrance, and followed the dusty road to the first temple.

"This one was dedicated to Hera and built around 400 BC, and there are older temples that were built hundreds of years earlier," said Luna, reading a pamphlet. "The city was also ruled by the Carthaginians, Romans, Byzantines, and, later, Christians. It is wonderful that the temples have survived for so many centuries. They have even faced earthquakes. Humankind and Mother Nature have not destroyed this wonderous location."

They strolled down the Via dei Templi to the Temple of Concord, which was similar to the Parthenon in Athens and could be seen from the Mediterranean Sea. It had remained largely intact because the Christians had turned it into a church.

"I have learned about these ruins in school," said Nico, "but I did not realize how huge this site was. Over there is the Temple of Heracles, or Hercules to the Romans."

"And up ahead are some Christian catacombs," said Luna. "They were carved out of the rock to house the bodies of the first Christians who lived here."

"Oh, Luna and Zia Catherine! That reminds me of a catacomb I want to show you in Palermo. It is quite unique."

"That sounds great. I'm looking forward to seeing your city."

"We should walk through the garden—the Jardin de la Kolymbethra. It is supposed to be one of the loveliest in Sicily," Luna said.

As the day grew unbearably hot, they decided to finish their tour of the Valley at the Temple of Olympian Zeus. They returned to the hotel in San Leone, and Luna and Nico headed for the pool. Cat decided to call Lisa for an update on Rodney's case.

"I miss you, Cat!" Lisa said when she answered her phone. "How's the trip going?"

"It's incredible! I know you've been to Italy, but for me this is a mind-expanding adventure. I love seeing the ancient sites."

"I'm so glad you're enjoying it. How are Luna and Nico?"

"Absolutely wonderful. I love them so much. It's a joy traveling with them. It's just sad that the meeting with Riccardo is hanging over our heads."

"When do you meet him?"

"In two days. We're driving to Palermo tomorrow. Nico wants to show me his hometown. I know it will be bittersweet for him to be there. Did you talk to Diana about her dad's computer?"

"Yes, and you were right. There were several files in the trash. I forwarded them to you, but I guess you haven't had a chance to read them."

"No. What was in them?"

"One was a file with the same flagged emails that were on Jim's computer. Another was a file on Anson Cassidy. It was like an investigation on the guy. The first entry was about Rodney seeing him at Emerson & Ritter. Cassidy had been hired by Giancarlo to give flu shots to the staff, and Rodney recognized him from Gamblers Anonymous meetings in Jax. I noticed that Rodney started the file the same day that Jim passed away."

"Didn't the police report say Cassidy was investigated for stealing drugs?" Cat asked.

"Yes, but the virus hit, and the investigation went away."

"Did Rodney mention that he spoke to him at E & R?"

"He wrote that Cassidy bolted when he saw him. Rodney said that he asked Brad why Cassidy was the one giving the flu shots, and Brad told him he didn't know. Giancarlo had arranged it."

"So, should we assume that Cassidy tried to steal drugs from the hospital where he worked to pay a gambling debt?"

Lisa sighed. "Could be. I shared this with Max, and he had a suggestion. Clever boy, my son. What if he communicated with Cassidy on an online gambling site, like a sports betting site? Max said he may be able to dig up some info on him and his relationship with Rodney."

"As long as Max doesn't put himself in danger and personally meet with him. Did Rodney mention anything else about the guy?"

"Not much. He had written out several questions, but there were no answers."

"Maybe he had the answers on his *new* computer. Is there a way that Max can contact Cassidy under a false identity? If not, then he should let it go. If Rodney was investigating Cassidy, he might be dangerous."

"I'll make sure it's safe," Lisa assured Cat.

"One other thing I wanted to mention was that Jerome emailed me about the real estate division, which is part of the Department of Treasury's investigation of E & R. Apparently, they got that info on a tip. I'm not sure where it will lead or if it has anything to do with Rodney."

"Don't worry about it now. Enjoy your vacation."

"Thanks, Lisa. I'll email after we meet with Riccardo. I miss you."

"I miss you, too. By the way, your fence is mended, and I planted a dozen rose bushes in your front garden."

Chapter 33

PALERMO

Another sunny day greeted the travelers as they headed west along the southern shore of the island. Catherine noticed miles of orange trees along the way. "I had no idea there were so many orange groves in Sicily."

"And they are navel oranges like yours in Florida. People from here immigrated to America, then returned to Sicily and brought the trees with them. So, you are seeing Florida oranges in Sicily."

"Amazing! There's so much to learn about your island, Nico."

Just past the town of Sciacca, they took the autoroute north through the interior mountains toward Palermo. Verdant peaks sped by, dotted with charming towns nestled in lush valleys and perched on hill-tops. Northwestern Sicily had been shaped by many civilizations, including the Phoenicians, Greeks, Arabs, Normans, and Spanish. Their influences continued to be felt in the architecture and cuisine. As they approached the city, Nico chatted away about his early life.

"Do you have any friends you want to see when we get to Palermo?" Cat asked.

"Thank you for asking, but no. I had two friends, but they have become involved with a bad group. I would like to see my mother's friend and neighbor, if she still lives in our old apartment building. And, of course, I would like to visit my mother's resting place."

"Absolutely," said Cat. "We can visit the cemetery and stop by and see if your mother's friend is still there."

On their way to the hotel, Cat attempted to guide Luna through the frenzied traffic with her GPS. "This is insane!" she said. "I've never seen such chaos. There are so many cars and motorcycles and bikes all jamming into every inch of the road. The constant blaring of horns is giving me a headache. And there don't seem to be any rules. They don't even stop at red lights."

"I thought the traffic in Rome was difficult, but this is much worse," Luna said. "Mamma mia! Please let us get to the hotel without an accident."

They finally located the Hotel Garibaldi, which was across the street from the theater with the same name. They missed the hotel's entrance and had to circle around several one-way streets and try again. Luna's hands were shaking as she parked the car in the driveway, and then they all started to laugh.

"That was quite the adventure! I think we should walk while we are here and not drive anymore."

"I agree, Luna. Let's get checked in and leave the car in the parking lot. I'm glad they have a lot on site, and it's behind a locked fence. I've heard that this isn't the safest city in Sicily."

The bustling streets were crowded with tourists. Nico led them on a tour of the port city on the Tyrrhenian Sea. They passed the beautiful Massimo Theater and went to the Quattro Canti, where four baroque palaces graced the square. The massive Fontana Pretoria, also known as the Fountain of Shame because of the nude statues, was next. They strolled through the historic streets to the Piazza Marina, the main square in the old part of the city.

"My mother used to take me to the bellissimo parco here before we would tour the museum of marionettes. There are puppets from around the world displayed there," Nico stated.

"Nico, would you like to go to the museum today?" asked Luna.

"No, grazie. My memories are enough. Would you like to visit the best market in the city?"

"Yes, please. I love outdoor markets," said Cat.

The Mercato della Vucciria was humming and lived up to its name: "the place of loud voices." Every type of vegetable, fish, meat, and cheese was available. There were jars loaded with aromatic spices and pre-prepared dishes from North Africa.

"There is a special dish they offer here made from boiled liver and spleen. It is fried in lard. Would you like to try it, Zia?"

Catherine groaned. "Definitely not! But I'd be happy to buy you some gelato."

"Limone, per favore. Then I will by some flowers. It is a short walk to the cemetery to see my mother."

Nico led the way into an ancient cemetery and quickly located the graves of his mother and grandparents. He fought back tears and brushed the leaves from the bronze plaques that marked the sites. He gently placed the flowers on the plaques and ran his fingers across the engraved names and dates. He whispered in Italian to his mother. Luna and Cat stood at a respectful distance. After twenty minutes, Nico stood, said farewell to his loved ones and slowly walked away.

The harbor was next place Nico wanted to take them, They were all silent as they walked. He led them through narrow streets to La Cala, where yachts and sailboats were moored. A large cruise ship was docked in the port, and masses of people were disembarking.

"I guess that's what we looked like in Málaga," said Cat. "A river of old people flowing from the mouth of a white metal beast."

"I am happy that travelers are on the move once again. The economy in all of Italy is dependent on tourists."

"It's the same with Florida. We need the tourists to thrive," said Catherine.

"Now it is time to show you where my mother worked. I have not been back since the fire," said Nico.

The young man's pace was slow as they walked up a road closed to car traffic. The pedestrian street was busy, and Nico stopped in front of an electronics store.

"Luna, non è qui! The ristorante is gone. Maybe that is for the best." Nico walked up to the building and placed his hand on the brick wall. His head dropped forward. A single tear escaped his eye. Luna placed her arm around his shoulders and silently stood beside him. Several onlookers stared at the woman and teenager frozen in place. Finally, Nico turned around and wiped the tear from his cheek. "I want to see if my mother's friend is at home."

Two blocks from where the restaurant used to be, Nico stopped and rang a buzzer beside a crimson door with a window fortified by iron bars. He rang several times before a woman opened a second-floor window and called out, "Cosa vuoi?"

"Ciao, I am looking for Reina Parlatore. She is a friend of my mother."

"Oh, caro ragazzo, she has passed on. The virus took her away."

Nico had been trying to be brave but this time the dam broke. He openly sobbed and tears flowed freely down his face. Cat handed him several tissues and Luna took his arm to lead him away.

"Grazie," Luna said to the woman.

With heavy hearts, they returned to the hotel. Nico said he didn't want to go out for dinner, preferring to rest. The women understood his need for solitude. They showered, changed, and asked the concierge for a restaurant recommendation.

"My poor boy," Luna said on the walk to the restaurant. "His soul has been battered and bruised so many times. And he may have a battle ahead of him with his father."

"I'm glad we're seeing Riccardo tomorrow. We've got to convince him to support you and not his brother. His uncle will see the depth of Nico's desire to be with you. I'm sure of it."

Chapter 34

CATACOMB

"Turn left and then a quick right," said Cat, following the GPS on her phone.

Luna followed the directions and ended up in a parking lot, with a guard yelling at them to turn around. Nico laughed in the back seat.

"We've been driving in circles for half an hour! This GPS sucks big time. How can it be so wrong so often? And the traffic is insane," Catherine said.

Luna sighed and turned the car around. "We are not giving up. Nico wants us to see the Catacombe dei Cappuccini, and we will."

After another ten minutes of crazy traffic and one-way streets, they arrived in front of a small church where a casket was being loaded into a hearse. Mourners were filing out and heading to their cars, and the wailful sound of a church organ came from the chapel. An elderly gentleman directed them to a parking spot and charged them ten euros for doing so.

"My mother would not take me to the Catacombe when I was young, but my friends told me about it. I believe I am old enough now," said Nico.

"I have read about the Convento dei Cappuccini and the catacomb. I had no idea I would ever visit such a macabre place," Luna said.

They paid the admittance fee and walked down a dim, damp, musty corridor to the first room. The monks and priests who once lived in Palermo remained, now corpses dressed in their hassocks and vestments. Skeletal faces—with gaping, silently screaming mouths and deep black eye sockets—greeted the visitors.

"Oh my God!" said Cat as they walked into the next rooms, where the remains of citizens were divided by gender, profession, and social standing. "Why are these skeletons dressed up and pinned to the walls?"

"It says in the brochure that it began with the monks who were placed in here. The natural preservation of these caves encouraged wealthy people to be memorialized this way. Some are skeletons, and others are mummified," Luna stated.

"This is selvaggio—wild!" said Nico. "Look at all the babies and small children over here. How sad. There are soldiers over there."

"They are soldiers from Napoleon's army. Look at their uniforms and tricorn hats," said Luna. "They stopped adding new residents in 1881. This is the most bizarre museum I have ever seen. Some faces look serene, but most are horrible, with their jaws hanging open and their skin a ghastly hue—when they have skin."

"Bizarre is an understatement," said Cat. "Nico, you said this would be unforgettable, and it certainly is. It's shocking how many bodies are here. The Grim Reaper must love this place. It was fitting that we saw a funeral outside. This is one place that I don't want a souvenir from. The images are permanently seared in my brain."

The morbid museum had been a good distraction from the anticipation of their next stop. Cat put in Riccardo's address on the GPS, and they headed out of the city. She turned and looked at Nico's ashen face, understanding the turmoil in his mind. Today's meeting with his uncle could determine the next chapter of his life. They pulled up in front of a wrought-iron gate flanked by stone walls covered in pale-pink climbing roses. Luna got out of the car, pressed the intercom button, and conversed in Italian. The gates swung open, and Cat's heart raced. Nico was visibly shaking as they mounted the stairs to the centuries-old stone mansion. The massive oak door swung open, and a younger, more well-dressed version of Salvatore greeted them.

Riccardo walked out and gave Nico an awkward hug. "Nico, it is wonderful to see you again. You probably do not remember me. You were a bambino when I last laid eyes on you. Please, all of you, entra." His voice was a deep baritone, rich and intimidating.

"Ciao, Zio." Nico's voice was close to a whisper.

Riccardo led them into a large drawing room. Catherine's eyes swept around a space filled with exquisite antiques that were displayed among mid-century modern furniture. Contemporary art was on the walls. It was a disjointed look that reflected a fragmented mind.

"Per favore, siediti. My governante has prepared this for you."

Everyone sat on the uncomfortable sofas arranged around a Carrara marble coffee table. It was laden with fruit, pastries, and sparkling water.

"I am happy to meet you, Luna and Catherine. Welcome to Sicily."

"I'm glad to meet you, too. It's a beautiful island, and Nico has done a marvelous job showing us around Palermo," said Cat.

"Touring this part of Italy is wonderful," said Luna. "It has been a lovely trip so far."

Riccardo cleared his throat and leaned forward, placing his hands on his knees. His eyes were laser focused on the young man. "Let us discuss the future of my nephew."

"Sì, Riccardo. It is Nico's future that we are here to talk about."

Nico's discomfort was evident on his face. He leaned forward and placed a slice of cake on a china plate. He nervously poked it with a fork, then took a big gulp of water. Finally, he met his uncle's gaze and said, "Zio Riccardo, I am happy to see you, and I would like to visit more often. But I want to assure you that my mother insisted that if anything should happen to her, I would live with Luna. Siena is my home. I have my school and my friends there, and I do not want to leave."

"Yes, Luna's lawyer has contacted me saying as much. And she vouched for the authenticity of Carlotta's wishes."

"Then why are you paying for Salvatore's lawyer to challenge custody?" Luna questioned.

"My incompetent brother has lost his job in Greece and no longer wants to return there with Nico. I have arranged for him to live with an acquaintance in Rome so he can find work and be closer to his son. I assure you, I have not been paying for his lawyer. I do not believe he is a dependable father, and I want to honor Carlotta's request."

"Thank heavens!" said Catherine. "We were so worried that you would fight us on Nico's custody. May I ask, then, who is paying for Salvatore's lawyer?"

"Salvatore would not reveal his benefactor. As long as he has the funds for the lawyer, he will continue to pursue custody. There is nothing I can do to prevent that. I am sorry, Luna."

"Grazie, Riccardo. I am grateful for your support. Would you be willing to sign an affidavit stating your concern about Sal's fitness as a father?"

"Sì. Please have your lawyer send it to me. Nico, would you like to see photographs of our ancestors? I have albums in the office."

Nico and Riccardo left the room, and the women sat in silence for a long while, each lost in thought.

"If not Riccardo, then who is paying? Viola questioned the other lawyer, and he said Salvatore was keeping it confidential. I was certain it was Nico's uncle."

"More unanswered questions," said Cat. "I'm glad that we have one more person in our corner, though. I was worried that Riccardo would be an adversary and not an ally. At least Sal is in Italy and not in Greece."

"Yet in some ways, that could be a problem. A judge may determine that I would be able to visit Nico in Rome if I lost custody. And that Salvatore has made the effort to find employment in Italy."

"I hadn't thought of that. Why is nothing ever simple?"

"We will face this challenge and make it as easy as possible for our dear boy."

As they waited for Riccardo to finish his visit with Nico, Catherine texted Sam with the good news. Sam replied right away saying he was delighted. He also said that he was just about to fly to Milan for an unexpected meeting and that he would connect with them when they were in Siena.

A little Tuscan romance?

Chapter 35

VENUS

Their final night in Palermo was extra joyful since a huge weight had been lifted off their hearts and minds. Riccardo's support gave them hope that Nico would be able to remain with Luna. When they returned to Siena, they'd look into who was funding Salvatore's legal quest to gain custody of Nico.

They walked the streets of the city, and Nico pointed out more places that he remembered from his childhood. They dined in one of Carlotta's favorite restaurants, sampling local specialties that included Pantesca salad and swordfish alla palermitana. They finished with cubbaita, an almond nougat, and cannoli stuffed with ricotta cheese and candied orange peels. Raising petite glasses of limoncello, they toasted Carlotta.

"What a beautiful evening," said Cat, "but I'm so full!"

"There is an old saying in Palermo. 'The stomach is sweet, the more you fill it, the more it stretches,'" said Nico.

"Well, mine is stretched to the limit," said Catherine. "Thanks for recommending this restaurant, Nico. Dinner was delicious, and I'm sure your mom would have approved."

"My pleasure, Zia."

Once they were back at the hotel, Cat checked her emails and found an update from Lisa. She'd written that Diana had learned the police had located Cassidy and questioned him about his relationship with Rodney. Anson had an alibi for the time before Rodney's body was found. The police were satisfied with his statements and were not pursuing him further. Lisa said that both she and Diana were convinced that Cassidy was still a person of interest.

Lisa also said that Max had been successful in tracking Anson Cassidy in an online sports betting forum. To punk his friends, Max had used a new online identity he had created months earlier. He went on several sites before he found Cassidy, and he was now thinking about developing an online relationship with him. Catherine sent an email thanking her friend. She insisted that Max not meet with Anson or reveal his true identity. She also gave Lisa an update on Riccardo's involvement in Nico's custody battle.

The drive out of Palermo the following morning was as harrowing as the drive into the city had been. Luna breathed a sigh of relief as they approached the autoroute and headed west toward Trapani. The breathtaking coastline sped by, and Nico chatted about more memories from his youth. Their first stop was the spectacular mountaintop town of Erice, where Carlotta had taken her son a few times. The narrow, winding mountain road tested Luna's nerves once again, especially as large tour buses passed by with only inches to spare. They drove up almost twenty-five hundred feet and parked beside the megalithic stone blocks that dated back to the Phoenicians who had occupied the area before the Greeks.

They passed through the Porta Spada, one of the three gates to the village. A combination ticket allowed them to enter half of the ten churches, the loveliest being San Martino, which had an elegant baroque interior. The quaint shops and restaurants lining the cobblestone streets were a visual delight.

"This town is spectacular, Nico," said Cat. "I'm so glad you suggested we come here. It's like something out of a historical movie. It doesn't seem quite real."

"Sì, it is a special place and untouched by the modern world."

They had a delicious lunch at a café in the Piazza Umberto, then walked down the many narrow streets and alleyways, stopping in tiny shops for souvenirs. When they approached the Castello di Venere, Catherine felt a strange stirring, as if experiencing an ancient memory of the place.

"'This Norman castle was built in the twelfth century on the remains of the temple to Venus Erycina,'" Luna said. "'There was a cult of the goddess of fertility, centuries before Jesus.'"

"Venus," Catherine whispered. She staggered over to a low stone wall and dropped down. Her shaking hands covered her face, and she gasped for air. In her mind's eye, she was witnessing a procession of young women converging on an altar, chanting in an ancient tongue. A marble statue depicting the flawless beauty of Venus Erycina was visible, and the women clothed in flowing white gowns were bearing offerings. Earthenware jars filled with essential oils, candles, and bouquets of wildflowers were placed on the altar in honor of the goddess.

"Zia Catherine, are you okay?" asked Nico.

Cat was jolted back to the present. This was a powerful vision, more of a remembrance than pure imagination. "I'm fine. Do you mind if we don't tour the castle? My nerves are a little frazzled." She then described her mental images in detail.

As they approached the nearby public garden, a fog descended on the castle and swirled through the towering pines. A chill ran down Catherine's spine as she spun around and saw an ethereal figure emerge from the haze. *Jim, is that you?* She blinked, and the apparition was gone. A shiver wracked her body.

"Catherine, what is the matter? You look like you have seen a ghost," said Luna.

"I think I did. It looked like Jim over there under the trees. I think he's trying to tell me something, but I can't figure it out. It's so frustrating. I wish I could talk to him."

Nico rushed over to the stand of trees, but only a damp mist filled the space. Luna put her arm around her sister. The fog continued to roll in and envelop them in its cold embrace.

"I think it's time to go," said Cat. "This place is beautiful but unsettling."

The swerving drive down Monte San Guiliano gave them spectacular views of the Egadi Islands off the coast. A ray of sunlight broke through the clouds and bathed the sea in a golden hue. Catherine tried to shake off the uneasy feelings she'd experienced in Erice. The intense vision of the maidens and possibly seeing her brother's spirit had been an unexpected part of her European adventure, and it was unnerving.

"Do you see the area of white in the distance, Zia?" Nico said, leaning between the two front seats and pointing toward the far side of the city.

"Yes. It looks like a snow-covered field. What is it?"

"It is the salt marshes. Salt has been harvested there since ancient times. It was sent to Europe in past centuries, including places as far away as Norway. Windmills were used to take water from one basin to another. Some have been restored."

"That's amazing. You're a fountain of information about the island. I'm looking forward to our next stop."

"I hope the traffic in Trapani is better than Palermo," said Luna, gripping the steering wheel.

"It can't be worse. I'm so grateful that you're driving instead of me," said Cat.

Chapter 36

PAOLO

The front of their trendy hotel, set in a historic building in Trapani, faced the stone breakwater and azure sea beyond. The back door opened onto a pedestrian street lined with shops and restaurants. The street led to the old town. Cat decided to take a nap before dinner and encouraged her sister and nephew to tour the city without her. Still shaken by the double visions in Erice, she took a long, hot shower and then slid under the duvet. The air conditioning was whirring, and she soon fell into a deep sleep.

Her dream was rife with images of water, including a mist-shrouded lake and then a dark river littered with floating debris. She dropped to her knees and reached into the swift current, searching for something but not having a clear idea of what she was supposed to find. The sound of heavy footsteps behind her made her jump to her feet. A menacing black-clothed figure rushed toward her and grabbed her arms. She struggled against the malevolent man, but it was to no avail. With a mighty shove, he sent her into the churning river.

Cat screamed and bolted upright in the bed. Hyperventilating, she tried to get her bearings. She went into the bathroom and ran a cool cloth over her face. *What the hell was that all about? I can understand dreaming about castles or Venus, but not a river. What does it mean?*

A short time later, Luna and Nico returned. They were so cheerful and talkative that Catherine didn't want to be a wet blanket. She decided not to mention her nightmare since she had no idea what it meant. Yet she felt it was a significant dream.

"I found the perfect restaurant for dinner, Zia. It is not too far from the hotel."

"Great. I'll get changed, and we can leave in a few minutes."

They strolled down Corso Vittorio Emanuele and went past the San Lorenzo Cathedral. The trattoria where Nico was taking them was down a brightly lit side street. Planters of red and yellow flowers surrounded an outdoor seating area. A gentleman in a crisp white shirt and dark pants stepped through the glass door and was about to greet his new customers when he raised his arms and called out in surprise, "Nico Alessi! Sei tu?"

"Sì, Paolo! È passato molto tempo. Luna, Zia Catherine, this a friend of my mother's. I saw the name of the restaurant and wondered if it was the same owner as the one in Palermo."

"Benvenute, signore. I moved to Trapani several years ago. It is much less hectic in this city."

"Nice to meet you, Paolo," said Cat. "From what I've seen, it's a lovely town."

"Paolo is an excellent chef, just like my mother," said Nico.

"I will bring you a sampling of Sicily's finest cuisine in memory of your bella mamma, Nico. Entra, per favore."

Paolo was true to his word and brought out plate after plate of delicacies. There were Sicilian wine pairings with each dish—Grillo whites, Nero d'Avola reds, and a sweet Marsala with dessert.

"I can't eat another bite!" said Catherine. "Paolo, this has been the best meal I've ever had. Everything was delicious. How can we thank you?"

"It was truly my pleasure, Catherine. Carlotta was the dearest of friends. It was unfortunate when she had to leave Sicily and was such a tragedy when she passed. She was beloved by all who knew her."

"Grazie, Paolo," said Nico. "I miss her every day. My plan is to study hard and become an excellent chef like you and mia madre."

"No doubt, my boy. No doubt."

A cool breeze welcomed them as they strolled back to the hotel. Two blocks from the entrance, they heard a commotion coming from a darkened alleyway. Cat ran toward the sound and saw two boys pummeling a smaller boy.

"Stop! Fermara!" she yelled.

The boys turned and laughed at the middle-aged woman running toward them. Cat rummaged through her purse and found the whistle that Lisa had given her. She blew it as loud as she could, hoping to get the attention of other passersby. The taller of the two boys stormed over to her, grabbed her wrist, and slapped the whistle out of her hand. He let out a stream of profanities in Italian, stomped on the whistle and strode away.

Cat fished around in her purse and found another item that her friend had given her: a can of pepper spray. She rushed over to the young man and hit him fully in the face with the spray. He screamed in pain as the other assailant ran to his friend's side. The boy who had been under attack ran down the alley and disappeared around the corner. Luna and Nico arrived as the pepper-sprayed boy was led away by the other young man. Luna insisted that they leave immediately. The three ran all the way back to the hotel, and once they were back in their room, they broke into nervous laughter.

"Zia, I did not know you were a badass! That was awesome," said Nico.

"I didn't know I was a badass, either. I have no idea what came over me. I'm usually a wimp, afraid of my own shadow."

"I am certain the boy who was being attacked is grateful you found your courage," said Luna. "I am glad you were not hurt. It can be dangerous getting in the middle of a conflict."

"You're right. It's the first time I've ever done something like that. What was I thinking?"

* * *

The following morning, the travelers headed east along the highway on the northern coast. Their destination was Cefalù, a vacation town beloved by Italians and the mafia. An American member of the renowned criminal organization had recently been arrested there while on vacation. It had happened during an international sting operation. Nestled under a massive cliff, the medieval city was one of the few beach towns untouched by modern blight. They found a parking lot across from the sea and walked along the promenade toward the historic area.

The public area of beach was jam-packed with families and groups of teenagers competing for a few feet of pebbled sand. Bright blue-and-white-striped rental umbrellas covered a vast area of the beach, where people could claim their spot for the day for a fee. Swimmers dove into the three-foot swells that splashed the sun bathers closest to the water. A tall, gangly man meandered through the crowd, calling out, "Coco, coco, coconuts," as he was selling fresh coconut milk.

They made their way to the row of medieval fishermen's dwellings that hugged the waterfront, and found a delightful restaurant that overlooked the sea. Through the open window, they watched swimmers frolicking in the waves. After lunch, they strolled the charming streets and went to the cathedral. It had two bell towers rising in salute to the massive crag, or Rocca, rising behind the church. Following clusters of tourists speaking several languages, they climbed the steps and entered the duomo. The highlight was the spectacular twelfth century mosaic depicting "Christ in the Act of Blessing." It was displayed over the altar. Leaving the church, they journeyed down the narrow passageways from the Arabic period, then went partway up the Rocca toward the citadel. They stopped at the fifth century BC structure known as the Temple of Diana. Catherine began to feel woozy again. *I don't need any more visions. My mind has done enough time traveling and glimpsing into the other side.*

"Do you two want to find the Airbnb? I think the heat is getting to me, and I've done enough touring today," said Cat.

Chapter 37

HANGAR BAR AND GRILL

After several attempts to exit the city through constricted one-way streets, and scraping the tire rims against the sidewalk, Cat directed them to the east side of the Rocca, where their lovely hillside Airbnb was. Their landlady, Astrid, was half Swedish, and she greeted them warmly. She took them to a second-story apartment with a spectacular view of the Tyrrhenian Sea, then showed them the infinity pool, which was just a short walk through a peaceful garden with ivy-covered fieldstone walls and dangling wisteria.

"Do you want to get changed and go back to the main beach?" Cat asked when they returned to the apartment.

"It was nice but so crowded," Nico answered. "What if we spend time at the pool and go into town for dinner."

"That works for me," said Cat.

"You two can go ahead. I want to get an update from Viola on Salvatore. I will join you in a while," said Luna, who was sitting behind the desk in the apartment.

After slipping into the refreshing pool and then settling on a bench, Cat began to relax. Nico swam several laps before joining her.

"Zia, what made you stand up to those boys in the alley? You acted so quickly."

"I'm not sure. I'm usually a scaredy cat. I've never tried to defend anyone like that before, but it just felt like the right thing to do. I guess I've led a sheltered life. I joined a few protests over the years, but they were always peaceful."

"Do you think that coming on this trip has made you braver?"

"I hadn't thought about that. I've definitely expanded my comfort zone. Maybe I'm becoming more of the person I can be in this life. Before we went out last night, I had a dream where a frightening person in a dark cloak grabbed me. I wasn't able to fight him off, and he shoved me into a raging black river."

"That is awful! I hate nightmares like that. I, too, have had dreams of being thrown into water. Do you think it is a common dream?"

Catherine sighed. "It could be. Perhaps because I failed in my dream, I was braver in real life."

"Do you think you are more open to the spirit world, too?"

"You're very insightful. That crossed my mind when we were at the Temple of Diana today, and my head started spinning. I wasn't ready for another apparition. It was strange enough having a vision of young maidens approaching the castle, then seeing Jim in Erice."

"You do have some good images for a novel. I would like to read about your visions. And about your courage in Trapani."

"Yes, Catherine, you were very brave," said Luna as she placed her bathing suit cover on a lounge chair and slipped off her sandals, joining them in the water. She walked down the pool steps and sat down on the bench in the shallow end. "The water is lovely, and the view of the sea is spectacular," she said as she took in the magnificent scenery. "This vacation has been wonderful in every possible way. Every Italian should tour Sicily as we have done. It is a unique part of the country, and the cuisine is distinctive and delicious."

"I know I've put on a few pounds," said Cat. "By the time we get to Tuscany, I'll be pleasantly plump. So, what did Viola say?"

"There is nothing new to report right now. Salvatore's lawyer will not say who is paying him, and that is to be expected. I am not certain what to do now."

"We'll figure it out when we get to Siena. We can hire a private investigator if we need to."

"Viola also found the location of my biological father. He lives in Montalcino, which is not far from Siena. He works at a vineyard there."

"Oh wow! That's where my friend William is renting a villa for six months. We should go there if your father decides to see you. That is, assuming you want to contact him."

"Yes, I will write him a letter. Many of our older people do not appreciate being contacted by email. Since this is a sensitive matter, I do not want to upset him."

"You're right. He has no idea you even exist. He would have been told that his baby died after birth. It would be a shock for him to learn that you're alive. It's unlikely that Angelina tracked him down the way she did with you. "

"She never said anything about trying to contact him. And I think she would have mentioned something like that."

"It's crazy that your family is expanding. First Nico, then me, and now your birth father," said Cat.

"And your father may have other children that will be your fratelli—your sisters and brothers," said Nico. "And I could have cousins."

"The past couple of years have been a rollercoaster in the world at large, and in our private lives," said Cat. "A global pandemic with unimaginable suffering and death, financial upheaval, and fights for equality around the world. And in the past months, we've personally had our ups and downs."

"There has been immense loss, and yet much has been found in the world," said Luna.

"It is up to my generation to continue the progress we have made," said Nico. "We can undo the bad parts and focus on caring for Earth and each other."

Cat and Luna smiled. "Yes, our generation has messed up the planet," said Cat. "You and your cohorts have to be superheroes and save this beautiful place so your children can inherit a better Earth."

Nico groaned and dove under the water.

"I suppose he does not want to think about having children of his own," said Luna. "Young men do not have fancies about marriage and babies like many young women do."

Nico swam laps until his limbs were like rubber bands. He climbed out of the pool and dropped into a lounge chair. The women watched him through the eyes of maternal love. Neither had to say a word, but both knew they felt the joy of shepherding the young man.

After they returned to their apartment, Catherine checked her computer and opened an email from Lisa. She read the first part of Max's report, thinking he could have a career writing thriller novels.

As my suspicion grew about Cassidy and his connections, I wanted to find a way to corner him in person—and get the answers. Figuring that Cassidy wasn't shy about his rambunctious social life, I spent hours combing through his social media and was able to find a spot where Cassidy would tag himself with frequent, and cringeworthy, posts on Instagram: the Hangar Bar & Grill.

This is a sleazy 1990s-era sports bar with—you guessed it—an airplane theme. It's located just east of the airport. It's hard to know why Cassidy frequented this location. Was it for the ambience of Dan Marino posters under the glow of neon Budweiser signs, complete with the stale smell of cigarettes and popcorn in the air? Or was it for the less-than properly clothed female bartenders and the sound of disgruntled college football fans arguing about Tim Tebow's true potential? It was most likely all of the above, and yet I knew this would be a perfect, nondescript location to get face to face with Cassidy himself.

By studying Cassidy's increasingly drunken posts on Instagram every Thursday night starting around 8:30 PM—kickoff time for Thursday Night Football—I knew this week would be a perfect time for the fateful meeting.

To blend in, I went through my closet and found an old, stained Florida State Seminoles sweatshirt and an Aerosmith hat that had belonged to Dad. I made the twenty-five-minute drive to an encounter that might change the course of Cassidy's life.

At just after 8:00 PM on Thursday, I pulled up to the dimly lit bar. It had an industrial, cold, warehouse feel. The parking lot was full of Harleys and F150s, and Cassidy's battered beige sedan was parked right in front.

As I walked in

Luna and Nico entered the apartment, chattering in Italian.

"I was telling Nico that his lovely friend Bria would be a wonderful mother to his future children," Luna said with a chuckle.

Nico groaned, then bounded into the bedroom to get changed. Luna went to the second bedroom to put on a dress for dinner, and Cat finished reading Max's report.

"It is fun teasing him sometimes," Luna said as she joined Catherine on the balcony. "Being the parent of a teenager is still new to me, and I will have to navigate my way through and figure out when to joke and when not to, how much leeway to give the young man, and when to reign him in for his own good."

"That's the challenge all parents have. I told you that Max, Lisa's son, was investigating Anson Cassidy over Rodney's death. He did what we asked him *not* to do and went to meet Cassidy in person."

"Oh no! What happened? Is he all right?"

"Yes, thank goodness. He tracked Cassidy down through an online gaming site and figured out where he might be during a preseason football game. He went to a bar near the airport in Jacksonville, and Cassidy was sitting at a table with two men. Fortunately, he decided not to approach him and instead sat at the bar so he could eavesdrop on their conversation."

"I did not know he was old enough to go to a bar."

"I think that was part of the appeal to Max. He turned twenty-one a few weeks ago, and I think he wanted to feel grown up. Anyway, he overheard Cassidy telling the men that he had a good deal working as a nurse for the clients of this rich Italian guy. He said he checks on the man's elderly mother every day and takes care of pregnant women in several condo buildings owned by the wealthy guy."

"Catherine, I do not understand. This sounds very odd."

"I didn't tell you, Luna, but when I went to check out one of the buildings owned by Emerson & Ritter and Riva Realty, I saw several pregnant women living there. The security guard said they were Russian. They were having 'anchor' babies, because if children are born in the United States, they automatically become American citizens."

"Yes, I remember reading about that. And buying real estate in America was also a way for Russian oligarchs to launder money."

"You're right. Our previous president and his grifter family laundered money that way. Max wrote that Cassidy never said how he got the job with the Italian guy. But he was bragging about it to these guys in the bar."

"I assume you believe Giancarlo made those arrangements."

"There's no doubt about it, because Riva had Cassidy give flu shots to E & R's employees. That's where Rodney saw Cassidy in the first place, and that's why we think there's a connection between the two. Both were members of Gamblers Anonymous. And there aren't many rich Italians in Jacksonville who own condominiums."

"The pieces of the puzzle are beginning to fall into place. What else did Lisa's son have to say?"

"Well, first of all, Lisa said the police aren't investigating Cassidy any further because he has an alibi for around the time Rodney was killed. But Max overheard him saying something about breaking his medical oath to 'do no harm.' That could be related to Rodney, or anyone else, of course."

"You would expect that a nurse would not be involved in harming people," said Luna.

"There are good and bad people in every profession. Obviously, he has some personal issues and a gambling problem that may have caused him to do something he normally wouldn't have done."

"I assume that Max is going to continue to investigate from a distance."

"I'm sure he will. His report sounds like a suspense novel, and I'm going to encourage him to keep writing. But he should never put himself in danger."

Chapter 38

LE CHAT NOIR

A short while later, they returned to the old town in Cefalù. Astrid had recommended a restaurant that gave a French twist to Sicilian food—called Le Chat Noir—and had made a reservation for them. The bistro was tucked in a corner, up a winding cobblestone street. They chose an outdoor table. The women each ordered a glass of rosé from Provence, and Nico ordered a soda. They watched the tourists amble by.

"So, Zia Catherine, what do you think of my home island?"

"It's more beautiful than I could have imagined. The diverse landscape, the mountains, a volcano, the lovely towns, and incredible ancient ruins. Exploring the island in person is so much more fulfilling than reading about it or seeing pictures on the internet."

"That is true, my dear sister. Actually, seeing places with your own eyes is quite different than looking through books."

"Many Americans traveled around their own country during the pandemic, which is great, but I hope more people expand their horizons and explore the world," Cat said.

"You are right. I learned so much on my visit to Florida," said Nico. "It makes me want to travel to many countries and learn about their culture and their food."

A lovely server—with silky dark hair in a high ponytail—came outside to take their order. She flirted with Nico. In Italian, he engaged the young woman in a conversation about Sicily and Palermo. Catherine didn't have to understand the words to read the body language. Luna and Cat exchanged amused glances before ordering their meals. There was a spring in the server's steps and a sway in her hips as she strolled back into the restaurant. Nico's smile remained on his face.

"Nico, do you know where you want to go to culinary school?" Cat asked.

"Sì. I have researched the schools, and there are many I will apply to. In Rome, there is the Italian Chef Academy and a modern school called Coquis. In Florence, there is the Florence Culinary School, the Cordon Bleu, and the Apicius International School of Hospitality. Any one of these would be amazing."

"I am certain you will be able to attend one of those fine schools," Luna said. "I will support your decision, even if you choose to go to a foreign institution. But I would be happy to have you stay in Italy."

"I promise to work hard, and I do want to go to school in Italy," Nico answered. "After I graduate, I will work for a time and save money so I can travel to foreign countries. I will come and stay with you in Florida, Zia, and learn Southern cooking."

"That would be great! And you and Lisa can cook and test recipes together," said Cat. "One day, we'll have a famous chef in the family."

After another outstanding dinner, they returned to the Airbnb, and Nico went to his room to text his friends. Cat took him a bottled water and found him sitting on his bed. He was wearing wireless ear buds and was listening to his playlist. She joined Luna outside, and they relaxed on the balcony and sipped a local Grillo white wine.

"That young waitress was quite smitten with our Nico," said Luna. "I am sure he will have many girls interested in him. I believe his friend Bria would like to be more than a friend."

"He's handsome and sweet and smart. I know many young ladies will pursue him. But I think he has a clear focus on what he wants to accomplish, and he won't settle down too quickly."

"I agree."

The shrill ring of Luna's phone startled them. She rushed inside to retrieve it from a coffee table. Catherine heard her sister cry out and hurried into the apartment. When Luna hung up the phone, she looked pale and shaken.

"What's wrong?" asked Cat.

"That was a call from my security company. My office and home were broken into tonight. They received alarms from both locations, and the police were dispatched. They want me to return immediately to investigate what may have been taken. Things have been strewn around, but they do not know if anything is missing. My office was violated first, and then, a short time later, the house was broken into."

"Oh my gosh. Who could have done it? Do you have cameras at either location?"

"No. I have never felt the need before. It is a relatively safe city."

Cat took her sister's hand and led her to the couch. "Do you think there are cameras on the streets near your home and office? Is the security company going to check with the police?"

"Yes. They will ask the authorities to check the public cameras."

Nico joined them and saw the distressed look on Luna's face. "Che c'è? What has happened?" he asked.

"It is fine, Nico. There has been an intruder at my office and our home. The police are investigating, so there is no need to worry," Luna said.

"Perché qualcuno dovrebbe farlo? Why?" Nico asked in a trembling voice.

"That is what we need to find out. I will fly from Palermo to Rome in the morning and return here in a couple of days. I will book my flight right away."

"I can drive you to the airport in the morning," said Cat.

"No, no. I will hire a car to take me there. You and Nico can continue your holiday, and I will rejoin you. We will ask Astrid if we can stay for an extra few nights. Perhaps you can go to the mountain town that she suggested we visit."

"Nico and I will be fine until you get back. Why don't you use my small carry-on suitcase so you don't have to check a bag."

"Thank you. I will book my flight and car service, then send an email to Astrid," said Luna. "What next?"

Chapter 39

GRETA

A visibly upset Luna left for the airport early the following morning. She'd hugged Nico, stroked his curly hair, and tried to soothe his fears. She told him that the police would find out who violated their home and that she'd FaceTime from the house to give them an update. He'd wanted to go with her but had agreed to stay with Catherine.

After breakfast, Nico headed to the pool while Cat sent several emails. The first one was to Jerome. She asked for an update on the FinCEN investigation into Riva Realty. The second was to Lisa, asking about Max's research into Cassidy. The third was to the Fernandina Beach police, asking about the destruction of her fence and garden. And the fourth was to Diana, asking whether the Jacksonville police had any news on Rodney's death.

Because of the time difference between Europe and Florida, she didn't wait for answers. She joined Nico poolside, dropped onto a chaise lounge, and soaked in the sunshine and the magnificent scene before her. *This vacation has had wonderful highs and stressful lows. We successfully overcame one challenge by meeting with Nico's uncle, only to face another a few days later. I hope it was a disgruntled client who broke into Luna's office and home. I know there's been ongoing problems with a couple of people.*

"Zia! You should come in the water. It is perfect."

"Coming."

The young man and his aunt swam a dozen laps, passing each other midway through the pool. Cat quit first and made her way back to the lounger. Nico did several dolphin dives before joining her. Wrapping a towel around his waist, he sat at the edge of the chair, let the water drip from his wavy hair, and asked, "Who do you think did it?"

Catherine knew exactly what he was referring to and knew that he was extremely upset about his home being violated. She wanted to comfort him but didn't want to dismiss his worries. He deserved to be kept fully informed about anything that happened. "It occurred to me that it might be one of Luna's clients who was angry," she said. "I know she's had several people upset about their taxes and the government. It could be someone who didn't think she handled their case well."

Nico grabbed a second towel and dried his hair. "The thought went through my mind, too. I have heard Luna argue with clients several times. I sent a text to my friend Remy, and he saw police at our house. He asked them for an update, but they would not answer him."

"Luna will call after she talks to the police. It's most likely that the break-ins are connected. Coincidences are rare."

"You are probably right. I trust our polizia to solve the crimes."

"I hope the Jacksonville police solve Rodney's murder soon. They dismissed the only person of interest we had, saying he had an alibi. And there haven't been any other leads that I know of. It's so frustrating, and I'm sorry for his daughter, Diana. Her children feel the loss of their grandfather, too."

"Sì. We know what that loss is like. It is with you every day. And it must be hard knowing that he was murdered."

"Very true, and the ongoing fear that his homicide hasn't been solved is difficult for them. Well, would you like to take a drive into the mountains? I think I can handle that better than driving through Palermo."

The narrow, winding roads into the lush Madonie Mountains, south of Cefalù, were challenging enough for Catherine. She gasped every time a speeding car dashed around her, especially when there were blind corners up ahead. She was certain she'd hear the sound of crashing metal, and she gripped the steering wheel tight. She was grateful that Luna had rented an automatic and not a stick shift.

They finally arrived at the mountaintop town of Castelbuono. Cat was anxious to park, and they found a spot on a side road. Parking was accompanied by the tire rims scraping against the sidewalk. Nico stifled a laugh and hopped out of the car. Cat took a photo of the cross streets with her cell phone so she could locate the car again—something she'd noticed that Luna did every time they parked in a new place. Many of the roads were so similar to one another that it was easy to lose your way.

While strolling past ocher-colored buildings with red-tiled roofs, Cat marveled at the abundance of lovely trees and flower boxes. The lively village was filled with restaurants, shops, and outdoor stalls selling cheese and other specialties. They toured the splendid church, then headed to the fourteenth-century Ventimiglia Castle, which housed the Francesco Minà Palumbo Naturalistic Museum. The museum had a combination of local and ancient artifacts, modern art, and a natural history section with cases of insects and taxidermy animals. Nico was excited to find a marionette in a plexiglass box, just like those he had seen as a child in Palermo. There was an exquisite Palatine chapel in the castle. Cat read that the skull of St. Anne, the patron saint of the town, was kept in a silver box behind the altar.

"I think I've seen enough skulls at the catacomb in Palermo to last a lifetime," she said.

"But when you come to Siena, you will want to see the marble box that holds the skull of your namesake."

"You mean the head of St. Catherine?"

"Sì. It is by the altar in the church of San Domenico. The remainder of her body is in Rome."

"Nico! I don't understand the devotion to bones. I remember reading about her influence on the Catholic Church, and the popes, during her lifetime. She ate very little, which probably led to her visions when she dictated her book. It was so unusual for a woman to have that power in the Middle Ages."

"Sì. I read part of her book, *The Dialogue of Divine Providence*, in school. It is a great work of early Tuscan literature."

"Today, we would say St. Catherine was anorexic. It's not surprising she died when she was quite young."

They finished the tour on the front steps, admiring the mountains in the distance, which were dotted with centuries-old homes. On their way to find a trattoria for lunch, they passed a banner that was hanging on a two-story building. There was a photo of the environmental activist Greta Thunberg, with writing below.

Nico translated. "It says, 'With Greta and her generation for the environment and for the future.'"

Cat took a photo of the banner. "As we were saying earlier, your generation must lead the way."

"You are correct, Zia, but for now I will lead you to a restaurant we passed earlier that looked very nice."

After ordering, the conversation turned to Greta and her success in generating interest in climate change and global action. "It still infuriates me that the last president attacked and mocked Greta on Twitter. He was worse than pond scum," said Cat.

Nico laughed. "That is a funny saying, but I agree that he was a nightmare. I would be most upset if a country's leader ridiculed me. There are good parts to Twitter and YouTube and TikTok, though. It is a way for the Green Movement to spread around the world and inspire people of all ages to protect the Earth from human activity."

After lunch, Cat located the car, and they began the journey down the mountain. Nico used the GPS to guide them on a different route from before. "It says to take a right on the next road. It is a small road, but I guess we should follow it."

Catherine carefully entered the roadway, and they descended down a gravel lane. Soon, the gravel ended, and it became a dirt road. Then the dirt ended, and they were bumping across a field. Nico laughed when two cows ambled toward the car.

"Good gracious! I can't turn around. I'll have to keep going. How can the GPS be so wrong!"

Finally, the car dropped over a curb and got on a road once again. Nico opened his window and yelled "addio" to the cows. Cat's nerves were frayed as they made their way back to Cefalù.

Chapter 40

LLADRÓ

Luna took a car service from Rome to Siena. She'd requested that her administrative assistant, Rita, meet her at the office. Luna's anxiety grew when she arrived and saw that the glass on the front door had been shattered. The historic building had a minimal security system.

"Who could have done this?" Rita said as her boss stepped out of the car. "We should have installed cameras inside and outside the building."

Luna's sense of security had shattered along with the glass. "That's something we need to do now. I feel so violated. Is anything missing?"

"Not that I could see."

Smashed glass on the front of the barrister bookcases and two damaged coffee tables greeted Luna in her office. Books, files, and papers were strewn around the room. Vases had been hurled against the wall, and wilted flowers lay in pools of water on the carpet.

"I'm overwhelmed," Luna said. "Rita, did the police have any theories about who would do this and why?"

"No. Because this is an isolated event. There haven't been any other break-ins in the area. They are still checking the street cameras and will update us. An officer said he would be at your house around seven tonight."

"Well, let's clean up in the morning. Right now, I want to go home and inspect the damage there."

"Do you want me to come with you?" Rita asked.

"No. Please go home. Viola is meeting me there in an hour."

With each step she took along the three blocks from her office to her house, Luna became more distraught. She kept running through who may have been angry enough with her to violate her property. Two former clients popped into her head, though neither would have done it themselves. A petty criminal would have been hired to do the deed. She arrived to find police tape strung across her front door. It caught Luna by surprise. She ducked under the tape and was grateful the door wasn't damaged. She dropped her bags in the front hallway and walked to the kitchen. The back door's glass was broken. She texted Viola and asked her to enter through the back when she arrived.

Slowly, Luna took stock of the damage in each room. Just like at her office, objects were smashed and tables were upended. At first glance, nothing appeared to be missing, but several cherished statues lay in pieces on the floor. She picked up the remains of a Lladró figurine, called "Mommy's Little Girl," that her mother had given her on her eighth birthday. She knelt on the floor and lifted the blue umbrella that had stood over the flower cart on the Lladró "Flowers of the Season" figurine. The statuette that her parents had given her on her twenty-first birthday was broken in two.

With a heavy heart, she placed the pieces of her past back on the shelf, then climbed the stairs to check the bedrooms. The two bedrooms on the third floor, which Carlotta had once rented, were not in use. The larger room only contained an old iron-framed bed and a couple of chairs. They were untouched. Upon returning to her bedroom on the second floor, she found that her cosmetics had been swept off her vanity, and clothes were lying on the ground. She checked the wall safe, which was hidden behind a painting of the Palio horse race in Siena's Piazza del Campo. She breathed a sigh of relief when she opened the safe and found everything was in order. She was grateful her important documents were untouched.

Next, she entered Nico's bedroom and found a similar scene. Nico's cookbook collection was on the floor, and his clothes lay in a heap. She sat on the edge of the bed and sobbed. After pulling herself together, she put everything back where she thought it had been, then rehung his clothes. Her phone rang in her pocket, and the face of her son and sister appeared on the screen.

"Nico, my love, I was just about to call you."

"I could not wait any longer to talk to you. We want to know what has happened."

"Yes, Luna, please fill us in," said Cat.

"Well, in both the office and the house, objects have been broken and thrown around. There does not seem to be anything stolen. Nico, your room seems fine," Luna said as she swept the phone camera around the room. "I am not certain that all of your belongings are here, so you will have to check when you return."

"I do not see anything missing, but I will know for sure when I am there," Nico said.

"What did the police say?" Cat asked.

"An officer called my assistant, Rita, and said he will be here soon to talk to me. At that time, I will get an update, and hopefully they will have made progress."

"I'm so sorry this is happening to you."

"I am, too. But I will clean everything up in the morning and return to Cefalù the day after tomorrow. We can continue our drive along the north coast of the island, then return to Siena." Luna heard a sound coming from the main floor and jumped.

"What's wrong?" Cat asked.

"It is fine. I asked Viola to join me here, and I think she has arrived. I must go downstairs. I will call you in the morning. I love you both." Luna descended the stairs and saw her lawyer standing in the living room.

"Why would someone do this?" Viola asked.

"That is what we need to find out. This is traumatizing," Luna said as she grasped the gold necklace she was wearing. Unexpectedly, the clasp gave way, and she held the rose pendant in her hand. "Oh dear! This was a gift."

"Here, give it to me. My daughter makes jewelry. She will be able to repair the clasp." Viola took the necklace and placed it in her change purse. She took a notepad and pen from her handbag. "Here is Anna's phone number. You can follow up with her about the necklace."

Viola insisted on helping her put the house back in order, so the women got to work cleaning up the mess in each room. The fragments of the figurines that were dear to Luna were gathered together and placed in a plastic bin. She would try to have them repaired, or she would replace them. Viola nailed a board across the broken glass on the kitchen door, and they checked the locks on all the windows.

When they had finished returning the house to normal, Luna went to the pantry for a bottle of her best wine. She took two of her finest crystal glasses from the dining room hutch, poured the ruby liquid, and handed one to Viola, saying, "It is so important to have good friends at a time like this. Thank you for helping me tonight. Saluti."

"Saluti. Let us hope the trespasser is found soon and punished." The women clinked the crystal glasses and inhaled the notes of plum, red current, and sweet balsamic in the wine.

"Yes, and discover why he committed the crime."

The front doorbell rang. "Let me get that," said Viola.

She returned a few moments later and was followed by an officer who was holding the police tape in his hand. Luna hoped he had some answers.

Chapter 41

SILENCE

The alarm startled Luna the next morning. A wave of anxiety washed over her, knowing that an intruder had been in her bedroom. Her sanctuary had been violated, and sadness wrapped around her heart. She hadn't been this despondent since Carlotta had died. Slipping into a robe, she ascended the stairs to the third floor. It was quiet and empty, and seeing the bedroom where her friend had slept only deepened her sorrow. A warm shower and hot coffee eased her anguish a little. She rummaged around in the freezer and found a package of cinnamon rolls. She popped one into the oven and poured a second cup of coffee. She was placing the warm pastry on a plate when her phone rang.

"Catherine, I was just thinking of you. The cinnamon rolls and coffee I am having remind me of your lovely kitchen."

"I'm glad. How are you holding up today? What did the police say?"

"I am doing well. Viola and I cleaned the house last night, and everything is in order. The police officer informed me that they do have camera footage of a man in a hooded jacket and mask on the streets by my house and office. But they were unable to get a facial recognition."

"Hopefully, they can get more video from the area and see him getting into or out of a car. That way, they might be able to track him down," said Cat.

"I have not found that anything is missing. The intruder created a mess in both locations, but I do not understand what the purpose of this crime was."

191

"I don't get it, either. I'm glad the police are following up. I meant to ask you last night if Viola had new information on Salvatore's lawyer."

"Oh, I forgot to ask her. I will call her and find out. I am going into the office soon to face that mess."

"This is mind boggling."

"Yes, it is. Do you have plans for today?"

"Nico and I are going to the beach this morning. We're renting umbrellas for the day and doing some people-watching."

"That is a lovely idea. Hug him for me."

"I will, sweet sister. Stay safe, and we'll see you tomorrow night."

Luna ended the call and sent a text to Viola asking about Salvatore's lawyer. When she didn't get a response after fifteen minutes, she decided to call. Viola's phone went to voicemail, and Luna left a short message. When she arrived at the office, she was pleased to see that Rita had been in early and had hired a handyman to replace the glass on the front door. She found another stranger installing security cameras in the reception area. Rita was in Luna's office and was sweeping the bookcase glass from the carpet.

"You are wonderful! Thank you for taking care of everything so quickly. You were right. We should have installed cameras before."

"Better late than never. How is your house?"

"Viola and I cleaned all the rooms. I feel despondent. I cannot imagine why someone would do this. I pray the police find the intruder."

"Break-ins are low on the priority list these days, but we can hope. How is Nico doing with all this?"

"I'm grateful he is in Sicily with Catherine. That child has seen so much heartache. He doesn't need to worry about this, too."

"I agree. When are you returning to Palermo?"

"Tomorrow afternoon. I'll take a car service in the morning and fly from Rome. They have the best flights on short notice."

"I can drive you. I'll visit my sister after I drop you off."

"That would be wonderful, Rita. You can pick me up at nine. Now, let's finish cleaning."

Luna returned home a short time later, and her call to Viola went to voicemail again. She contacted Viola's law partner, but he hadn't heard from her since yesterday. On the walk over to her lawyer's house, a sense of uneasiness flooded Luna for the second time that day. She spotted Viola's next-door neighbor peeking out from behind a curtain as she walked up the front steps.

Her knock on the door went unanswered, so Luna walked around the back to the kitchen door. Again, there was no answer, and her anxiety turned into fear. Viola's daughter had informed her earlier that she hadn't spoken to her mother since noon the day before, and she was concerned. She told Luna where the spare house key was hidden and gave her the code to the security system. Returning to the front of the house, Luna located the key and entered. She quickly turned off the alarm and called out Viola's name.

Silence.

Luna swiftly checked every room, and nothing seemed disturbed. There were no dishes in the sink, and her bed had not been slept in. She sent a text to Viola's daughter saying all looked well in the house but that there were no signs of her mother. Just as she slipped her phone in her purse, it rang. The officer they'd met with said he hadn't been able to identify the man in the hooded jacket.

"Thank you for keeping me updated. On another matter, I've been unable to reach my lawyer, Viola Mancini, whom you met last night. I'm at her house right now, and I do not believe she came home last evening. Both her daughter and I are very worried."

"Since it has been a short time, a missing person's file cannot be opened. If you send me a photo, I can put it into our system. Let me know immediately if she contacts you."

"Thank you. I will get you her photo right away."

Luna went into the office and found a recent picture of Viola. She took a photo and sent it to the police. While locking up the house, she noticed the neighbor peering at her again. She walked over and rang the bell. An elderly woman cracked open the front door.

"Ciao, signora. Do you know Viola?"

"Sì."

"Did you see her come home last night?"

"No, but I heard a ruckus. It may have been a scream. I looked out my front window, but I did not see anyone."

"Did it sound like a woman? Could it have been Viola?"

"Si. It was a woman, but I could not tell who it was."

"Grazie. Here is my number in case you remember anything else."

The woman hesitantly took Luna's card and ducked inside. On the walk home, Luna kept glancing around for any signs of being followed or for suspicious-looking characters. She'd never felt more paranoid or alone.

Chapter 42

AMARO

Before heading to the beach, Catherine sat on the bed and opened her laptop. She wanted to check her emails before they left for the day. There was one from Jerome saying that the accountant had recommended that the Department of the Treasury search for a second set of "books" at Riva Realty. They were suspicious and suggested that offshore bank accounts should be investigated, including those in the Cayman Islands and Cyprus.

"Nicosia," Cat said.

Nico bounded into the room. "Did you call me, Zia?"

"No. I said Nicosia. It's the capital city of Cyprus."

"I would like to go there some day. Sam said it is very nice."

"He told me his recent trip there was canceled."

"Maybe it was another time that he went there. Are you ready for the beach?"

Cat turned off her computer. "Let's go, buddy."

They parked near the shore and rented an umbrella and lounge chairs. Watching the sunbathers on the public beach in Cefalù was entertaining. They shared amused glances when chubby men in tiny swim suits paraded by. There were gaggles of girls in equally skimpy suits, and families tried to rein in their offspring while juggling beach gear.

Cat's phone chimed, and there was a text from Luna. She said she was worried because Viola was not responding to texts or phone calls and wasn't at her home or office. She also added that Viola's neighbor had heard what she thought was a disturbance the night before. Luna stated that she'd asked the police to follow up when the appropriate amount of time had passed.

Cat texted back, *Do you think you should stay until you find out where Viola is?*

No. I will return tomorrow. Her daughter is searching for her, and she will keep me updated. There is nothing more I can do until I hear from the police. I have a new security system in the office, and my assistant, Rita, is looking after things for me.

Whatever you think is best. I hope Viola contacts you soon.

I do, as well. Please do not tell Nico about this.

Okay. Good idea. No sense in upsetting him until we know more.

The break-ins at our house and my office are troubling enough.

I agree.

Love you, Catherine.

I love you, too. Cat slipped the phone into her purse.

"Were you texting with Luna?" Nico asked. "Is everything okay?"

"Yes, and she's still planning on coming back tomorrow. Oh my gosh! Look at that huge man over there with the bad toupee and the tiny red speedo."

Diversion, Cat thought. *I don't want Nico to worry unnecessarily.*

"Do you want to go in the water?" Nico asked.

"Not right now. You go ahead, and we can get some lunch later. I think I need some of those great French fries we had the other day."

Nico bounded across the sand and jumped into the sea. Cat smiled when she noticed several teenage girls watching him. Closing her eyes, she tried to get a mental image of Viola, but her mind was blank. *I wish I could contact her telepathically. We need some paranormal help.* Cat drifted into a light sleep. She jumped and squealed when her nephew shook his head and a cascade of water drops splashed onto her, waking her up.

"Thanks! I was getting a little hot."

Nico laughed and flopped into the chair beside her. "The water is bellissimo. I love swimming in the sea."

"It's been great traveling around the island, but it's also nice to spend some time in one place and relax. And I'm glad we've been able to stay in such a beautiful place. I think Cefalù is one of my favorite cities."

"It is spectacular, or spettacolare, as a local would say."

Cat reached into her purse when her phone chimed. *I bet Viola has contacted Luna. Everything out of the ordinary is unnerving these days, especially after the break-ins. I'm sure Viola is sorry she caused Luna and her daughter to worry.* The text wasn't from her sister, however; it was from Diana.

"Is that from Luna?" Nico asked.

"No. It's from Rodney's daughter, Diana. She wanted to update me on her father's case. How about we have lunch on the beach? Would you like to run up to the restaurant and order? I'll have a salad and an order of fries, and you can get anything you want."

"I am so hungry."

Cat took out her wallet and handed several euros to Nico. The young man threw on a t-shirt, shorts, and sandals, then headed up the beach. *Wow, a teenage boy is so hungry. He lives in the moment, and I absolutely love how he brings me into it with him. If only reality didn't keep rearing its ugly head.*

The text from Diana was disturbing. She'd heard from Peter, her dad's replacement, who said that the Customs and Border Protection agents had arrived with a warrant to search the warehouse for counterfeit goods two weeks prior. Diana hadn't wanted to ruin Cat's vacation but had decided it was important that she know about this. The agents had opened every shipment and taken samples of a variety of products.

Peter said he was sure it was all a mistake, and he was confident in the authenticity of their imports. He told Diana that Bradley had freaked out when they arrived. Now they were waiting to hear back.

Products like leather wallets and Parisian face cream? Cat wondered. *Is that what Rodney was investigating and what Jim's flagged emails were about? If Hazel was still there, I'd contact her. I don't want to talk to Bradley. I'm sure this doesn't have anything to do with Rodney's death. Fake goods aren't worth killing someone for. Are they? And I'm involved because I own part of the company! Maybe it's time to cut my ties with E & R.*

Nico's arms were loaded down with containers of food when he returned to their beach chairs. Cat took bottles of Perrier from her fabric bag, and they spread out the feast.

"Thanks for getting lunch. I didn't realize how hungry I was," said Cat. "This looks great."

"I am having French fries, too. And pasta."

"These fries are delicious. It's a good thing that you're young and slim, Nico. You can get away with a carb-loaded meal."

Several hours later, they left the beach and stopped at a grocery store before returning to the apartment. Cat was intrigued by the variety of food and picked up a bottle of Amaro liqueur that Astrid had recommended. Future chef Nico offered to cook dinner, and he carefully chose the ingredients, along with a few sweet treats.

Once again, Nico proved his culinary chops and created a memorable dinner by using the freshest local seafood and produce. The warm evening breeze called to them, and they sat on the patio and ate gelato after the kitchen was cleaned.

Cat poured Amaro into a glass and sipped the bittersweet liqueur, trying to decide how to ask Nico an important question. "You know that Luna, Viola, and I will do everything in our power to have you stay in your home. Luna wants nothing more than to be your parent forever."

"Sì. I know."

Catherine took a deep breath. "What if a judge gives your father full custody?"

"I have been thinking about that, of course. It would not be my choice, but I will respect the law and live with him until I am eighteen. It will be easier if Papa stays in Rome. Then I can see Luna often."

"That's a mature answer."

"In three years, I will legally be an adult and can make my own decisions. If Luna agrees, I can return to Siena and live with her."

"Don't ever worry about that. I know she'll always want you."

"If I do have to live with Papa, I will insist that I remain in school. That will need to be part of the legal agreement."

"That's a great idea. And Luna and I will always help you financially with your schooling. When I sell my share of Jim's company, I'll have more than enough money to travel and help you with your education."

"I can work while I go to culinary school and pay my way."

"Well, let's worry about that in a few years. Right now, I think we need more gelato."

"I will be happy to get you more. And some for me, too."

Cat's phone chimed, and she read a text from Diana. The investigation done by Customs and Border Protection went well, and they didn't find any counterfeit products among the inventory at Emerson & Ritter. Cat breathed a sigh of relief. *I wonder if they knew they were under scrutiny and got rid of any fake goods? At least it's one less problem.* Her phone dinged a second time, and she was relieved when she read another text from Diana. A contact at the Jacksonville PD had informed her that Anson Cassidy had been arrested. Diana had no knowledge of the charges, but she'd text again when she knew more about what was happening.

Chapter 43

MISSING

Pacing like a caged tiger, Luna called Viola again. She'd informed the police of the neighbor's comment about a disturbance the night before, and they were investigating. Viola's daughter had contacted all her mother's friends and acquaintances, but no one had any information. Luna was at her wits' end and didn't know what to do. She sent a goodnight text to Nico. She texted her sister and told her that Viola was still missing but that she wasn't panicking just yet. Cat sent back a message saying she hoped Viola would be in contact soon.

Luna's go-to stress reducer, a hot bath, was what she needed to calm her frayed nerves. She took out her best bath salts and hyacinth essential oils, then turned on the water in the old-fashioned clawfoot tub. After heading to the kitchen, she poured prosecco into a flute. A faint noise in the backyard startled her. She opened the curtains and peered out the window. She turned on the patio light and looked out again, but the night was calm. Remembering the running water in the tub, she shut off the kitchen lights and dashed upstairs. Luna closed the ceramic taps and swirled the water to dissolve the salts as she sipped the sparkling wine. She inhaled deeply and began to relax, and for a brief moment, she felt at peace.

Bang! A loud crash came from the floor below. A chill ran up her spine.

Luna placed the glass on the floor. With fear wracking her body, she tiptoed down the darkened stairs. She rounded the corner but stopped when she thought she heard footsteps. Treading softly on the runner, she inched toward the kitchen. The dim hallway nightlight cast an eerie glow. Luna froze. The board that had covered the broken window was on the floor. The back door was wide open.

She spun around to race upstairs. Luna only made it up a few steps before a masked figure dressed in black grabbed her from behind. She let out a blood-curdling scream and struggled to get free. She elbowed her assailant and fought like a mama bear defending her cub. A fist struck her on the side of her head. She fell forward on the step as the pain shot across her temple. A gloved hand holding a chloroform-laced cloth covered her mouth.

Then all went dark.

* * *

At nine o'clock the following morning, Rita rang Luna's doorbell, ready to take her to the airport. She was looking forward to visiting her sister afterward. When there was no response, Rita called Luna on her cell phone, but it went to voicemail. She walked around to the back of the house and gasped when she saw the open door.

"Luna! Are you home?" There was no answer. She entered the kitchen and noticed that the security system had not been activated. Luna's purse was on the counter. At a snail's pace, she walked down the hall. She stood at the base of the stairs and called out again. "Luna, are you here?"

Rita climbed the stairs and stiffened when an ancient wooden step creaked. She held her breath and listened for any sound from the floor above. All was quiet. Step by step, she climbed to the landing, gripping the bannister. The bathroom door was open, and she saw that the antique tub was filled with water. Candles had burned down to the base of their wicks, and a floral scent lingered in the air. A champagne glass filled with wine was on the floor next to the bathmat, but there were no bubbles rising from the bottom. She dipped her hand into the tub, and the water was cold.

In the main bedroom, she found a perfectly made bed and an open suitcase on an ottoman. Quietly, she called Luna's name again, expecting no answer. She looked for Luna's cell phone and couldn't locate it. Panic washed over her, and with quivering hands she rummaged in her purse for her cell. She opened her keypad and hit 112. Help was on the way.

She returned to the kitchen and searched Luna's handbag, finding her wallet and passport but not the phone. Rita called everyone who might know where Luna could be. She knew she had to call Nico, but she was delaying that as long as possible. She went out the back door and walked down the alley to where her boss parked her car. The Fiat was there. She rushed back to the house when she heard a car approaching.

Two police officers arrived, and she welcomed them inside. She explained her relationship to Luna and described the recent break-in at the house. She showed them that the wood board that had covered the broken window on the door now lay on the floor. She also mentioned the disappearance of Luna's lawyer and friend, Viola, who had vanished after leaving Luna's home two nights earlier. The officers proceeded to search the house. They questioned Rita about Luna's movements the day before and asked her if she knew of anyone who might pose a threat.

"Luna was in the process of adopting her deceased friend's son. The boy's birth father was fighting for custody, but I don't think he'd harm her. The young man is in Sicily with Luna's sister at the moment."

"Have you spoken to him?" the officer asked.

"No. I have been dreading the call. I should do it now."

"It might be best to speak to the sister first. If Ms. Bianchi does not appear in the next twenty-four hours, we will file a report and send in a forensics team," said one of the officers before they left.

Rita closed the front door, pulled up Nico's contact information, and tapped the number.

"Ciao, Rita. How are you?"

"Fine, Nico. Is Catherine there? I would like to speak to her."

"She is sitting by the pool. I will take my phone to her."

* * *

202

"Rita is on the phone," Nico said as he handed his cell to Cat. He sat on the edge of the chaise beside her.

"Hi, Rita. I left my phone in the apartment. Did Luna ask you to call us about her flight?"

"No. I was supposed to pick her up at nine this morning, but she was not at home. I am here right now. The back door was ajar when I arrived, and I do not believe she slept here last night."

Catherine jumped out of the chair. "Oh my God! Where could she be?"

"Zia, what is it?"

"Rita, did you call her friends? Did you call the police?"

"Yes, Catherine, and no one has heard from her. The police are waiting twenty-four hours to file a missing person's report."

Fear vibrated in every cell of Cat's body. "Was her purse there?"

"Yes. Her handbag, wallet, and passport are all here. But I cannot find her cell phone or keys. I am very concerned because Viola is still missing, as well."

"Thank you for letting me know. We're on our way back to Siena. I'll be in touch." Cat ended the call and gave the phone back to Nico.

"Zia!"

Cat took his hand. "Luna was not at the house this morning when Rita arrived to take her to the airport. She doesn't know where she is."

Nico's face drained of color, and he looked as if he was about to cry. "Oh no! No! We must go immediately. We must find her!"

"Yes, of course. You're right. Let's pack, and we can start the drive. I'll look up the ferry schedule so we can get back to Calabria."

"NO! It will take too long to drive. We must fly!"

Cat dropped into the chair. She began to hyperventilate. After several minutes, she got ahold of her breathing. With tear-filled eyes, she looked up at Nico. "I can't do it! I can't get on a plane."

"Yes, you can. You must. We have to go. You have to find your sister!" Nico pulled Cat to her feet and began to drag her toward the apartment. They bumped into Astrid on the garden path.

"What's wrong?" Astrid asked, looking at Cat's tear-streaked face.

"Luna is missing. We have to fly to Siena to find her," said Nico.

"But I can't get on a plane. I'm afraid of flying," Cat moaned.

"You can and will fly, Catherine. My mother has anxiety about flying. It's not uncommon. I have Valium I can give you. I'll bring it right over." Astrid ran toward her apartment.

"Let's go, Zia! I will pack while you book the flights."

They ran to the apartment, and Cat went on the internet and booked two tickets from Palermo to Rome. She called Luna's number, but there was no answer. Her follow-up text had the same result. She got Rita's number from Nico's phone and sent her a text with the flight information, requesting that she pick them up at the airport. Cat threw her clothes and Luna's into the suitcases and went to the bathroom to pack their toiletries.

She closed the door and barely made it to the toilet before vomiting. Gasping for air, her body shook like an earthquake, and she slumped to the floor. She wiped her mouth and sobbed. *How can I do this? How can I face my fear? But how can I not when my sister is missing? I know something's wrong. Viola has disappeared, and now Luna. I have to make my feet get on a plane.* Pulling herself together, she grabbed their toiletries and put them in the suitcase. Nico had already finished packing, and she could hear him answer the door when Astrid arrived.

"Please tell Catherine that this medication will help her. I hope you find Luna."

"Thank you," Cat said, entering the room. "You've been very kind, Astrid. I'm sure there's a good explanation. Sorry we don't have time to clean the apartment."

"That is the least of your worries. Now go, and Godspeed."

Chapter 44

AIRPLANE

They threw their bags into the car and sped down the highway. Nico navigated, and Cat was grateful they didn't have to drive through the center of Palermo to reach the airport, which was located west of the city. Focusing on the road was difficult as a cyclone of possible scenarios spun around Catherine's mind. She went through every logical reason for Luna's disappearance, and with each mile she became more afraid that it was foul play.

They located the car rental company, and Catherine agreed to pay the additional fees to drop the vehicle off at a different location. Her marvelous Sicilian adventure had come to an unexpected and unnerving end. Her hands shook as they checked in at the kiosk and took their luggage to the drop-off point. On rubbery legs, she made her way toward security.

"Have you been through security like this before?" Nico asked as they waited in a line that snaked back and forth.

"Not at an airport. They did have something similar on the cruise ship, but we didn't have to take off our shoes."

"This line reminds me of Disney World. That was a great trip. I am glad we stayed at Animal Kingdom. And I got to go on all those rides. It is a magical place."

Catherine smiled at the young man, knowing he was trying to distract her from the impending trauma of boarding a plane, and he was distracting himself from what they might face in Siena. When they got to the front of the line, Cat's passport and boarding pass danced in her trembling hand. She grabbed her right wrist with her left hand, then finally slid the documents through the slot at the bottom of the plexiglass.

The genial older man smiled at her as he inspected her passport. "You are American. I am happy you have traveled to Italy."

"I am, too." *And right now, I'm traveling to save someone's life. I can do this. I must do this.*

"Have a good flight," he said, handing Cat her passport and boarding pass. He took Nico's documents, and the young man chattered in Italian to the security officer. *Nico is as nervous as I am, but for a different reason. He must be frantic about Luna. I can't add to his distress. Pull it together, Cat.*

When they arrived at the gate, Nico dropped his backpack on a chair and offered to buy Cat a bottle of water. Cat slumped in the next chair. "That would be great. Thank you."

"Are you going to take the pill that Astrid gave you?"

"I'm not sure. I've never taken Valium before, and I don't know how it will affect me. I need to have all my wits about me when we land, and it's a not a long flight."

"Sì. I don't want to have to carry you off the plane," Nico said with a sad smile. "I will buy us some water."

Cat closed her eyes and clenched her fists. *Catherine Emerson on a plane. Can this be real? Mom, Dad, Jim, please help! Give me the courage to face the biggest challenge of my life. I can't abandon the people I love. I can't desert my family. Luna and Nico need me to be fearless.*

"They called our group number, Zia Catherine."

Beads of sweat appeared on Cat's forehead. She took the water from Nico and pressed the cool bottle to her cheek. She forced her feet to move, one step at a time, then stopped.

Behind her, Nico gently gave her a nudge and whispered in her ear, "It will be fine. You are stronger than you know."

The walk down the jetway to the plane seemed to take forever. She felt like she was marching to her execution. Nico continued to encourage her until they arrived at the airplane door. Cat was glued to the floor, and the sweat began to drip down the side of her face.

A flight attendant saw her distress and touched her arm. "Buona giornata. Can I help you find your seat?"

"Sì," Nico said, standing behind Cat. "This is my aunt's first flight. Here are our boarding passes." Nico took the pass out of Cat's hand and gave it to the attendant.

"Per favore follow me."

Luna needs me. Luna needs me. Cat repeated her mantra as she forced herself to walk down the aisle. Nico slipped in first and sat by the window. He closed the blind and placed his backpack under the seat in front of him. Cat sat in the middle seat and quickly tightened her seat belt, trying to gain control of her nerves. She gulped the water, clenched her eyes shut, and fought against a rising tide of fear. She was grateful the seat beside her remained empty. It was embarrassing enough to have Nico see her like this.

Before putting her phone on airplane mode, Cat texted Lisa and said she was on a plane, about to take off, and that she and Nico were going to Siena to find Luna and Viola. Lisa texted back that she always knew Cat would be brave when she had to be, and she said she was proud of her. Cat placed her phone in her purse and put it under the seat.

Nico held her hand. "Breathe, Zia. You will be fine. Pretend you are on a train and it is about to leave the station. You are excited about your journey."

This is crazy. I'm ridiculous. A fifteen-year-old boy is trying to keep me from jumping out of my seat and running off the plane. At least I'm diverting Nico's attention from his own concern about Luna. I was brave before. I have to be brave now. I can't let Nico down. I can't let my sister down. With eyes squeezed tight, she listened to the flight attendant review the safety information in Italian and then English. Moments later, the plane pulled away from the jetway, and Cat cried out. She rocked back and forth and silently repeated her mantra: *Luna needs me.*

After rumbling down the tarmac, the plane lifted into the sky and banked to the right. Nico released Cat's hand, and she started counting her breaths—five seconds in, hold for four, and five seconds out. The hum of the engines actually eased her nerves just a little. *I'm flying, and I'm not dying! Jim, please watch over us as we take this historic flight—historic for me, anyway. I hope you're proud of me. I did what you asked in your final letter. I've faced my greatest fear and embraced adventure.*

She looked over at the young man who had gotten her to this point. His eyes were closed, and tears streamed down his face. "Nico, what's wrong?"

Wiping his cheeks with the sleeves of his t-shirt, he paused and seemed to decide if he should voice his concerns. "What if my father has something to do with Luna's disappearance?"

"Oh, dear boy, don't even think about that. I'm sure Salvatore had nothing to do with Luna going missing. He'd never take that chance now that he has a lawyer to work on his behalf."

"But what if he does not trust the law to get him what he wants. And he wants me." Nico opened the blind and peered at the massive white clouds in the clear blue sky. He shut it again when Catherine gasped beside him. "Sorry."

"It's fine. I just need a little more water." Cat pushed the call button for the attendant and requested another bottle. She continued her deep breathing for another ten minutes, trying to keep her anxiety in check. Nico stared blankly ahead.

"There could be a simple explanation for why we can't reach Luna," Cat said. "Maybe she got a call from Viola and rushed out to help her. The fact that she has her phone with her is encouraging. Her battery might be dead, and that may be why she's not answering. By the time we land, I'm sure we'll have a message from her."

Nico nodded but didn't respond.

Chapter 45

SIENA

The announcement that they would soon be landing produced another wave of dread in Catherine. The fear of landing was as intense as the fear of flying. Her mother had crash-landed, and Cat wasn't convinced the same thing wouldn't happen to her.

Nico sensed her agitation and held her hand again. "You are right about what you said earlier. There is probably a good explanation for why Luna has not answered her phone. But soon we will know for sure."

"True. I'm grateful that Rita's picking us up at the airport. She'll probably have good news when we land. I'm just starting the second part of my Italian vacation a little early."

Beads of sweat formed on Cat's brow once more, and she gently rocked back and forth. Nico continued to hold her hand as the plane descended and finally hit the ground with a thud. Catherine let out a cry, then laughed nervously as they taxied to the terminal. She smiled weakly at her young companion and said a prayer of thanks. Nico took his phone from his backpack and texted Rita that they'd arrived. He also asked if she'd been in touch with Luna. She texted that she hadn't. She said to text her again when they had their luggage.

On wobbly legs, Cat exited the plane, and they located the luggage carousel. Nico grabbed their bags from the belt and led Cat outside. He flagged Rita down as her car approached, and she pulled to the curb. She jumped out of the car and wrapped her arms around the young man, holding him for a long moment.

"Catherine," she said, releasing Nico and then hugging Cat. "It is very nice to meet you. And you are surely Luna's sister. I can see the resemblance. Let's get the bags in the car and be on our way."

"It's lovely to meet you, too."

They loaded the suitcases into the trunk, and Cat sat in the front beside Rita. Nico hopped in the back.

"How was your flight?" Rita asked her passengers.

Cat and Nico looked at each other and laughed. "This was my very first flight. And I wouldn't have made it through without Nico helping me every step of the way. He had a shaky old lady to deal with."

"Oh my. Luna mentioned you did not like to fly, but I did not realize you had never flown before."

"My mother—actually, Luna's mother, too—died in a plane crash, and it deterred me from ever wanting to fly. It was the exact opposite with my brother, Jim. He flew whenever he could and chose a profession where he traveled all the time. He always wanted me to go with him. I really wish I had."

"But you were brave today, Zia," said Nico. "We could not take the time to drive. It is difficult to get here quickly on the ferry from Messina to Calabria."

"Yes, Nico. It is a long drive," said Rita. "There is probably a good reason why we haven't been able to reach Luna, and I hope she is at home when we arrive in Siena."

Once again, Cat felt the panic hit her like a tidal wave. *Breathe. Just breathe.* She watched the outskirts of Rome pass by as the possible explanations for Luna's disappearance galloped through her mind. The best case was that her sister was following Viola's trail and was unable to call or recharge her phone. *Luna, where are you? This is not how I envisioned my first view of Rome. When we find Luna, we can return and tour the historic city.*

Silently, they traveled north through lush countryside. It was so familiar to Catherine from books and movies. She was following her mother's path from Rome to Siena over half a century later—not as a young woman, but as a mature woman on a mission to find a sister she'd only recently met. *A sister found and lost. I must find her again.*

Recalling her mindfulness training during meditation classes, Cat intently focused on the rolling hills dotted with ancient towns perched above olive groves. Vineyards—heavy with fruit and with glorious roses at the end of each row—filled Cat's heart with a momentary sense of peace. *This land is where my mother's family came from. It was part of her and is a part of me. Tuscany is in our heritage and in our blood. I wish I had traveled here before. I'm happy that Jim had been here several times before he passed. But I really wish he were here with me now.*

Country roads winding up mountainsides were flanked by towering, pointed cypress trees, and they led to massive stone villas. Church spires rose above the charming villages, and sheep and cattle grazed below.

"It's so beautiful here. Sicily is amazing, too, but different. Both parts of Italy are incredible," said Cat. "There's nothing like seeing the world with your own eyes."

"That is correct," said Rita. "I only wish you had arrived under different circumstances. But please do not worry. We will find Luna, and all will be well."

"I'm sure you're right. We have to keep the faith and figure out where she went and why."

"We will be in Siena soon, and I will take you directly to the house, but I do not think you should stay there. I have two guest rooms, and you are welcome to stay with me. I live only three blocks from Luna's house."

"Grazie, Rita," said Nico, "but would it be all right if I go to my friend Remy's house? We have been texting, and his mother has agreed."

"That's a great idea. You should be with your friend. I can stay with Rita until—until we find Luna," Cat said. "Remy is an unusual name for an Italian boy."

"Si. He was named after his father's best friend, who moved from Nice, France, to Siena as a child," answered Nico.

"Nico, do you want to go home first, or do you want to go directly to your friend's?" Rita asked.

"I think I prefer to go to Remy's. I will return home when Luna is there. Here is the house key." Nico took out his key ring and handed it to Cat.

Remy was on the sidewalk when they pulled up to his house. Cat got out and thanked him for letting Nico stay with him. She hugged her nephew after he retrieved his suitcase from the trunk. She said she'd let him know if she heard from Luna and that he should do the same. As Rita pulled away from the curb, Cat got a text from Sam asking how she was enjoying Sicily. She replied that Luna had returned to Siena because her home and office were broken into and that now she was missing. She explained that she and Nico had flown to Rome and that she was on her way to Luna's house. She'd contact him with any news. Sam responded that he was shocked that Cat had gotten on an airplane. He added that he had important meetings the next morning, but afterward he'd rent a car and drive from Milan to Siena. He'd arrive late in the afternoon and hoped Luna was found by that time. Cat thanked him and said she was looking forward to seeing him the next day.

"Catherine, do you want me to come in with you?" Rita asked as they arrived at Luna's house.

"No. I'll be fine. I'll let you know when I'm on my way to your place."

"The security system has not been turned on, and everything was left as I found it. I will contact the police and give them your cell number in case they have any information. I know this is difficult for you, but be strong."

"Thanks for everything. You're right. I need to believe that all will be well."

Catherine was about to carry the suitcases up the front steps when she looked around and saw that Rita had stopped her car in the middle of the road. She rushed over and tapped on the window. Rita rolled the window down as she continued to talk on her phone.

"What's wrong?"

Rita hung up the phone and stared at Cat.

"Rita, what is it?"

"Sorry, Catherine. It is my mother. She has fallen and is at the hospital."

"Does she live here in Siena?"

"No, in Cristallina in Chianti, a town north of here. I must go immediately. Do you still want to stay at my house tonight? I can give you a key," Rita said.

"No. I'll stay here or with Nico at Remy's. Please, go and take care of your mother. I'll be fine."

Chapter 46

LOVELY WELCOME

Catherine gazed up at the medieval stone house, taking in the time-less beauty of her sister's home. She unlocked the heavy wooden door and placed the luggage in the front hallway. The air was still and warm, and she trembled as perspiration trickled down her sides. *I feel like I'm in a scary movie. I don't know what's lurking in the attic or under the stairs.* She began to quiver and dropped onto the bottom stair. Finally, she got her breathing under control. Reaching deep inside herself, she found a spark of courage and stepped into the living room. She was lightheaded and queasy.

"Luna, are you here?"

Silence.

She walked through the dining room to the kitchen and gasped when she saw the broken glass in the back door, the wooden board lying on the floor. Daylight was beginning to fade, bringing a somber mood to the room. Her dream of experiencing the exquisite evening light of Siena with her sister, each of them holding a glass of wine, was replaced with a growing sense of dread.

She crept back down the hallway and climbed the stairs, stopping after each creak on the steps. Fear rushed through her when she entered the bathroom and spotted the full bathtub and champagne glass on the floor. Cat walked down the darkened hallway to the main bedroom and grew even more concerned when she noticed that the carry-on suitcase she had loaned Luna was still full. *Luna didn't unpack before she disappeared. Dear Lord, where can she be?*

She looked into Nico's bedroom, then went into the guest room. After turning on the light, she saw that the room had been prepared for her arrival. There was a white wicker basket on the dresser, and it was filled with soaps, lotions, chocolate, and two novels. A pastel floral comforter covered the queen-sized bed, and several colorful, flower-shaped pillows had been placed along the carved headboard. *What a lovely welcome. Luna, why aren't you here to share this moment with me?* She climbed the stairs to the third floor and peeked into the dark, musty bedrooms. The smaller room was empty, and the larger room had an iron bed and two overstuffed chairs. She scurried back to the ground floor and was about to carry Luna's suitcase upstairs when her phone rang in her pocket.

"Rita, is your mother okay?"

"I am on my way now, but I got a call from the police."

"Oh God! Not Luna!"

"No, it was not about Luna. A woman's body was found floating in the Arbia River, which is east of the city. There was no identification, but Luna had sent the police a photo of Viola, and they believe it is her. Viola's daughter is on her way to identify the body. An officer will soon be arriving at Luna's house with a forensics team. With this new development, they are not waiting until the twenty-four hours are up tomorrow."

Catherine slumped to the floor, her heart pounding in her chest. "Thanks for letting me know, and please keep in touch." *My terrible dream of being pushed into a river. Was it a premonition of what would happen to Viola? What if Luna ends up in the river, too? I can't lose her, and neither can Nico!* The doorbell rang several minutes later. Cat slowly rose to her feet and opened the door.

"You must be Ms. Bianchi's sister," the officer said. "I am Detective Luciano."

"Yes. Please come in."

"Our team will be as quick as possible."

"Thank you. I'll stay out of your way."

The team moved with efficiency, taking photographs and dusting for fingerprints. Cat slumped on the sofa, trying to tamp down the rising panic. When the authorities left, she went into the kitchen and found a hammer and nails. She placed the fallen board on the broken door and pounded nails into the wood. The sound echoed through the house, and it gave her a feeling of action, of doing something.

She put Luna's suitcase in her bedroom, then took her bag to the guest room. The bathroom was next on the list. She emptied the tub and took the wine flute down to the kitchen. After grabbing a bottle of red wine from the rack on the counter, she perused the kitchen for the first time. The white stucco walls contrasted with the dark beams of the ceiling and window frame. A wall of field stones added to the ambience, and framed photos of Nico cooking were a delightful personal touch. Decorative ceramic tiles behind the burners provided a touch of color, as did the drapes that were hung below the farmhouse sink and over the window. Cooking utensils were crowded into glass jars on the counter, and beside them was an ornate wooden box. *This is exactly what I pictured Luna's Tuscan kitchen would look like. It's so warm and inviting.*

After locating a wine glass and a box of crackers, Cat returned to the guest room and locked the door. She anchored a chair under the doorknob, just like she'd seen in movies. She poured a glass of wine and picked up the chocolates and one of the novels. She climbed under the covers and texted Nico to say that she was staying at his house because Rita had to leave town for the night. Nico offered to come and stay with her, but she said she was fine. She didn't mention Viola or the police who'd been there earlier. Then she sent a text to Lisa, who would read it the following morning.

Sorry that you will read this terrible news first thing in the morning, but I know you'll want to know. Luna is still missing, and Viola was found dead. The police have no leads. I'm terrified I'll never see my sister again, but I have to keep hoping. I'll keep you posted. Just going to bed.

She plugged in her phone on the bedside table to make sure she didn't miss a call. While sipping the deep red wine, she began to read the novel, but nothing was registering. After reading the first page three times, she gave up and picked up a book on the nightstand that had photographs of marvelous Italian villages. By the time she finished the book, she was three glasses into the bottle of wine, and her head was swimming. *Luna is fine. She has to be. Rita will be back tomorrow, and Sam will be here, too. We will find her!*

Catherine corked the bottle and turned off the lamp. Slowly, the wine lulled her into sleep, but disturbing dreams had her tossing and turning. Her phone chimed at 11:00, and she bolted upright, praying it was Luna contacting her. However, it was Nico saying he couldn't sleep and wanted to make sure she was okay. She responded that she was good and would see him the next day.

Eventually, she fell into a deep sleep and dreamed she was traveling in a high-speed train. The Tuscan countryside was whizzing by. The train screeched to a halt, and a conductor entered the car. He grabbed her arm and screamed at her to leave. She broke away and ran off the train. Instead of a train station, though, she found herself in a medieval chapel next to the tracks. She opened the creaking door and stepped inside. Sunlight was pouring through a stained-glass rose window and shining over a white marble altar. Several people were seated in the front pews. While gliding up the aisle, she saw a figure shrouded in darkness in an alcove to her right. A woman with dark wavy hair that fell to her shoulders raised her arm toward Cat.

"Mom?" she called out, but the lady vanished before her eyes. She approached the worshippers and shrieked. Their faces were skulls, with black holes where their eyes should be, and their jaws were grotesque and gaping.

Cat woke suddenly and screamed aloud, almost tumbling from the bed. She was shaking, and her body was covered in perspiration. After taking a moment to calm down, she got out of bed, moved the chair away from the door, and then unlocked it. She turned on the lights and walked unsteadily to the bathroom. Splashing cold water on her face, she tried to get the images out of her mind. Cat got herself a glass of water and checked the time. It was still the middle of the night. She trudged back to the bedroom and slipped back into bed. *Mom, Dad, Jim, please help me find my sister!* She closed her eyes and hoped to telepathically connect with Luna.

Chapter 47

PROFETA

The shrill ring of the phone jolted Catherine from her sleep. The haze from good wine and bad dreams clung to her brain. "Nico. Hi. Good morning. How are you?"

"Okay. I could hardly sleep last night, and I am sorry for calling so early. We should have heard from Luna by now. I am very worried."

"Don't give up hope. We'll find her. I'm sure of it."

"I just wish—"

"I know, I know. It's so frustrating not being able to do anything constructive. What are you doing this morning?"

"That is why I called. Remy's mother would like for you to come for breakfast. I can text you the address and directions."

"Oh, that sounds good. It is just what I need. I'll shower and be over soon. I love you."

"I love you, too, Zia."

Cat checked her messages and then got out of bed, showered, and quickly dressed. When she arrived at Remy's, the boys were waiting outside. She was so glad he had his friend for support, but it was as if a dagger pierced her heart when she thought of how devastated Nico would be if he lost another mother. He rushed over and hugged Cat for a long moment.

"Please come inside, Ms. Emerson," said Remy.

An elderly woman with steely gray hair pulled back in a tight knot was standing by the sink. Dressed all in black, she grinned at Cat and pulled out a chair for her. "Siediti, per favore."

218

"Grazie," Cat answered, smiling at the petite lady. She slipped onto the red, vinyl-padded, metal chair that was beside a mid-century Formica table.

"This is my Nonna C," said Remy. "My mother will be down in a moment. Would you like some coffee?"

"A pleasure to meet you," Cat said. "And yes, Remy, I'd love some coffee."

Nonna C settled in a chair opposite Cat, her dark eyes locking with Cat's.

Wow! She has an intense gaze. I feel as if she's peering into my soul.

A younger woman bounded into the kitchen and rapidly spoke to Remy, who placed the coffee and a platter of fruit and baked goods on the table. The boys grabbed plates of food and went out to the back patio.

"Benvenuto, Catherine. I am Elena, and I see you have met my mother. Please have something to eat. We have the boys' favorite pastries today in honor of Nico."

"Thank you for inviting me, Elena. It's wonderful to be in your lovely home."

"It is our pleasure to have you here and to meet a friend of Nico's. I just wish you were here under different circumstances," Elena said. "May I ask if you have received any new information?"

"I wish I had good news this morning, but I still haven't heard from Luna." Cat nibbled on a croissant and a cluster of grapes, then drained the mug of coffee.

"It is such a worry for everyone," Elena said. "I am certain we will hear from her today. Nico and Remy are close friends, and we have known him and Luna for a long time. He is welcome to stay with us for as long as needed."

"Yes, I'd love it if Nico could stay here while we search for Luna. I know it will be the best thing for him." The strong coffee started to clear the cobwebs from Cat's head, and the food was helping, too. "Luna's assistant, Rita, should be back soon—she had to leave yesterday to help her mother—and I have another friend arriving from Milan this afternoon. The forensics team came to the house last night and did a thorough scan of all the rooms. I'm hoping to hear from the police soon, probably today."

"We have been praying for her safe return," Elena said, nodding at her mother. "My mother's name is Catherine, as well," she added. "She was named after our patron saint and had planned to follow in her footsteps and enter the convent. But one day she heard God speak to her, and He said she should marry and have children. She has fulfilled that obligation, and since that day she has also become a profeta, a seer, as you would say."

The elderly woman smiled at Cat and took her hand. The bony, wrinkled hand of Nonna C was surprisingly strong.

"Do you mean she's psychic?"

"Precisely," Elena answered. "But she does not use tarot cards or a crystal ball. She relies on a person's energy to read the situation. If you would like, she could do that for you now, and I will translate."

Cat's jaw dropped, and she nodded. "Yes, please. I would like that very much. Grazie."

Nonna C's eyes closed, and her breathing slowed. After what seemed like forever to Cat, Nonna C began to speak.

"You have been brave, yet there are more trials ahead." Elena translated her mother's words. "You see yourself as the hunter as you search for Luna. But you are also the braccato, the hunted. You are the prey."

Cat shuddered at the alarming words. Nonna C continued, still gripping Cat's trembling hand.

"One has crossed over, and one remains. Time is of the essence," Elena said.

Nonna C slumped in the chair and released Cat's hand. Elena brought her mother a glass of water and stroked her hair. "Grazie, Mama." The old woman struggled up from the chair, gave Cat a quick smile, and shuffled out of the room.

It took Cat several minutes to respond. "I haven't told Nico yet, but Viola, Luna's lawyer, was found floating in a river. Her daughter confirmed it was her. She must be the one your mother said crossed over. Which means that Luna is still alive."

"Oh, dear God, that is so tragic! I hope you are right that Luna remains with us. Poor Nico. He has already had so much sorrow in his short life."

"That's for sure," Cat said. "Thank you so much for your hospitality. I'm going to be on my way. Will you thank your mother for me? I'll go outside and say goodbye to Nico, then head back to Luna's. Maybe I can find a clue as to where she went."

Cat hugged her nephew, telling him not to worry and that Rita would soon be back to help her. Nico said that he and Remy were going to play video games, and she was glad that he would have a fun way to spend the day. She retraced her steps back to Luna's, but before she'd gone a block, her phone rang.

"Hi, Rita, are you driving back to Siena?"

"No. My mother had a blood clot this morning, and I am going to stay with her for at least another day."

"I'm sorry about your mom. I'll let you know if—I mean, when—I hear from Luna. Nico is staying at Remy's, so he's fine for now. I'm going to contact the police again and find out what they know. Did you give them a list of clients who might be suspects? Or anyone else who might harm Luna?"

"Yes, and as of yesterday, they have not identified anyone suspicious. I cannot imagine Luna having enemies who would be a threat to her. I am sorry that you have to face this alone. I will return as soon as I can."

On the walk back to Luna's, Cat played over in her mind anything she could have missed. *Someone broke into Luna's office and house. She was obviously the target, and it was personal. Nothing was taken, but property was damaged. The only enemy I can think of is Salvatore, but I don't think he'd risk losing custody of Nico.*

Stepping through the front door, Catherine felt a rush of cool air. The hair on the back of her neck stood straight up, and goosebumps dotted her arms. "Hello? Is anyone there?" Nothing. Making her way down the hall to the kitchen, she noticed a scent that was strangely familiar. It was similar to the perfume her mother wore, but with an undertone of gardenia. *What is that fragrance? Oh my gosh, it's my nonna's perfume!*

"Nonna, are you here? Did Remy's grandmother send you? Can you help me find Luna?" she whispered.

Memories of her nonna's kitchen crystalized in her mind. In many ways, it was similar to Luna's, and just as homey. She'd always felt safe in her grandmother's presence and wished she was there now for support. After pouring a glass of water, Cat went to the guest room and turned on her laptop. Once again, she called Luna's phone, and her heart sank when it went to voicemail. She checked her email and smiled when she saw one from William. He was asking how she was enjoying Sicily. She responded that Sicily was an amazing island and said that she'd update him soon. She didn't want to get into the frightening events of the past few days. The next email was a lengthy one from Diana, who gave a full account of Cassidy's arrest.

Anson Cassidy was charged with the attempted murder of a loan shark to whom he owed money. They had been arguing at a bar in Jacksonville when the man appeared to have a heart attack. A young woman at a nearby table saw Cassidy smirk, and she reviewed a cell phone video she'd taken of her girlfriend at the time. In the background, Anson was putting something in the man's drink while he was in the restroom. She showed the video to the bartender, who immediately called the police and then stopped Cassidy from leaving the premises. The drink was tested later, and it was discovered that it contained a drug called aconite, which can cause heart attacks. Fortunately, there had been a paramedic "in the house" at the time, and the bar had a defibrillator. The paramedic was able to get the man's heart going again before the ambulance arrived.

Diana asked Cat whether she thought Cassidy was responsible for her father's death, though he had been hit on the head and wasn't drugged. She wondered if he would change his MO. Cat responded with an email and said that she wasn't sure if Cassidy would change his modus operandi, but it was possible. She added that evidence against Cassidy was mounting. She asked Diana to keep her updated. She forwarded the message to Lisa and said she was grateful that Max hadn't engaged with the obviously dangerous Cassidy.

Cat was about to look up aconite on her search engine when she got a text from Sam. *Sorry, I've been delayed. Be there in the morning.*

Rita's not here, and now Sam's not coming. What am I going to do? She closed her computer and called Detective Luciano. She was disappointed when she learned he had no news.

Chapter 48

THE TOWER

With no clear idea of what to do next, Catherine Emerson decided to walk the streets of Siena. She imagined her mother strolling beside her, pointing out places she remembered from her year in the medieval city. The fan-shaped Piazza del Campo was her first stop. Cat envisioned the pageantry of the Palio—the flag throwers in their costumes and the crowds cheering on the jockeys dressed in colorful silks.

She walked past the Fonte Gaia and wondered if her mom had thrown a coin in the fountain. Had Maria wished that she'd find true love after her boyfriend had deserted her? Did she mourn the death of her baby and dream of having another child someday? *Mom, I never thought I'd be standing here where you lived and loved. You still had to care for other children even though you'd lost your own. And now I'm afraid the baby that you bore is lost again.*

She mindlessly roamed the cobblestone roads and alleyways for hours, trying to come up with a plan to find Luna. Eventually, she made her way back to the house, praying her sister would be waiting for her. An empty house greeted her, but this time there were no cold breezes or wisps of perfume. She sent a text to Nico asking how he was doing, and he responded that he was fine.

The next text made her drop to her knees. It was from Luna's phone.

Catherine, help me.

Cat phoned her sister immediately, but it went to voicemail. She texted back, *Luna, where are you?*

Luna can't talk right now. She's tied up.

With shaking hands, Cat typed, *Who is this?*

It's time for a game. Do you like games? I do.

WHERE IS LUNA? WHO ARE YOU?

It's a treasure hunt, with Luna as the prize.

Let me talk to Luna.

You have to play the game first. Let's see how smart you are.

Proof of life!! Cat answered.

In time. If you can follow the clues, you'll find the treasure and save your sister's life.

Why are you doing this?

You'll find out soon enough.

I want to talk to Luna!

Let's begin. Go to the place that holds your namesake's head for the next clue. And if you call the police or tell anyone, Luna is dead.

Don't you dare hurt her! Cat typed and yelled out loud at the same time.

When there was no response, Cat jumped up and paced the room. *Should I call the police and risk it? Rita and Sam, why aren't you here to help me?* Cat was shaking like a poplar leaf in a wind storm. A decision had to be made, and quickly. *Can I do this? Am I brave enough to face a kidnapper by myself? Am I a badass?* A shock of energy shot up her spine. She was being infused with a feeling of strength she'd never experienced before. *I am fierce and brave.* Cat took deep breaths and gathered her wits.

My namesake's head. St. Catherine. The Duomo! No, it was somewhere else. Where the hell did Nico say it was. Another church. Saint Dominic's!

Cat typed *Basilica Cateriniana San Domenico* into the map search on her phone. The church was several streets away. She locked the house and began to run toward the Basilica. *What if there's no clue? What if I can't find it?* She ran down the Via della Sapienza to the piazza and gazed up at the austere Gothic structure. She was expecting a spectacular, ornate church like the Duomo, but the simplicity of the building surprised her. Her fifty-year-old legs were aching, but adrenaline was coursing through her veins.

There was a large group of chattering tourists outside the Basilica, and she skirted around them and entered. She was shocked by the massive size of the largely empty interior. She rushed past small clusters of people until she heard the word "skull" and stopped in her tracks.

"Are you talking about the skull of St. Catherine?" she asked a guide.

"Sì. It is in the chapel to the right of the altar. Straight ahead," he answered.

Cat ran to the beautiful chapel. Detailed frescoes of the life of Catherine Benincasa covered the walls. The carved-wood gate, which led to the altar and the gilded marble tabernacle where the saint's remains were housed, was chained shut. Cat peered through the marble banisters beside the gate, searching for anything that might be a clue. She ran her hands around the inside of the banisters and the round posts until she located a small envelope taped to the base of one of the posts. She grabbed it and jumped up just as a Dominican priest came up behind her.

"Cosa stai facendo? What are you doing? That area is closed off, as you can see."

"Thank you, Father. I dropped this when I was looking into the chapel," Cat answered. "I'd better be going. Have a good day."

Catherine power-walked out of the church, and the bright sunlight momentarily blinded her. She blinked until her eyes adjusted to the light, then nervously glanced around the piazza to see if she was being watched. When she didn't notice anyone suspicious, she slipped her finger under the flap and pried open the envelope. Typed on a slip of paper was, A *heavenly view. Will you rise to the occasion?*

What the heck does that mean? A view of the stars? Is there an observatory nearby? A view from a religious place? The bell tower in a church? I hate this game! Who can be so cruel to make me go through this?

In the search engine on her phone, she typed in *best views in Siena.* The first one on the list was the Torre del Mangia, the bell tower beside the Palazzo Pubblico, the town hall, and the museum. The tower was on the south end of the Piazza del Campo, where she had toured earlier. It was another long sprint, but she gathered all her strength and followed the path indicated on her phone. After rushing down Via del Galluzza, she stopped to catch her breath.

I'd better be right about the tower. But what if it's all a lie? What if this maniac doesn't really have Luna? What if she... No, I'd know in my heart if she was gone. Cat inhaled deeply and noticed a scent in the air. It was similar to Jim's favorite cologne. A tingling sensation permeated her body, and an upsurge of confidence infused her. Her run became a quick walk, but she forged ahead.

It was after 6:00 PM by the time she reached the ticket office of the Torre del Mangia. There were only minutes before they closed for the day. The crowds were thin, and many people were leaving instead of arriving like she was. She paid her ten euros and began the climb up more than four hundred stairs. She squeezed by other patrons, repeating "mi scusi" several times. People complained about her rudeness, but she didn't have time to waste.

Every twenty steps, she stopped and gasped for air. "I must find Luna" became her mantra during the climb. She tried not to think about her fear of heights or of what she'd face when she arrived at the top. When she stepped out into the open air, the view was breathtaking. The evening light was filtered through high clouds, bringing a golden hue to the spectacular city below and the verdant hills in the distance. For Cat, the whole experience was terrifying. She clung to the wall as panic overtook her. She did not want to look down. Two young women approached her and asked her in English if she was okay.

"Not really," Cat said honestly.

"Then why are you up here?" asked one of the American teens.

Cat contemplated before answering, searching her mind for a reasonable explanation. "A friend thought he could make me overcome my fear of heights if I saw how beautiful it is looking out over Siena."

"He's not a very good friend," said the other teen. "But the view is amazing."

Cat averted her eyes from the rooftops and rolling hills, instead looking down at her feet to get ahold of her anxiety. To make matters worse, she had to locate another envelope up here somewhere. *What kind of sick joke is this jerk playing?* Cat turned to the teens and told them she was looking for an envelope.

"If you want, we can look for it," said one of the girls.

"That would be great! It probably looks like this one," Cat said as she took the first envelope from her purse.

Within five minutes, the teenagers returned with the envelope and the next clue to the life-and-death game in which Cat had reluctantly been participating. She thanked the girls and inched against the wall next to the exit. She gripped the railing and bolted down the stairs.

"Scusi, scusi," she repeated as she tried to get past the tourists making their way down. She was blocked by an elderly man whose bulk took up the entire stairwell. He looked into Cat's face and, seeing her distress, flattened himself against the wall to let her by.

"Thank you so much," she said, then continued her swift decent.

Chapter 49

CASA DI SANTA CATERINA

Once she was back in the Piazza del Campo, she opened the envelope. On the paper was, *Do you like this game? I'm enjoying it. You're not the coward I thought you were.*

Who is this? Who thinks I'm a coward? Salvatore? Who else lives here who would want to hurt Luna and who also knows about me? The second part of the note held the next clue. *You found her head. Now find her house.* Cat typed in *house of St. Catherine in Siena* on her phone. The Casa di Santa Caterina was back toward the Basilica. She wasn't sure if it would be open at this time of the day, but she had to try. On aching legs, but with an iron will, she headed to the birthplace of St. Catherine. She asked for all of her loved ones on the other side to give her the strength to see this through. Her ringing phone startled her.

"Ciao. How are you?"

"Hi, Nico. I'm okay. I'm walking around the city and waiting for the police to call me back. Don't worry, I'll let you know when I talk to Luna. Enjoy your video games with Remy."

"I know you will call me if you hear from Luna. I just wanted to make sure you were all right."

"I'm doing fine, sweetheart. I'll talk to you soon."

Cat arrived at the fourteenth-century house of Catherine and was flustered when she discovered it was closed for the day. She peered up at the two stories of balconies above the main door. Deep-red roses were

228

flowing from window boxes that were placed above the four arches on each level.

"Now what?" Cat said out loud.

The front door squeaked open, and a tiny nun peeked out. "Are you Catherine?"

Cat jumped back, startled by being personally addressed by the wizened woman. "Um, yes, I am."

"This is for you." She handed Cat an envelope like the other two, then hurriedly shut the door. It took a moment for Cat to take in the unexpected encounter. *How did she know I was here? Oh, there's a camera on the balcony. She must have been waiting for me.*

When she opened the envelope, she was puzzled by what was written on the paper inside. *Your quest ends where it began.* Cat leaned against the wall and clenched her eyes shut, trying to figure out the clue. A breeze caressed her face, and the fragrance of roses descended on her. She looked up at the flowers in the boxes above and knew in an instant what the note meant. *Thanks, Mom.*

In the growing twilight, she jogged toward the place where she'd first received the text that initiated this mission to find her sister. Out of breath, but determined to face whatever lay ahead, she arrived at Luna's darkened house. She ran up the front steps and pulled back when she saw that the front door was slightly ajar. As she reached for the doorknob, her heart was beating a mile a minute.

She stepped over the threshold and used the flashlight on her phone to illuminate the front hall. Leaving the door slightly open so she could make a quick exit if necessary, she held her breath and strained to hear any sound. In the stillness, she swung the flashlight toward the front parlor and jumped when the light bounced off a mirror. *Get it together, Cat! Keep going. Why would the monster who created this game send me here if the house was empty?* Walking through the dining room, she paused again and listened. Silence. She entered the kitchen, and the light caught the metal head of the hammer she'd left on the counter. Jim's voice sounded in her mind, saying, "Arm yourself." She picked up the hammer, and then her eyes moved to the wine rack, and she wondered if a bottle would be a better weapon.

In the eerie glow cast by the flashlight, she spied the wooden box next to the wine. *Nico's knives!* She put down the hammer and opened the box that had been a gift to Nico from Luna. Cat picked up a large chef's knife, eying the glint of the blade and feeling the weight of the handle. She then spotted a slim six-inch fish knife. She lifted it from the box and slid it into the back waistband of her jeans, under her shirt. With her phone in one hand and the chef's knife in the other, she tiptoed down the hall to the stairway. She froze when the front door slowly creaked open. Cat sprung around and ran toward the kitchen.

"Catherine! It's me."

Cat stopped in her tracks and turned to see Sam standing in the doorway. "Oh my God! Sam! I didn't think you were coming tonight. Thank goodness you're here." She rushed down the hall and wrapped her arms around his neck.

"Careful with that knife! You don't want to stab anyone."

Cat let out a nervous laugh and placed the knife on the hall table. "I'm being tortured by some madman who's playing an evil game with me. I've been all over the city. The clues led me back here, but there's no one in the house. I'm afraid I won't find Luna in time."

"Don't worry. Calm down. Tell me what's happened." Sam listened patiently as Cat filled him in on the last couple of days. Seeing her anxiety, yet knowing she was being extraordinarily brave, he hugged her tightly and said simply, "We'll find her." Then he turned around and closed the front door.

"I need some water." Cat headed down the hall, turning off the flashlight on her phone. She flipped on the overhead light, placed her phone on the counter, and grabbed two bottles of water from the fridge. She handed one to Sam.

"I'm so grateful you're here," Cat said in a quivering voice. "Luna's assistant, Rita, had to stay with her mother for another day or two, and I thought I'd have to do this alone."

Sam walked over, lifted her chin, and gazed into her eyes. Finally able to relax, Cat smiled at him and leaned against the counter. "This is not the way I thought I'd tour Siena."

"So, whoever he or she is knows about your relationship to Luna. Is there anyone you suspect?" Sam asked.

Cat paced the kitchen and downed the water. "The only person I can think of is Salvatore. But what I don't understand is why he'd risk doing something that would mess up his custody fight."

"You're right. It doesn't make sense, but crime is often rash and can make no sense at all. Have you had an update from the police?"

"I haven't talked to them today. The text from this maniac said not to. I didn't want to jeopardize Luna's safety. After what happened to Viola, I know this person is dangerous and capable of murder."

"Are they sure Viola's death was a homicide?"

"Why else would she disappear and then be found floating in a river?"

"Do they have any suspects?" Sam questioned.

"Not that I know of. This is unbearable," Cat said as tears welled in her eyes. "What am I supposed to do now? The house is empty."

"Have you looked upstairs?"

"No. That was where I was going when you appeared."

"Come on. Let's check the whole house just in case."

Chapter 50

WOLF

Cat took the lead. They crept up to the second floor, turning on lights to dispel the darkness. The bedrooms and bathroom were just as Cat had left them that morning. She listened again for any sound as they mounted the stairs to the third floor. Partway up, a foul smell assaulted her. It was a mixture of metal and urine. She stopped. Sam gave her a nudge from behind, and she continued her ascent.

She flipped on the light switch in the smaller of the two rooms, but there was nothing inside. The odor became stronger, and fear gripped Catherine. *It smells like blood.* Her feet were glued to the floor. She knew she had to face whatever was in the next bedroom, but panic overtook her. She could feel the bile rise in her throat and slumped against the wall. Sam took her arm and gently led her forward. He reached ahead and turned on the light. A primal scream escaped Cat's lips when she stepped from behind him. On the bed, her sister lay motionless, her eyes closed. She was gagged, and her hands and feet were tied.

Cat rushed to her side and began shaking her. "Luna! Dear God! Wake up."

Luna moaned, and her eyes flickered but didn't open. Cat scanned her sister for any wounds, then reached over to take the gag out of her mouth. But before she could help Luna, Cat was yanked backward by her hair. She cried out in pain. With a muzzled cry, Luna tried to sit up and open her eyes, but she fell back on the bed, unable to overcome the drug in her bloodstream.

Cat reached behind and grabbed the hand that was holding her hair. She was able to turn partway around and was shocked to see it was Sam who was assaulting her. The malevolent sneer and the pure evil emanating from his dark eyes almost made her heart stop. He picked her up and threw her down on the chair beside the bed. Her head was spinning, her mind whirling, as she tried to make sense of the unimaginable. The soul-crushing reality finally hit her.

"Sam, please tell me what's going on," she whispered.

Sam reached into his pocket and took out a pistol. She jolted backward, fear racing through every cell in her body. It was then that Cat noticed the origin of the awful smell. In the far corner, a young man was slumped against the wall, a bullet hole in his forehead. Blood dripped down his face, and his vacant eyes spoke of the horror of his demise.

"I told you I like to play games. This has been an epic one, don't you think?" Sam said as he pulled up the other chair and sat down. "And now the game is almost over."

Cat was trembling, but she held his gaze, refusing to cry.

"It's all your fault, Catherine," he said, his tone implying that she had hurt him. "If you'd just sold your shares of E & R to Brad, none of this would have happened. But you had to go and get that accountant to meddle in the business."

Quivering but laser focused, Cat tried to put together what was happening. "I don't understand any of this."

As if speaking to a child, Sam said, "You opened a Pandora's box we thought we'd closed when your brother and Rodney—shall we say—left us. The lowlife nurse we'd hired to 'handle' Jim screwed up, and his removal of Rodney was a complete mess."

Cassidy. Not natural. Finding her voice, she said, "You had Jim and Rodney murdered? Because of the counterfeit goods? That makes no sense." Cat was beginning to get a grip on her emotions, and she could feel her anger rise.

"Since you won't be talking to anyone ever again, I guess I can fill you in. The fake goods were the least of it. They were removed from the warehouse before the Feds arrived. Rodney and Jim stuck their noses into things they shouldn't have. Your brother was getting close to uncovering the money laundering side of our business. Riva had been successful in washing cash for Russian and Italian oligarchs, and they were putting pressure on Giancarlo to put an end to Jim's meddling. So what could we do?"

"Did Brad know about this?"

"No. Brad's an idiot. Riva was brilliant at hiding his illegal business, but Jim stumbled on the truth. He found the bank account in Cyprus, along with the second set of financial records."

"But you just met them. How did you get involved in this?"

"Ah, that's the part of the game you missed. Riva and I met years ago in Cyprus and have worked together in the past. When you started making waves, we were going to have you taken out, and the company shares would revert to Brad. But then you found out you had a sister and changed your will."

"So, both Luna and I had to be 'taken out,' as you say." Cat was horrified.

"I had never imagined that you'd come to Italy, but it was perfect. A fatal car accident in Sicily was the original plan. But I have a soft spot for Nico."

"Oh my God. I can hardly believe this. Was Salvatore involved in this?"

"No, but Nico will have someone to live with when you two bitches are gone."

Cat slumped in her chair, her heart in anguish and her mind in turmoil. *This is the end. I can't save us. At least Nico's safe.*

"So, you had someone break into Luna's office and house to lure her back to Siena."

"You are absolutely correct. Smart lady. Unfortunately, the moron working for me was supposed to nab Luna, but he grabbed that lawyer instead. I told him to follow the signal."

"What signal?" Cat asked.

"The one in the tracker." Sam sneered as he stood up and approached Cat, the gun trained on her chest. She shrieked as he grabbed the gold necklace from around her neck—the necklace that he had given her. Brutally, he yanked it off. "There are tracking devices in these necklaces, and I've been able to follow your every move. It was hilarious watching you run around Siena today. I was surprised by how fast an old lady like you could move. For some reason, the lawyer had possession of the necklace, not Luna. Then Franco here," he said, gesturing to the dead man in the corner, "had to get rid of her, but he did a lousy job. That's why I had to take over."

I fell for a homicidal sociopath. He spared Nico, but Luna and I will die here. There's no point in asking him to reconsider. Cat's mind was racing. *I need the full picture before I go.*

"So, I'm assuming that *meeting* Luna and Nico on the airplane to Florida wasn't by chance."

"Now you're getting in the game, Catherine. Riva got the name of your sister from Hazel, and he booked me on the same flight from Rome to Miami. I paid off the agent to change my seat so I'd be next to Luna. Hazel had been working with Riva to keep Brad in the dark about what was going on."

"Hazel? What? Why would she betray me?"

"For the money," he answered, as if the answer was obvious. "She needed cash for her daughter's experimental drug treatment, and Riva gave it to her in exchange for info on you, and for her promise to keep her mouth shut."

Just when I think I can't be more surprised or heartbroken. The wolf in sheep's clothing Jim wrote about was Hazel. Mrs. Santa Claus. He probably knew he couldn't trust her.

"And for you, it was all about the money, too," Cat whispered.

"Of course. What else?" Sam barked as he stood menacingly over her.

Chapter 51

GAME OVER

Salty tears flowed down her face. *How could I have been so blind? Did I trust him because he looked like Zach? I feel horrendously guilty that because of me, Luna has become involved in this deadly situation.*

"You actually believed I'd be interested in someone old like you." The obnoxious laugh that came out of Sam's mouth made her skin crawl. His kiss, their dance in the moonlight, and the enchanting evening together had all been a cruel hoax.

"Just so you know, the women I date are stunning—young and sexy. Not old and decrepit. You're pathetic." Sam sneered at her, knowing he had hurt her. Cat thought she could hear her phone ringing. She'd left it in the kitchen, and she hoped it wasn't Nico trying to contact her.

Sam continued to drone on about how stupid and gullible she was, but she shut out the words meant to destroy her soul. Suddenly, she noticed a fragrance that overpowered the stench emanating from the body in the room. It was Jim's cologne. In her mind, she heard her brother say, "Ready, set..." and then the doorbell rang. Cat and Sam both jumped and turned toward the door.

"CAT, GO! THE COPS ARE HERE," Jim yelled in her head.

Cat leapt out of the chair and crashed into Sam. They tumbled to the floor, and the gun flew out of his hand and skittered across the floor. Sam struggled to reach it while Cat was still piled on top of him. She pulled the fish knife from the waistband of her jeans and plunged the weapon into the back of his outstretched hand. Sam screamed and shoved Cat off of him. He grabbed the handle of the knife and yanked it out of his right hand. Catherine scrambled up and picked up the pistol, firing one shot through the front window. Glass showered down on the police who were waiting on the front porch. She backed up and aimed the gun at Sam's head.

Cat heard a huge bang on the first floor as the police threw open the front door. Cat sidled to the bedroom door, the gun clenched in her fist. She called out to the police. The pure hatred in Sam's eyes bored into her. *I'm not going to die today. Sorry, Sam.* Pounding footsteps, dancing flashlights, and loud voices filled the house.

"Ms. Emerson, are you all right?" Detective Luciano asked as he dashed into the room.

A wave of relief washed over Cat. "I'm okay, but my sister needs an ambulance. She's been drugged. This man here is Sam Lawrence. He kidnapped Luna and murdered Franco over there. And Franco murdered Viola."

The second officer went to the deceased man to check for a pulse. He called in to his precinct to request two ambulances as well as the forensics team.

"Let me take that," Luciano said, gesturing to the pistol. Cat gladly handed over the gun and went to her sister's side. She gently removed the gag and then retrieved the fishing knife, using it to slice the ropes around Luna's wrists and ankles, drops of Sam's blood remaining on the cords.

"Luna, can you hear me? Please wake up," Cat said softly, caressing her sister's forehead.

Sam remained silent, gripping his bleeding hand and being helped to his feet. The officer cuffed his hands in front and shoved him into a chair. The absolute evil in Sam's eyes shocked the veteran Luciano.

The wail of sirens grew closer, and the ambulances screeched to a halt in front of the house. Paramedics with stretchers rushed up the stairs, and they first checked Luna's vital signs, then placed her on a stretcher. The second crew would wait for the forensics team before they removed Franco's malodorous corpse.

Luciano grabbed Sam by the arm and dragged him toward the door. The detective said, "I called you, Ms. Emerson. When you didn't pick up, I had the feeling you were in danger."

"Your intuition was dead-on," she answered. "Thank you for arriving in the nick of time."

"Catherine," Sam hissed as he was led from the room. "This isn't over."

"Oh, Sam, yes, it is. I won the game," Cat spat back.

She waited until Sam was out of the house before she called Nico. She told him that Luna was fine and that they'd be on their way to the hospital in a few minutes. Cat gave him a brief description of the course of events and the crushing news that Sam was behind Luna's kidnapping. Nico cried out when he heard of Sam's involvement and began a profanity-laced tirade in Italian.

When he finally quieted down, Cat asked, "Do you think Remy's mother can drive you to the hospital? I'm riding in the ambulance with Luna."

"I am sure she will. Oh, Zia! We are all safe."

* * *

The next few days passed in a blur. Only this time, Catherine wasn't planning a funeral; instead, she would be attending one for Viola. Luna's physical recovery from the drugs Franco had given her had been swift and complete. However, she was still badly shaken by what had happened to her and to Viola. Franco had held her captive in a nearby warehouse, waiting for word from Sam to take her back to her house and administer the sedative. She was horrified when she learned that Sam knew of Catherine's every move through Siena, planning both their deaths all the while.

Luna and Cat made several trips to the police precinct to make statements. Sam was moved to a high-security prison in Rome and denied bail. Nico was distressed by Sam's betrayal but was grateful that his father hadn't been involved in the scheme to kidnap Luna and murder both her and Cat.

Cat called Lisa and gave her the details of the abduction of Luna, the murder of Franco, and the arrest of Sam. "Jim helped me to leap at the right moment. I never thought I'd be grateful to hear a ghost talking in my head."

"Oh my God, Cat, I can't believe all this has happened! Thank goodness Jim did contact you, or you might not be alive today. I've been texting with Diana, and Cassidy is singing like a bird. Riva was the mastermind behind everything, and Brad was a dupe. Jim had been working with Kirk, Riva's assistant, to hunt down the truth behind the money laundering and other aspects of Riva Realty that were outside the law."

"I guess I can say that I'm not surprised. Bradley always thought he was a lot smarter than he actually was. He's smart in the book sense, but his street smarts aren't so impressive. He can be gullible, but I am glad he had nothing to do with any of this. It's all so tragic. Jim, Rodney, and Viola are all dead. My heart is broken."

"When are you coming home?" Lisa asked.

"I'm not sure. Viola's funeral is tomorrow. What a stressful time this has been. I haven't made plans to get home yet."

"I completely understand. How are you getting home?"

Cat sighed. "I haven't decide that, either."

Chapter 52

HOME

Driving rains pummeled Siena the morning of Viola's funeral. After arriving at the sixteenth-century Baroque Church of St. Martin, Cat silently wept as she and Luna and Nico slid into a pew near the front. She averted her eyes when Viola's daughter, Anna, and her family walked down the aisle. The palpable grief in the church was unbearable, and her guilt overwhelmed her. The mournful sounds of crying echoed throughout the church.

It's all my fault that Viola's dead. My decision to have Jerome hire an accountant to look into E & R has led to this moment. I never could have imagined that an action in Jacksonville would have such dire consequences in Italy.

After the service, Cat parted ways from Luna and Nico. She decided to stroll the damp streets of Siena alone instead of attending Viola's internment and wake. The dreariness of the day began to lift, but the gloom in Cat's spirit remained. Crossing the Piazza del Campo, she stared up at the tower she'd reluctantly climbed. *I faced my fears of flying and climbing the heights to save my sister, and now I have to confront the rest. This difficult chapter of my life has to end. Diana deserves my support, and I must help with the case against Riva. I need to go home to Florida, and I don't have time to take a cruise.*

Later that evening, after Cat booked her flight to Florida the following day, she and Nico sat at the kitchen table.

"Zia Catherine, I understand why you want to go home, but I will miss you. And I will always be grateful for your bravery. You saved Luna's life."

"I'll miss you so much, Nico. I only wish I hadn't put Luna in danger in the first place."

"The criminal acts of Giancarlo and Sam are not your fault," Luna stated, entering the room. "You were a victim and could have lost your life, too."

"Thanks to Jim, I was able to seize the moment and stop Sam. I can't believe I didn't see the evil inside the man. Love can be blind, and so can infatuation."

"We were all fooled," said Nico. "It will be hard for me to trust strangers again."

"We will be more cautious in the future," Luna said. "I spoke with Viola's law partner a few minutes ago, and he is taking over the custody case. He learned that Riccardo *is* the one funding Salvatore. He lied right to our faces."

"How can I trust anyone!" Nico cried. "Why would he betray his own nephew?"

"I am so sorry. But his deceit may help us win the case. There is a pattern of dishonesty in that family as well as neglect," Luna said.

"We're your family, Nico. Now and forever," said Cat.

"Let us celebrate Catherine's last evening in Siena. I have the perfect restaurant."

There were tearful farewells at the Rome airport the next morning. Catherine promised Luna and Nico that she'd return at Christmas and they'd finish their tour of northern Italy. This time, she had to confront boarding the airplane on her own. As a distraction, while she waited at the gate, she wrote a long email to William and Charlotte detailing the events that had happened since they'd disembarked from the cruise ship all that time ago.

Cat realized that reliving her wonderful tour of Sicily only made her want to travel more in the future. The pandemic had underscored the fact that no one is guaranteed a long life. She'd take to heart Jim's final words in his letter to her: to embrace life. She definitely planned to do that, but she was turned off embracing a future romance. *Maybe I do have the basis for a novel in everything I've experienced—a mystery, but not a romance, that's for sure.*

Cat's boarding group was called, and she forced her feet to move toward the entrance to the jetway. *I need to get home* became her mantra until she was seated in the airplane. Sweating and chugging water, Catherine decided the Valium in her purse would be the answer to the long flight and her all-consuming anxiety.

* * *

"I'm so happy you're home!" Lisa called out, rushing toward her best friend, who was exiting security at Jacksonville airport. "And I'm so proud of you for flying."

They hugged for a long moment. "What a crazy time it's been since I last saw you. Oh Lisa. I was such a fool to trust Sam."

"Oh, my dear friend. Don't think about that now. Come on. I'll take you home, and we can deal with everything tomorrow."

The following weeks were filled with depositions, lawyers, authorities from Customs and Border Protection, FinCEN—the Financial Crimes Enforcement Network—and the Jacksonville and Fernandina police. The pieces of the puzzle were slowly falling into place. Giancarlo Riva was arrested for murder, and the money laundering through real estate and high-end artwork was still being investigated. He had been under pressure from the Italian and Russian Oligarchs to get control of the business and silence Catherine after she'd hired the accountant.

Cassidy had poisoned Jim with aconite the same day the staff received flu shots. He'd given Jim an energy drink laced with the drug. Anson Cassidy first met Giancarlo when his mother was taken to the hospital where Cassidy worked. Rumors swirled concerning Cassidy's gambling problem, and Giancarlo knew immediately he had a patsy to do his dirty work. Anson had also been the one who searched Jim's apartment, looking for his laptop, any flash drives, and paper documents related to the investigation.

Cassidy had intended to kill Rodney at his apartment, but the big man had most likely seen him enter the apartment and fled the scene. He'd probably been worried about his safety and had money and clothes stashed in his car. He didn't need his ID and credit cards to survive. Eventually, Anson tracked down Rodney and finished the job with a blow to the head, then submerged Rodney's car in the river. Sam had told Cassidy to frighten Cat and had arranged for him to shoot up her front yard, then send the warning email. It was all part of Sam's twisted game.

The scandal was extensively covered on local and national news broadcasts as well as on social media. Emerson & Ritter lost much of its business. Bradley was determined to restore the company's reputation and finally welcomed Catherine as a full partner, knowing he couldn't have a better business partner. Needing something to keep her busy, Cat agreed to help run the business. She wanted to do her part to save the jobs of E & R's employees.

Chapter 53

ROSE GARDEN

Cat threw herself into the business her brother had co-founded and was surprised at how successful her negotiations with international importers were becoming. Brad shut down the commercial real estate side of the business and focused on exports. Both of them had been fundamentally altered by the events of the past several months, and they were determined to work in harmony. Cat even went with Bradley to buy more flattering eyeglasses.

The heat of summer gave way to the cooler days of autumn. Cat settled into her new routine working for E & R during the day and writing a novel in her spare time. Her editing days were behind her for now. The daily texts she exchanged with Luna and Nico kept them close, and the sisters decided to put their attempts at telepathy on hold for the time being. She booked a flight for a month in Tuscany; she would leave on December 8. Lisa was going to join her for the first two weeks, then return to Amelia Island in time for Christmas with her family.

Late one evening, the doorbell rang. After opening the door, Cat peered through the screen and gasped. "Zach! What are you doing here?" She stepped through the screen door and let it bang shut behind her. "Please, sit down," she said, gesturing to the Muskoka chairs on the porch. "How did you ever find me?"

Cat and her high school sweetheart sat quietly for a long moment. She lit the candle on the table and inhaled the floral-scented air, trying to banish the thoughts of the last time she had sat on the porch with a man who looked so similar to the one seated beside her.

"You haven't changed a bit, Catherine. You still have the most beautiful eyes."

Cat blushed and was grateful for the dim twilight. "I never imagined I'd see you again."

"I moved from Denver to Jacksonville a year ago. After my wife and I divorced and our twin girls left for college in New York, it was time for me to come home. The mountains are great, but I missed living near the ocean."

"But how did you find me? I'm not listed in the phone book, and I took down my website and all social media connections."

Zach smiled—the same magnificent smile from so long ago, not the pale imitation that Sam had given her. "I read the article in the Jax newspaper about Jim's death and your misadventures in Italy. That was quite a complicated series of events."

"That's an understatement," Cat said.

"The article mentioned that you live in Old Town Fernandina. I thought I'd drive up and hopefully run into a local who could tell me where you lived. But when I drove by this cottage and saw the garden full of roses, I felt positive it was your home. So I thought I'd take a chance and knock on the door."

"The Tuscan roses are in honor of my mom, and now my Tuscan sister, too. A lot has happened since we last saw each other all those years ago."

Zach took a deep breath. "One of the reasons I wanted to find you was to say I'm sorry about breaking up with you. I was too young back then to make a commitment. But I thought about you all the time. I even had dreams that we were married."

Smiling at the first love of her life, Cat said, "I had dreams about you, too. And now that we're both older and wiser, maybe those dreams will come true."

La Fine

ACKNOWLEDGMENTS

I'm grateful to the very talented Kristen Jaques for designing the book cover, as she did with my last two novels. Thanks to Tom Jaques for his valuable insights and edits.

A special thank you to Valerie Gray for her masterful editing. The novel is much richer for your revisions and recommendations.

A heartfelt thanks to my husband Mike, and our children Matt, Becky, and Tom, for their encouragement and unconditional love and support.

ABOUT THE AUTHOR

PHOTO BY MATTHEW COSBY

E. Louise Jaques and her husband, Mike reside in Amelia Island, FL, the setting for all of her novels. Louise and Mike's driving tour of Sicily shortly before the COVID-19 pandemic was the inspiration for the Sicilian section of *Her Tuscan Sister*. They are looking forward to traveling the world again, in addition to their trips to Northern California to see their wonderful grandsons.

www.ingramcontent.com/pod-product-compliance
Lightning Source LLC
Chambersburg PA
CBHW031214260626
47169CB00007B/2058